REVIEWS & ACCOLADES

"GRIPPING AND INTENSE! GENUINE HEART-FELT CHARACTERS...A MULTI-LAYERED LITERARY THRILL RIDE!!!"

—Danielle L. *TV/Film Production New York, NY*

"Masterfully crafted from the life and experiences of author AL-GERNON, 'Just Another Innocent Life' fuses fact with fiction to embroil readers...While Algernon's 'Just Another Innocent Life' may look like the work of a fearless team of Hollywood script writers, its author is brave enough to admit that the story is wholly based on reality."

—NY Media Press Release

"A gut-wrenching story of justice delayed and finally attained. From the early days of the investigation to the final courtroom scene, you will be on the edge of your seat until the last page."

—Colleen L. *Senior Editor NYC P.A.*

"Best fiction book I've read in a very long time! I literally could not put it down... readers will always want to know what is coming up on the next page."

—Michelle W. *Business Owner San Diego, CA*

About J.A.I.L.

The death of a police detective's young daughter rocks a town and creates a scandal, which exposes many dark secrets as the lover of the cop's wife is charged in the unthinkable crime.

Defense Attorney Michael Petagnas – a former Prosecutor who now practices on the other side of the aisle, represents the young man who claims to have no involvement in the first-degree murder. Preparing to go head-to-head against his former understudies in this very high profile, David versus Goliath trial, Petagnas hires Private Investigator Nick McLean. The street savvy investigator believes that there is much more to the story, and begins to uncover multiple layers of corruption and police misconduct. He vows to discover the truth and prevent the young minority defendant from becoming the second victim of a heartless cover up, and just another innocent life.

Based on Actual Events

J.A.I.L.
JUST ANOTHER INNOCENT LIFE

By
ALGERNON

JUST ANOTHER INNOCENT LIFE
A fictional work based on, and inspired by the actual
events surrounding the life of the author.

According to the Federal Bureau of investigation, in 2011 there were 3,991.1 arrests for every 100,000 people living in America. That means over the course of a single year, one in 25 Americans was arrested.

About 10,000 people in the United States may be wrongfully convicted of serious crimes each year.

J.A.I.L.
JUST ANOTHER INNOCENT LIFE

PART I
DUE PROCESS?

CHAPTER 1

"I never really liked my name. Especially now, seeing it here in the newspaper ... the name the teachers couldn't pronounce and the other kids made fun of ... there it is in black and white ... Algernon!"

A weary-looking, young African-American man turns from staring out of a small rectangular window. His eyes blood red and glossy from lack of sleep and anxiety. His full birth name is Algernon Flowers. He holds a folded newspaper page that bears the date: *December 7*. He crumples it into a ball and drops it to the ground as he moves away from the window. The sound of his brown rubber sandals shuffling along the floor is almost deafening as he makes his way toward the rusty iron table in the center of the dimly lit room. He looks down at all the various carvings embedded into the aged tabletop before taking a seat on a cold, round metal stool that is bolted to the concrete floor. As he sits, he rests his elbows on the table, allowing his weight to be absorbed by the semi-sturdy tabletop that creeks to his every movement. He places his palms together and interweaves his fingers. The fluorescent light beams slightly as it deflects off the bright white plastic band on his right wrist. It catches his eye as he reads to himself the contents written in black marker. He continues to speak aloud—his voice periodically breaking from emotional stress.

"I suppose this makes it official. Written in black ink and delivered hot off the press. The name none of my Catholic school teachers could pronounce, let alone spell, there it is, correctly spelled in bold print: A-L-G-E-R-N-O-N, right under my photo ... my mugshot."

He looks down at his dingy, orange Local County-issued jumpsuit and lets out a half laugh of disbelief, accompanied by a slight sarcastic smirk as he continues his monologue.

"It was only a few months ago that I actually decided to embrace the uniqueness of my name. I figured that as a recording artist and music producer with such an uncommon name, I would be another one-name star like Madonna, Usher, Beyoncé, Jewel, or Bono. I even imagined a public address announcer at some large venue with an excitable voice bringing me out to the main stage during a major concert as the crowd erupts; Ladies and gentlemen, ... welcome to the stage ... ALGERNON!"

Algernon Flowers pauses momentarily to swallow the mass of ruptured emotion lodged in his throat before continuing.

"That was before seeing my name plastered all over the morning newspaper. Not for record-breaking ticket sales, or chart-topping hits, but for first-degree murder! How did I get here? How could this have happened? Once again I am ashamed and embarrassed by the very uncommon name I was given at birth ... only this time, it is the least of my worries."

After a brief pause in his oratory recount to look down once again at the department of corrections band attached to his wrist, he looks up with tears in his eyes at the well-dressed gentleman seated across from him and addresses him intently.

"I did NOT do this! I didn't do ANYTHING! I don't even know what happened!"

The man on the other side of the table nods affirmatively as he places his shiny silver ink pen onto the canary yellow legal notepad that he had been using to keep an account of this young man's story. He leans back in the black plastic chair as he crosses his legs and places his hands onto his knee. His crisp navy blue suit is flawless. Not a wrinkle. His shirt is immaculate, and his necktie knotted to perfection. Unlike the frightened and fatigued young man whose wrist bears an inmate number, the well-dressed man sports on his wrist an expensive watch that boasts of his success and prosperity. His slightly tanned olive skin and strong Greek chin are almost statuesque. His stern, dark, confident eyes mirror his posture and demeanor. His name is Michael Petagnas—former state attorney and chief of homicide who retired with a one hundred percent conviction rate. Now he is on the other side of the aisle as a criminal defense lawyer with a firm that he shares with his partner, Steven Didia Sr. He looks at this petrified young man and calmly addresses him in an almost parental tone.

"Al, I have to say that this doesn't look good. You know the father is a local police detective, and we *are* talking about a child here. A little girl was beaten and somebody has to pay for that, and they want that somebody to be you."

Algernon drops his head as the gravity of the situation weighs heavily upon him. He looks up and again pleads with his attorney.

"Please! I swear, I had nothing to do with this!"

Mr. Petagnas uncrosses his legs and leans forward toward his anguished client.

"Hey, I believe you. I've prosecuted many, many homicide cases when I was with the state attorney's office. I have looked into the eyes of murderers, and I can tell that you are not one. I wouldn't be here if I thought or felt otherwise. The reason I decided to take your case is because I see a young man with little to no resources being railroaded by a system that will crush the strongest of men. It's not me that has to believe you. You are facing an uphill battle against the district attorney with unlimited resources."

Algernon takes a deep breath, and releases it as he attempts to deal with this monstrous weight looming over him. He closes his eyes and braces himself as Petagnas continues to break down the severity of the moment.

"I spoke with the D.A. and they want to put a deal on the table. They are offering fifteen years for a manslaughter plea."

Algernon opens his eyes in disbelief and quickly rejects the idea. "No way! I didn't do this!"

Petagnas interjects: "Calm down. I'm not suggesting that you take the deal, but as your attorney I have to let you know that there is an offer, and if you decide to take it to trial and roll the dice with an unpredictable jury..." he pauses and makes certain that he has his client's full attention before continuing. "The evidence is only circumstantial, but during my time on the other side of the aisle, I have won many trials based solely on circumstantial evidence. I just want to you know that if you decide to take this to trial and lose, you face life in prison, or the death penalty."

Algernon leans in further and in almost a whisper restates his claim, "I had nothing to do with the death of that child."

Petagnas sits back in his chair and once again crosses his legs as he nods affirmatively and pauses before continuing.

"All right then. I will let them know that you aren't interested in any deals."

"Absolutely not," agrees Algernon.

Petagnas reaches to his left and retrieves his leather briefcase from the floor next to him. He opens it and places the legal pad into it and slides the shiny pen into his inner jacket pocket. He stands and extends his hand toward his client. Algernon also stands and shakes Petagnas' extended hand as he looks nervously at his very confident attorney.

"What happens next?" asks Algernon.

Petagnas picks up his briefcase with his right hand, and places his left hand in his pocket before responding.

"They have nothing actually tying you to anything, so the next thing we need to do is get some actual evidence that does NOT tie you to this. It should be innocent until proven guilty, but you're getting a raw deal here, kid. You, my friend, are guilty until proven innocent."

The well-polished attorney turns and signals to a corrections officer standing outside the room behind a blue metal door with a large glass window. At this prompt, the officer jingles his large ring of keys while unlocking the door from the outside, as Petagnas turns back to his client.

"I know you can't afford one, but we are going to need to hire a private investigator."

Algernon nods affirmatively.

"I know a guy who is an absolute bloodhound and somewhat closer to your budget," Petagnas states as the officer enters the room and steps aside for him to exit. While continuing to walk toward the door he completes his thought.

"Don't worry, I will pay him out of the retainer! Trust me, he's the best!"

Mr. Petagnas exits down the dark corridor lined with grey metal bars and earth-tone tiles. The heels on his black leather dress shoes click rhythmically toward the visitor's security entrance. He approaches the front desk, signs his name on a clipboard, and retrieves his ID from the officer on duty. As he walks to the front exit toward the parking lot, he reaches into his pocket and pulls out his cell phone. He pushes open the heavy iron door and squints as his eyes readjust to the sunlight. After dialing a contact, he holds the phone to his ear and begins to speak.

"Yes, this is Michael Petagnas calling for Nick McLean."

CHAPTER 2

Private investigator Nicholas McLean enters his tiny office and sits in a cushioned office chair behind his cluttered desk when his phone intercom beeps. He is tall and intimidating in stature, with broad shoulders and large hands. Comfortably dressed in denim jeans, a blue button-up shirt and brown shoes. His haircut and clean-shaven face suggest that he's former military or law enforcement. He navigates his way through a variety of randomly strewn colored case folders as he attempts to locate the telephone. After a few beeps he picks up and holds the receiver to his head as he answers.

.　　　.　　　.

"Yes, put him through," McLean says politely into the phone.

.　　　.　　　.

While he waits for his caller to be patched through to his line, he clears a section of space to take any notes needed during this conversation.

·   ·   ·

"Michael, good to hear from you. What's going on?" McLean listens intently and proceeds to write down a name and an address on a small notepad. "You got it. I will get on this right away." After a pause he continues, "Not a problem at all. We can discuss my rate later. Thanks, and I am glad to be on board with this. OK, bye."

McLean hangs up and tears off the page from the notepad. Opening his desk drawer, he takes out a leather-bound binder and places the loose page inside of it. He stands up and pats himself down as to make certain that all his personal items, wallet and keys, are on him before heading toward the door. Before exiting he retrieves a light brown jacket from behind the door and carries it on his forearm as he pulls his door closed.

·   ·   ·

The rain clouds begin to roll in as the typical afternoon thunderstorm is expected daily this close to the beach. Several cars and trucks speed by his black sport utility vehicle as McLean slows down to pull into a daycare center driveway. The vehicle kicks up dust and gravel as he comes to a stop in the unpaved parking lot at the rear of the building. He shuts off his engine and gathers his jacket and binder from the front passenger seat. As he exits the vehicle he can hear the sound of children playing. He proceeds to walk around the side of the building toward the front, passing a fenced-in playground. From his vantage point he can see several children, from toddlers to pre-teens, taking part in various playful activities while a couple of adults supervise and keep watch over them. One of the adults, a short, older woman with salt-and-pepper hair, wearing an apron and holding a sleeping baby, makes eye contact with him. McLean acknowledges her with a smile and polite wave. The woman nods to him, and motions toward the front to indicate to him to meet her at the front entrance as she gently hands the sleeping baby to another daycare employee. McLean continues to walk along the side the building to the front. When he gets to the front, he takes the three steps onto the wooden porch, and walks to the door where he sees a sign that reads: EMMANUEL DAYCARE CENTER. Before he can ring the bell, the woman opens the door. Her name is Hazel Flowers, the mother of the defendant in this case. She attempts in vain to appear chipper, but the heaviness in her heart is far too much and her eyes reveal anguish. Ms. Flowers opens the dialogue with a nervous, awkward greeting.

"Hello, Nick?" She is half shielded by the door.

"Yes. Are you Ms. Flowers?" replies McLean.

She nods affirmatively as she steps back and out of the doorway, inviting him to enter. McLean steps inside and Ms. Flowers closes the front door behind him. She speaks softly as not to wake any sleeping children, and begins to walk down the hall to a front office area.

"This way. We can talk in my office. Can I offer you something to drink, water, coffee?" offers Ms. Flowers.

"No thank you, I'm good," McLean replies.

Ms. Flowers gestures for him to sit on a small couch inside the office as she closes the door to give them privacy. She takes a seat on a chair beside a metal desk. McLean realizes that he has yet to formerly introduce himself.

"I'm sure Mr. Petagnas has already informed you that I will be leading the investigation for your son's defense," states McLean.

Ms. Flowers nods affirmatively as McLean opens his binder in preparation to take notes. He continues, "I just need to ask you a few questions about Algernon." A large photo on the wall behind Ms. Flowers catches his eye.

"Is that him?" he asks.

Ms. Flowers looks back at the photo as she responds, and for the first time since their interaction, she smiles genuinely.

"Oh, yes. That was last Christmas. He dressed up as Santa and all the kids took photos with him. He was always so great with all the children. He loved them and they loved him. They all called him Uncle Al," states Ms. Flowers.

She turns back to face McLean, and almost immediately her countenance returns to the distressed, worried look. McLean jots down something in his book and then continues.

"Have the police or anyone from the DA's office contacted you for a statement or deposition yet?"

"Yes, well they asked me if I ever saw him with the little girl, or if he has ever been violent with any of the children here at the daycare center. I told them no way. He was always great with them," Ms. Flowers replies assertively. "Plus, I never saw him with that little girl," she adds. "As far as any relationship with that woman … Ms. or Mrs. Howell, I never even knew he was dating anyone. He was mostly traveling and promoting his CD or playing music at various venues around town. They really didn't ask me much else. I don't think I could be of much help to them. I only know the young man that I raised, and he would never, ever put a hand on a defenseless child to cause harm … Never." There is not a trace of doubt in her voice. She pauses and then remembers something.

"Oh, they asked me one more thing. They wanted to know where he got the money to retain an attorney like Michael Petagnas."

This gets McLean's attention. He inquires for clarity.

"Wait, the detectives asked you that?" he asks.

"Yes," she replies. The private investigator continues to take notes as Ms. Flowers speaks. "I thought it was strange that they would ask me that …"

McLean interjects. "Well sometimes when a case is not a slam dunk for either side, the prosecution would offer a plea deal in which an overworked, underpaid lawyer, fresh out of law school and working for the public defender's office, would jump on, as not to have to face off with more experienced attorneys during a trial." He pauses while Ms. Flowers waits, listening, for him to continue. "My guess is that they were hoping your son wouldn't have retained such an experienced attorney, and then been forced to take the lesser of two evils— some bogus plea deal—and they could make this go away without a lengthy trial. By retaining a defense team like Petagnas and Didia, essentially Al is saying he's prepared to fight for his life and freedom."

Ms. Flowers takes an exaggerated deep breath, and then exhales slowly and dramatically. McLean looks over his notes before continuing.

"Ms. Flowers, is there anything else you can think of? Do you remember the night he went over to ... " he searches his notes before continuing, "Mrs. Howell's apartment?"

Ms. Flowers pauses to think before responding.

"I only remember that he got in maybe around 9 o'clock that night from Nashville. He drove there with the pastor and deacon from my church. He was there at a music conference selling his CDs. They dropped him off, and he brought in a suitcase and a box, which he took to his room. I could see the driveway from the window in my bathroom. When I got out of the bathroom about twenty minutes later, I walked into the kitchen to ask him about his trip, but he was gone. I looked out the kitchen window and saw him get into a dark colored vehicle," she recalls.

McLean hands her his notebook and pen. "Can you write down the names of the people Algernon was with in Nashville?"

She obliges, and then returns the notebook and pen back to him. He closes his binder and stands up to indicate the end of the meeting. McLean slides a business card from his wallet and hands it to her.

"Well, Ms. Flowers, if you think of anything else that you feel is important, feel free to call me anytime."

Ms. Flowers shakes his hand and then walks him to the front door. "Thank you for helping my boy. I pray that the truth will come out," Ms. Flowers states as she opens the door. McLean nods affirmatively. "Well, finding the truth is my specialty. Have a good day, and I will be in touch."

Upon reaching his vehicle, he notices the adults in the playground gathering the children back inside as large raindrops from the darkened skies begin to pound the roof of his car.

"Wow, Florida weather is the worst," he mumbles.

He quickly enters his vehicle, starts his engine, and drives away.

CHAPTER 3

It is late in the afternoon and the streets are still wet from the recent downpour, yet the sun shines brightly. The scent of rain is mixed with the smell of freshly cut grass from the well-maintained lawns and beautiful landscaping of this gated suburban community located in an upscale Almond Beach neighborhood. McLean exits one of the homes and walks to his vehicle parked in the curved driveway. His jacket is still wet from the rain. He takes it off and tosses it into the back seat. After removing his cell phone from his jeans pocket, he enters his vehicle and starts the engine, dialing a number as he backs out of the driveway. He immediately notices a silver sedan, resembling an unmarked patrol car, parked across the street. The engine is running, he can tell, but he cannot see inside through the dark tinted windows. At the end of the driveway, he puts his vehicle in drive and continues through the gated community of large homes. He peeks in his rearview mirror to see if there is any activity regarding the silver sedan. He loses sight of it as he continues along the bending street. Someone comes on the other end of his phone and McLean diverts his attention to his phone call.

"Hey Mike, I just left the pastor's house, and they both confirm that Mr. Flowers was, in fact, driving the van for the entire trip from Nashville ... approximately eighteen to nineteen hours, including stops for shopping and meals."

McLean briefly glances in his rearview and sees nothing. He continues to speak. "According to the deacon, when he suggested that they stop in Jacksonville, Algernon appeared to be texting something while driving and this caught his attention. He, the deacon, pointed it out and made a statement about it not being safe. He went on to add that during the entire dinner at the Chinese restaurant where they stopped, Algernon was constantly texting back and forth, and almost seemed annoyed."

McLean's attention is diverted as he notices the silver sedan is now cruising behind him. He is not quite sure if this is merely a coincidence, so he pulls over to the side of the road. He waits as the suspicious car drives by. Unable to see inside the passing car through its dark tinted windows, he tries to see the license plate, but only gets a partial number as the car disappears around the bending road. McLean drives forward and around the bend, but the car is no longer in sight. He continues his phone call.

"Anyway, now we have to get a witness list and discovery from the D.A. In the meantime, names came up of some people I should talk to. I also want to pay a visit to the school where Mrs. Howell works, and speak to some of her coworkers."

He listens to the other line before continuing.

"OK, will do. See you then."

McLean hangs up and continues to drive toward the exit of the gated community. When he approaches the highway he drives under a sign that reads: HOLLIS HILL – 20 MILES.

McLean merges to the right to exit. He comes to a stop at a flashing red light and checks the intersection before crossing. Now with the sun beginning to set, streetlights and driveway lanterns illuminate the streets and homes in this modest and quaint neighborhood. McLean checks his notes as he searches for a particular house. He sees the one he is looking for, *1219 Flomich Street*. He turns into the short driveway and pulls up behind a red pickup truck that is parked outside the garage. This gives him hope that someone is, in fact, home, and that his trip wasn't a waste of time. He exits his vehicle and walks to the front door. Before he even touches the doorbell, he can hear a small dog barking just on the other side of the door. Although the inhabitants of this dwelling are surely aware of his presence by now, thanks to the yelping canine, McLean presses the doorbell anyway. The dog's barking escalates. McLean can hear a man's voice scolding the animal, immediately causing the barking to cease. The door then slowly opens and a tall, heavyset African-American man in his mid-to-late sixties fills the doorway. He is wearing denim overalls with a white T-shirt underneath. The small dog nestled between his feet attempts to sniff the new visitor from a distance. The old man looks past McLean to see what he is driving and if he is alone before addressing him with a heavy Southern drawl.

"Yes, can I help you?" inquires the old man.

McLean extends his right hand, which is ignored by the husky gentleman.

"My name is Nick McLean and I am a private investigator working a case for Michael Petagnas."

After realizing the man is not accepting his handshake, McLean takes a business card from his wallet and offers it to the man, who examines it before saying another word. He looks past McLean skeptically once more before he responds.

"And what is it that you want here?"

"I'm looking for a Deborah Long?" replies McLean while referencing his notes.

The untrusting old man looks at the business card once more, and then back to McLean. "What is this in reference to?" asks the old man.

"I'm with the legal team that is representing Mr. Algernon Flowers in a first-degree murder case," states McLean.

The old man seems intrigued.

McLean continues, "Deborah's name came up as someone we should talk to. Is she home?"

The man appears to be contemplating if he should lie or not. After a brief but awkward pause, the old man steps aside and allows the mysterious private investigator into his home, as he yells out in the direction of the back of the house.

"Debbie, there's someone here that wants to speak to you!"

He shuts the door and gestures for McLean to move into the living room.

"Deborah is my granddaughter. She isn't in any sort of trouble is she?" asks the man.

"No, not at all. I just want to see if she has some information that can assist in our investigation," replies McLean.

Soon a tall, athletic young woman in her late twenties enters the room. She was clearly having dinner as she still has a mouthful of food. Noticing this, McLean addresses her apologetically.

"Pardon me if this is a bad time ..."

The old man interrupts with his deep southern drawl. "Aw hell, this isn't a bad time, she's always eating."

The woman, Deborah Long, gives her grandfather a scolding look as she tries to quickly chew her food. McLean politely continues the dialogue.

"Ms. Long, I just have a couple of questions to ask you about your friend, Mrs. Brenda Howell," announces McLean.

The mention of that name causes Deborah to quickly and forcefully swallow her food, as she clearly wants to respond. She obviously knows exactly what this is in reference to. After clearing her mouth, she shakes McLean's hand and offers him a seat on the couch. Once they are all seated, Deborah begins to speak before McLean can ask his first question.

"Let me start off by saying that Brenda has been a friend since we were freshmen in college. I don't want to get her in any trouble or anything."

McLean interjects, "She is not in any trouble as far as I know. There is a young man sitting in the county jail right now facing a serious charge, and if there is any information that you have that may be of any use to me, I need it. I'm not here to bring charges or anything against your friend. I just need you to share the incident in ..."

Before he can get it out, Deborah completes his sentence.

"The incident in the bathroom at church!" she exclaims.

McLean is now convinced he has correct information. This woman is going to be quite valuable to this case.

"Yes, can you tell me about it?" he asks.

Deborah looks at her grandfather seated next to McLean. The old man gives her a positive nod as encouragement to go ahead.

"Now this was around January when the baby, Deja, was about twenty-two months old ..." Deborah begins to recount her story. McLean takes careful notes as she continues. "I was in the church bathroom. It was first Sunday, I remember because the entire choir wears white on communion Sundays. I was in one of the stalls when I heard Brenda storm into the bathroom."

Deborah pauses as if to carefully choose her next few words before continuing. "I heard the baby crying. Brenda placed her on the changing table next to the sink and began ..." again Deborah pauses.

McLean urges her on. "She started what?" he asks.

Deborah closes her eyes and exhales before going on. "She was beating her. She was beating the baby because she spilled juice from her juice box all over Brenda's white suit ... AND Brenda was leading a song that morning so she now had to stand up in front of the entire church with a big juice stain on her clothes. Sounds silly and petty, but maybe she was in a bad mood. She gets cranky when she and her husband argue."

McLean writes in his notes as he asks a question. "So she was pretty upset by the child spilling juice?"

Deborah Long continues. "Yes. At least that's what she was saying. 'Look at what you did, look what you did to my new suit!' That's when I stormed out of the stall and had to physically pull Brenda away from little Deja."

Deborah stops, becoming emotional. It is overwhelming to speak this of her long-time friend. She abruptly leaves the room, in tears. The old man stands up and starts to walk toward the front door. Clearly this interview is over. On his cue, McLean stands and follows the old man to the door.

"Please give her my card," McLean says to the old man, "Have her call me if she has anything else she thinks …"

The old man cuts him off in mid-sentence and almost shoves him out the door.

"I think you've upset her enough," huffs the old man.

McLean pleads, "Sir, we could use her as a witness. Her story could really help our client."

The old man creates enough space in the doorway to get McLean out and then barks back, "She is not testifying against her friend and I don't want you coming back around here!"

With that he slams the door shut in McLean's face. McLean walks toward his vehicle with his cell phone now in hand and to his ear. He won't allow his frustration to deter his optimism. The same silver sedan with dark tinted windows from earlier is parked on the street two houses down. He notices it as he gets in his car and is very doubtful this is just a coincidence. As he backs out of the driveway, someone on the other end of his phone answers. McLean speaks calmly into his phone, "Hey, grab a pen and write this down." He backs up slowly so he can see the plates on the suspicious vehicle. He then reads it clearly, "P-W-Q-4-1-9 … got it?" He pulls away but the car doesn't seem to follow him. He continues with his phone call, "Do me a favor and run those plates for me. I'm heading back to the office now." He hangs up and drives toward the highway, periodically checking his rearview mirror.

CHAPTER
4

At the Local County Jail, lockdown time is approaching and inmate 174988 in A-block of unit three has not yet gotten his half hour out-of-cell time. Due to his special lockdown custody status, he remains locked within an assigned six- by eight-foot cell for twenty-three and one-half hours daily. At any given time, decided by the on-duty corrections officer, the heavy iron door is rolled open remotely, and the inmate can take a shower or use the payphone to make collect calls to his family. The inmate is Algernon Flowers. He stands against the cold iron door, which is solid and has a rectangular slot cut out up near chest level for two purposes: for officers to observe the inmate without mechanically rolling open the door, and the other as a means of passing trays of food to the inmate. Algernon Flowers uses this for a different purpose. He leans over and watches the officers every thirty minutes to see which door will be opened next. He hears one door close, indicating that an inmate has exceeded his out-of-cell time and has been sent back to his assigned cell. Algernon waits with anticipation, hoping his door is rolled open next. Although he hasn't showered in several days, his main objective is to use his entire time, all thirty minutes of it, to call his family. He has limited contact with anyone other than jail officials, and he wants updates, any word at all, as to what is going on with his case. The double buzz-like horn sound is heard, which provides the inmates warning that the large iron door, with the ability to crush human bones, is about to get in motion. Algernon backs away as the rumble of a door opening on the tier directly above him causes his door to vibrate. This is very disappointing. Now at the least, he will have to wait another half hour to hear a loving voice on the telephone.

Exhausted and frustrated, Algernon leans his forehead against the cold metal door. The smell of copper, iron, and lead is nearly too powerful to bear. The light green paint is almost entirely rusted and worn away on the inside. To his right, a heavily scratched metal toilet, with a sink attached. To his left, cold brick walls painted the same bright green as the door was likely at some point. Behind him, an iron twin-size slab, approximately two feet high, is bolted to both the brick wall and the concrete floor. A flat plastic mattress barely covers it, resembling an animal bed at any local zoo. There is also a two-foot square metal table attached to the wall in the left corner next to the bed, with a metal stool bolted to the ground in front of it. This can be very challenging for a left-handed person to eat, or write on, with it being attached directly to the left wall. The inmate assigned to this cell just so happens to be left-handed. Not that he has attempted to eat since arriving here almost a week ago. His stomach rumbles from hunger, yet his loss of appetite will not allow him to even touch the almost inedible slop that is tossed into the cut away of his cell door three times per day. The officer monitoring each inmate's diet has listed him as a possible "suicide by voluntary starvation" risk. It is for this reason, the very next time that heavy green iron door is rolled open, it is not for Algernon Flowers to enjoy a half hour of telephone privileges, but to be escorted by two officers to the suicide watch unit.

. . .

Here in the suicide watch unit, the air conditioner is cranked up high, and blows ferociously, as frigid air pumps out of the vents attached to the ceiling. Before entering a cell, Algernon is stripped naked, thoroughly searched, and given a paper, hospital-style robe. He is then sent into the cold cell that has the county standard twin-size slab, but no mattress, as it could possibly be used to injure oneself. The same goes for any blankets or pillows. It is here that Algernon is instructed to spend the night, as a specially assigned officer paces throughout the hours, periodically ordering the inmate to stand and respond to random questions to show coherence and mental state. As he lies in the fetal position, shivering from the cold air blasting directly onto him, inmate Flowers begins to feel this is more of a punishment for refusing to eat—a sign of rebellion—rather than for his own safety. All through the night there are violent screams from other inmates on the suicide watch unit. Some, mentally ill and being tormented by their demons—while others kick the iron doors, and bang on the metal beds to draw attention, or to keep annoying the officers.

At 5 o'clock in the morning, Algernon is awakened once again for a final head count before the guard shift takes place. Shortly thereafter, a new officer, just beginning his shift, comes bearing a breakfast tray. The beige cardboard tray offers two cold, flat slices of French toast, a slice of dark-colored stale bologna, and a small paper cup of red juice. Not a very appetizing meal in the least, but one that this inmate dare not refuse, for fear of being kept in this torturous unit another horrific night. His eyes blood red and puffy from lack of sleep ... his body still shivering uncontrollably, he accepts the tray from the officer, and while still standing by the cell door, scarfs it all down with little effort or hesitation.

CHAPTER 5

Private investigator Nicholas McLean sips his morning coffee as he pulls his SUV into the first available parking spot. He chugs the remaining liquid contents from a Styrofoam cup, and then looks to place it into the cup holder. However, both cup holders are full of half-filled cups, so he throws the one in his hand onto the floor in the back seat, which is already littered with similar gas station coffee cups. He turns off his engine, grabs his binder from the front passenger seat, and exits his vehicle. He makes the short walk to a side entrance of the Law Offices of Petagnas & Didia. Upon entering the foyer he is greeted by a young female receptionist who acknowledges him by name, and informs him that the meeting he is attending is about to begin in the conference room. He thanks her, then starts down the familiar hallway.

In the main conference room, a discovery meeting is underway as several legal assistants sit near and around a large, oval-shaped, glossy oak table. At one end sits Attorney Michael Petagnas. His partner and co-council, Steven Didia Sr., is seated directly to his right. Across from him sits Petagnas' senior paralegal, Sandy Ward. She is a slim, middle-aged woman with blonde hair and freckles. She removes her reading glasses as she completes her verbal presentation of a written statement from Mrs. Brenda Howell, given to the Rocky Beach Police detectives concerning her daughter's death.

"We are currently awaiting the photos taken by detectives of Mrs. Howell's right hand with the large diamond cluster rings, and broken fingernail on her middle finger. Apparently the homicide detectives felt that the shapes of the rings matched the bruises on the child's lower abdomen," Sandy Ward concludes before taking her seat.

Michael Petagnas speaks next. "Thank you, Sandy. Those will be very helpful to our defense, I'm sure. Now let's hear from our lead investigator, Nicholas McLean."

With his hand, he gestures toward the other end of the large table where McLean sits with his binder of notes already opened. All eyes and heads turn in that direction, and are now on the tall, clean-cut private investigator.

"Thanks, Michael," says the visibly sleep-deprived McLean. "Although I've only been on the case for less than forty-eight hours, I have obtained several leads. The most promising, yet least likely to cooperate, is Mrs. Howell's long-time friend Deborah Long, who actually witnessed a possible incident of physical abuse between Howell and the deceased child."

This seems to pique the interest of those listening as some make note of that point.

McLean continues. "According to unofficial phone records that I obtained from a contact at Mr. Flowers' cell phone provider, there were several text messages between him and Mrs. Howell."

"Very good," says an impressed Michael Petagnas.

McLean continues with his presentation. "According to the transcription of the texts, Mrs. Howell sent a barrage of messages asking Mr. Flowers for his ETA on the night in question. As the evening went on, and the times kept getting pushed further, Howell's texts seemed to become accusatory and angry."

"How so?" Petagnas asks as he gestures for Sandy Ward to take note of this particular point.

"Well, I couldn't get a copy without a court order, but I wrote down some of them ..." McLean reads directly from his notes: "OK, at 6:43 P.M., Howell sends a text: *Well?????*–With four question marks. A minute later Flowers replies: *Sorry, Deac wanted to stop for dinner*, to which Howell replies: *Wow, do you think I'm an idiot? You're out with the pastor and deacon selling CDs or are you out there screwing some whore?* Flowers then responds: *In Jacksonville at dinner. Will let you know when we're back on the road.* After this Mrs. Howell called Mr. Flowers' phone six times in a row. None of the calls lasted more than two or three seconds."

Michael Petagnas interjects, "My guess is that he didn't want to have that embarrassing argument in front of the clergy he was at the table with. If he had a flip phone, then probably opening and closing it would stop the ringing or vibrating, thus he was hanging up on her. Perhaps that's why the deacon said he seemed annoyed at dinner. It was probably during this series of back-to-back calls."

Everyone at the table seems to be taking notes at this point, as Petagnas gestures back to McLean, who continues to read the exchange of text messages.

"Yes, so following the series of calls, a text from Howell's phone came in: *LIAR! If you're not with a female why don't you answer your phone?* After that, there is a short phone call to Howell's phone from Mr. Flowers. It is not again until 7:22 P.M. do we see any other recorded activity between the two. He texted her: *Leaving J-Ville now. Hopefully with no traffic we will be in Rocky Beach by 8:30.* The next few texts are from

Howell with no response from Flowers, who was driving at this point. She writes: *You've been gone a week and I miss you.* Four minutes later she writes: *You don't seem very excited to see me,* and includes a sad face. After that, a couple of question marks only. The next activity doesn't take place until 8:58 P.M.. Flowers calls Mrs. Howell, and that call lasts twenty-seven seconds."

McLean closes his binder, as that concludes the information he has thus far. He wraps up his presentation. "So, I am going to the elementary school where Howell teaches to speak with some of her coworkers this afternoon."

"Great work, Nick," offers Petagnas. He then addresses the entire room. "Well folks, we have a lot of work to do. Let's get to it."

With that, the entire staff scrambles quickly, yet in an organized manner.

Steven Didia, a stocky Italian-American man from New York City, remains seated. He wears a professional gray suit, but no tie. His full, thick black hair is brushed back with a small part to one side. He quietly summons McLean using his hand and a slight nod of the head. McLean makes his way around to the far end of the large conference room table, shaking hands with some of the others who appear happy to see him again. As he reaches the other end of the table, Didia stands up. He is much shorter than the towering McLean. They wait for a moment as the last few staff members exit the room, leaving McLean, Didia and Petagnas alone.

"What's up?" asks McLean.

Didia speaks with a strong New York City accent. "Nicky, first of all, good to see you again."

The two men embrace in a manly hug. McLean has to bend down to the shorter Didia.

Didia continues to address McLean, "Remember that plate you asked us to run for you? Well it came back without a hit." McLean is puzzled.

Petagnas adds, "Yeah but Mr. Personality, Steven here, knows everybody."

Didia, who seems to enjoy the minor stroke to his ego, smiles before continuing.

"So I have this contact in the Rocky Beach PD," states Didia. "Turns out it's one of theirs. Unmarked undercover—assigned to the detective's squad."

McLean is a bit disturbed by this news. Didia shakes McLean's hand, holds on a bit longer than normal, and looks him directly in the eye before continuing.

"The deceased child's father is an active Rocky Beach Police Detective, and I don't think you will make his Christmas list by digging up evidence to help defend the man that's charged with her murder ... not to mention the fact that same man was sleeping with his wife. Watch your back out there," cautions Didia. With those words, he exits the room leaving only Petagnas and McLean.

"Well, looks like you've got a busy day ahead of you," says Petagnas to his lead investigator, who picks up on the hint to get going.

"Oh, yes. Lots to do. I will be in touch," replies McLean. He exits and goes directly to his vehicle. Once inside the safety of his sport utility vehicle, he presses the automatic locks, and then checks his rearview mirror before pulling off.

CHAPTER 6

It is shortly after 12 noon at the Richard M. Weinstein Elementary School and Ms. Angela Crowell sits alone in her classroom working on a lesson plan. Her sixth-grade students have all gone to have lunch in the school cafeteria. She munches on her own lunch as she works. Her short auburn hair is complemented by her blue pants suit, small-rimmed glasses and matching jewelry. Her left hand sports a modest, single diamond engagement ring. She takes a bite out of her sandwich as a male school staff member knocks on the open classroom door. This appears to startle her as two men fill the doorway and enter. The first man, a school campus employee, is a young Hispanic male. The second man following closely behind him is private investigator Nicholas McLean.

The young staff member makes the introduction. "Ms. Crowell, sorry to disturb you, but Principal Miller asked me to escort this gentleman up here."

Ms. Crowell politely brushes crumbs from her mouth with the back of her hand as she stands and walks to the door to meet them.

The young man continues, "You have a visitor ... this is a private investigator ..."

McLean jumps in with his hand extended toward the attractive young teacher and introduces himself, "Nick McLean."

Ms. Crowell shakes his hand and introduces herself, "Angela Crowell."

The young man exits the classroom, leaving Ms. Crowell and McLean to speak alone.

Angela Crowell continues to engage the friendly private investigator, whom she has spoken with briefly prior to his visit. "When I got your call, I was shocked that you would even want to talk to me. I mean, what possible information do you think I would have that will help your murder case?"

McLean gestures at a chair beside the teacher's desk. Ms. Crowell duplicates the gesture as an invitation for them both to be seated. McLean opens his binder and readies his pen as he addresses her, "Ms. Crowell ... is it Ms.?—Mrs.?"

"It's Mrs.—Well, soon to be," replies Crowell as she holds up her left hand to display her ring.

Not allowing his disappointment to belie his professional demeanor, McLean moves on. "Well, soon-to-be Mrs., your name came up several times as someone who knows Mrs. Brenda Howell pretty well. I know she hasn't been back to work since the passing of her daughter. Are you and she very close?"

Crowell thinks of the best way to answer. "Let's just say that she tends to always find her way into my classroom during breaks ..."

Ms. Crowell seems as though she isn't sure she should go into any more detail. Picking up on this, McLean presses a bit.

"Oh, do you two usually spend break time together?" he asks.

"No, not really ..." Crowell replies.

Before she can complete her thought, they are interrupted by a tall, very handsome man dressed in a local county sheriff's uniform. He walks in looking down at his cell phone.

"Hey Angie ..." blurts the man in uniform.

As he looks up from his phone, he makes direct eye contact with McLean, and stops in mid-thought and mid-stride.

"Oh, sorry," offers the handsome man apologetically. "I didn't know you had company. I will catch you later," he concludes as he makes a b-line out the door.

McLean can tell that the very awkwardly nervous display he has just witnessed was excellent timing, and more than likely has something to do with Ms. Crowell's illusiveness. McLean looks at her and allows her to continue.

"THERE is the reason Brenda is always in my classroom," says Crowell reluctantly.

McLean looks back toward the now-empty doorway, and then back again to Angela Crowell. She lets out a sigh, and then realizes that she may as well just explain further. She opens up a little more to McLean.

"That is Ron Garzero. He's the local county deputy assigned to our school. He and my future husband just so happen to be old high school buddies."

McLean writes in his binder as Ms. Crowell continues.

"Brenda and Ron sort of have, or had, a fling ... a mutual attraction, or whatever."

By his look, Crowell can tell what McLean wants her to admit. "What?" she asks. "Do you want me to say that they were sleeping together?" She hesitates, diverting her gaze. "I don't know. I can guess ... Yeah maybe, but she is married, and he is my friend so please don't drag his name into this."

"Relax, let's back up," suggests McLean.

Crowell gently bites her lip in a slight nervous fit. She takes a couple of deep breaths before continuing.

"A few months ago, Brenda and Ron were hanging out in her classroom during a break ... You know, the usual flirting or whatever. Then her husband, who is a police officer, drops by unannounced to take her to lunch. Well, it was awkward to say the least. Brenda says that when her husband got her alone, he threatened to make her life miserable if he catches her flirting with Ron again. The county police make a lot more money than the local city police, so this was a major blow to her husband's ego."

McLean continues to write almost every word from this potentially valuable source as she continues her recount of an interesting series of events.

"Anyway, she swore to her husband that she and Ron were just friends, and he was interested in another teacher, and was only there asking her for advice on how to ask that teacher out. Not sure if hubby bought it or not, but ever since then, Ron and Brenda have used my room for their ... " Crowell uses air quotes, "break time."

McLean has to try not to smile as he realizes that this woman has just given him pure gold.

"Anything else you want to add? Anything else strange or unusual with Mrs. Howell's behavior?" he asks.

Crowell is visibly nervous. She obviously feels she has said way too much already. She is seeking an end to this interview.

"Look, I can't get caught up in this. I'm busy planning my wedding, and I really don't need the extra stress."

McLean plays on her emotional state. "Well, here's the thing, Ms. Crowell. We have a murdered toddler that can't speak up and say who caused her death. I am working hard for an innocent man that is sitting in the county jail facing life in prison, or the death penalty. Neither one of them will ever plan a wedding, or do any of the wonderful things that you feel are more important than uncovering the truth here."

Crowell looks down and shakes her head, indicating her understanding of what's at stake. McLean puts his hand on her shoulder and pleads with her. "Please, the woman you are protecting, she wasn't only cheating on her husband with your friend Deputy Ron ... she was also with our client, Mr. Flowers." Crowell looks up to defend herself.

"I am NOT protecting her!" she exclaims.

McLean continues, "Well OK, perhaps you don't want your name, or Deputy Ron's name to come up. Is there anyone else that you think I should talk to?"

Crowell is hesitant, but eventually speaks.

"Ms. Richardson. She works in the main office. You should go talk to Ms. Richardson."

McLean writes down that name, and then closes his binder. He pats Ms. Crowell on her shoulder as a symbol of gratitude. She looks to the ground and refuses to make eye contact with him. He stands and begins to exit without saying another word. He then stops in the doorway and addresses the emotionally stressed teacher.

"You did the right thing. You should be proud," says McLean.

Ms. Crowell still doesn't look up. She gives only a sarcastic half-chuckle.

"Thank you for your help, and good luck with the wedding planning," McLean offers sincerely.

As he waits for a response from her, the bell rings, indicating that lunch period is over. McLean turns to exit as hyper children run past him and begin to fill the classroom. Ms. Crowell gathers herself, throws her half-eaten lunch in the trash, and gets back into teacher mode by settling her class.

CHAPTER 7

The last of the big yellow school buses is pulling out of the Richard M. Weinstein Elementary school parking lot as the school day has ended. A few parents wait in idling cars and minivans as several stragglers scurry out to the various buildings on the campus. Most of the staff parking area is still full. One black SUV is parked at the far edge of the lot, near the sports field. From this vantage point, McLean can see each staff member as they walk to their vehicles, while remaining somewhat inconspicuous. He keeps his eye on a particular car—a white, late-model coupe. Periodically, McLean drinks from a large Styrofoam cup, but never loses site of his target. He grows optimistic as a clump of adults exits the main office building. He keeps his eye out for whomever goes to that little white car. The group disperses, biding farewell as they walk to their respective vehicles. A petite, casually dressed African-American woman walks to the white car, and opens the driver side door.

She carries a large purse on her arm, which she transfers to the floor on the passenger side as she gets behind the wheel. After starting the engine, she changes from her work shoes into more comfortable sandals before putting her vehicle into reverse. She looks in her rearview mirror and notices that she is now blocked in, and the driver is exiting the vehicle. She rolls down her window and yells in frustration, "Hey, come on, move your car!"

Before she realizes it, Nick McLean is leaning down into her window.

"Audrey Richardson?" he asks.

After getting out of her car to speak with McLean, Ms. Richardson has a question for him before he even asks her anything.

"So you're defending that guy?" she asks.

"Yes, Mr. Flowers," he replies.

Richardson appears to be looking around anxiously as she speaks, almost afraid to continue talking with him. Recognizing this, he makes an offer. "If you want, we can go somewhere else and talk?"

She simply shakes off the suggestion and asks him another question. "Do you think they will find him guilty and send him to the electric chair?"

McLean finds her line of questioning rather peculiar, but continues to engage her. "I'm not sure what will happen but ..."

She cuts him off, "Do *you* think he really did it? You think he hurt that little girl?" she asks. Ms. Richardson continues to look around suspiciously as if she is not comfortable even talking about this case.

Trying to remain politically correct, McLean chooses his words carefully.

"I feel that there is more to the story, and that's why I'm here trying to fill in some of the blanks, and unanswered questions."

Richardson nods in agreement as if she is finally speaking with someone who shares her opinion.

"I think there is *A LOT* more to the story," she interjects in almost a whisper.

"What do you mean?" asks McLean.

"It just doesn't add up," she replies. "I think they got it all wrong."

McLean calmly opens his binder and prepares to get whatever he can from this woman. Again she looks around nervously before continuing.

"Listen, every morning I am the first one in the office. I turn on the office lights, AC, copier, and even start the first pot of coffee. You see that window right there?"

McLean looks over to where Richardson is pointing. One of two windows on the west side of the main office building that overlooks the staff parking area. She continues, "That's my office. So I see all the teachers and staff as they come in." She leans into McLean almost shoulder to shoulder and whispers out of the side of her mouth, "Did you know Mrs. Howell was playing *friendly* with the school deputy?"

McLean takes a step back in an attempt to regain his personal space. "I was told something along those lines, yes," he replies.

Richardson realizes that she is way too close to this man whom she doesn't even know, and also takes a step back.

"My bad," she offers apologetically before continuing. "Well, anyway, when I tell people that something is not right with this whole situation, they say I shouldn't make assumptions."

McLean inquires further for clarity. "What is it, exactly, that makes you say that?"

"Not just one thing," she replies. "It's when you put it all together ... when you sum it up, things just doesn't make sense."

McLean attempts to steer Ms. Richardson into being more direct. "So why don't you tell me what you mean? Things like what?" he pries.

Richardson places one hand on her hip, and uses the other to count off a list of items with her fingers. "Well first of all, she came in extra early the morning that her baby was found … you know …"

McLean sees that it is difficult for her to even say the word *murdered* so he tries to move her along.

"Right, OK," he acknowledges.

Richardson continues. "Right, and she's never in that early. None of the teachers really get in until closer to 7, 6:45 at the earliest. She was getting out of her car at 6:20. Not only that, do you notice that *all* of the staff members park their cars with the front toward the curb? That morning, not only did she *back* her car in, but she also took the very first spot, closest to the entrance. We usually leave the closer parking spaces for our older staff, like Mr. Cohen."

McLean writes this all down in his binder as she continues.

"Now she usually parks closer to the center of the lot next to the deputy's portable over there. I imagine this is so she can easily sneak in and out, if you know what I mean?"

McLean smiles, but only to appease Ms. Richardson. Another car drives past behind McLean's car and Richardson waves to one of her fellow coworkers before continuing.

"So, after backing her car into the parking spot, she stared at her phone for almost an entire two minutes before walking toward the main office … which, by the way, is *also* another thing that she has never done. I walked out into the reception area and there she was."

"Mrs. Howell?" inquires McLean.

Richardson nods affirmatively as she proceeds to give her account of the events as she remembers.

"I looked at the time, and I even made a comment as to her being in quite so early … before 6:30 even. She told me that she forgot to turn the clock back in her classroom before leaving for the weekend on that Friday."

McLean speaks out loud as he writes in his binder, "Daylight savings."

"Yes," Richardson continues. "We did gain an hour of sleep over the weekend, but she was still extra early. During that interaction, Mrs. Blake, the principal's secretary, came into the reception area. I left to go into my office, but I was still in ear shot and heard her."

"Mrs. Howell?" McLean asks for clarification.

"Yes," Ms. Richardson replies. "Brenda Howell asked Mrs. Blake if she knew what the time was. Not only did she and I just have a conversation about the exact time, but there is also a huge clock on the wall in the reception area. About two other people have also said that she asked them for the time that morning, and then she mentioned having to go take her daughter to daycare." Ms. Richardson refers to McLean's notes, "Are you getting all of this?"

"Yes, I am. Thank you," he replies.

Realizing that she has concluded her account, he asks her to write her contact information down. After she complies, he closes his binder and hands her his business card.

"Thank you. You have been very helpful. Here is my card. If you think of anything else, please don't hesitate to call me."

Richardson takes the card and replies, "No, thank *you*, sir. I've been saying something isn't right for weeks now, and finally found someone who doesn't think I'm crazy."

The two shake hands and return to their vehicles to go their separate ways—Audrey Richardson feeling like she has a huge weight lifted from her chest, and Nicholas McLean realizing how much heavier the weight of his workload is.

McLean pulls off from behind Richardson's vehicle and exits the school parking lot. As Richardson puts her car into reverse she is startled to see another car now blocking her. It is a silver sedan with dark tinted windows.

CHAPTER 8

It's another busy Thursday evening at the Local County Jail. All inmates receive visitation according to last name. Mondays and Thursdays seem to be the busiest of the week. With the visitor's waiting area almost completely maxed to capacity, the room is filled with chatter, crying babies, and the occasional yell from the correctional officers as they call out the last names of the next group of inmates up for scheduled visitation. Almost all of the visitors are female; mostly young minority mothers with their small, active children in tow. They wait patiently, listening to hear the name of their loved one to be announced. Almost all of them will be heading into the family room for contact visitation. Here they will sit at a table across from their family member, and the inmates can hold their young children. These are special privileges usually reserved for the inmates awaiting due process for minor, nonviolent offenses. For those with more serious charges, they must see their families in a locked booth with three-inch-thick glass between them, while speaking through an unsanitary telephone. It is here Ms. Hazel Flowers will be shuffled off to await when her son's name is called. She sits nervously in between a couple of heavyset women, who possess very little fashion sense, style, or class. Ms. Flowers clutches a small piece of paper that she tore from a notebook. On it she wrote down some encouraging words to read to her son. Words of encouragement and support from parents whose children attend her daycare center. Although she wants to see her son, Ms. Flowers gets major anxiety from the process. The very smell of this facility gives makes her nauseated.

As her son's name is called, Ms. Flowers walks up to the desk to be identified and screened—a process similar to airport security, with the added humiliation of a criminal-like frisking. As the correctional officer pats her down, a tear rolls down the anguished mother's face. After her screening, she is allowed to proceed down the hallway to the single booth where she then waits to see her son. She sits on the cold metal stool and clutches the piece of paper she brought with her. As she awaits the arrival of her son, she prays silently for strength. She needs to try to be upbeat as to not discourage him any further. It was only this past summer—less than six months ago—she was attending her son's college graduation ceremonies, followed by the live recording of his first music album. She recalls the happier, prouder moments to find inner peace in this time of emotional turmoil. When her son was only five years old he contracted a severe inner ear infection that rendered him legally deaf. Yet two years later, when he was only seven years old, she enrolled him into one of the most prestigious music schools in New York City, where they lived at the time. Algernon Flowers excelled in piano, and went on to not only win several awards for performance and original compositions, but he later earned himself a full music scholarship. The album he recently recorded was something he dreamed of and prepared for his entire life. His entrepreneurial nature inspired him to write, record, de- sign, produce and market his music by starting his own small entertainment label. He was a real mamma's boy who, even up until his arrest, lived in a room in his mother's suburban home. He loved his mother's cooking and would often bring friends over on Sundays when she would cook extra-large meals after she got home from church.

Ms. Flowers sits with her eyes closed as she continues to reminisce about the happier times in search of anything that will make this ordeal any less torturous. She has yet to see her son draped in the orange-colored, county correctional jumpsuit. She attempts to mentally prepare herself for that moment. Her eyes open and she immediately perks up as she hears the jingle of keys. She can see the doorknob turning inside the booth. She reaches to her left and retrieves the telephone from the wall. As the door opens, she is startled to see a man who is not her son. She is confused as the man sits down in the booth on the other side of the thick glass. She is frozen still in the awkwardness. The officer behind the inmate points behind Ms. Flowers, trying to indicate for her to look behind her. She obliges, and observes a woman with a small child walking up behind her. Down the short hallway, a husky female officer signals for Ms. Flowers to return to the screening area. Still confused, Ms. Flowers returns the telephone to the wall, gets up from the stool, allowing the woman with the small child to sit, and makes her way down the hall toward the female officer. As she gets within a few steps of the female officer, she is informed that her son cannot have visitation because he was just released from the suicide watch unit. This news is too much for the normally well-balanced woman. She requires medical assistance as she passes out underneath the stress.

After waking up on a stretcher in the visitor's foyer of the jail, Ms. Hazel Flowers is given cold water to drink. Two members of the jail's medical staff are present along with a male correctional officer.

"You are going to be fine ma'am," says one of the medical techs.

"Wait, why was my son in the suicide watch unit?" asks Ms. Flowers while trying to sit up and stand.

The medical technician assists her in sitting up. "Just take your time. Don't try to get up too quickly," he suggests.

Once back on her feet, she can see that a small crowd has gathered. She is slightly embarrassed, but her focus is elsewhere. "Can somebody give me any information on my son? Is he all right?" she cries.

The male corrections officer steps in closer. "He is, yes ma'am," he assures her. He looks at a clipboard with various inmate information as he continues. "Sorry, but I don't have any further information as to exactly why he was transferred to the suicide watch unit. It's only listed here as precautionary."

"Well when can I see him?" she asks.

"Looks like his next scheduled visitation is not until next week, Monday between 7 and 8 P.M.," he replies after checking the chart.

Under the dark, cloudy sky Ms. Flowers exits the Local County Jail. Tears roll down her face as she walks through the visitor's parking lot. When she gets to her vehicle, she sits in the driver's seat with the doors closed and windows up, clutching the steering wheel with the piece of paper still in one hand. She can't even muster the energy to start the engine. In the distance, past barbed wire fence, she can see what appears to be an area where the inmates are housed. Some small windows bear light. She wonders if her son is on the other side of one of the illuminated windows, and if he is being strong. She unfolds the piece of paper and reads the contents out loud in her car, as if he could hear the words. Her hope is that they would somehow supernaturally reach his heart and bring him peace. After reading the last of the encouraging messages, she concludes, "I love you, son ... we are all behind you." She wipes away her tears, starts her engine, and begins her drive home, where she will have to now put on another show of strength for the family waiting for a positive update on their beloved brother, uncle, nephew and friend.

CHAPTER 9

The clock on the dashboard of Nick McLean's SUV turns from 8:59 to exactly 9 P.M. He begins to drive. He maintains the speed limit, but occasionally goes five to seven miles above it. This is his third run this week. He is timing the driving distance between Mrs. Brenda Howell's apartment in South Rocky and the Rocky Beach residence where she picked up Mr. Algernon Flowers. Understanding that traffic times may vary, he makes his usual run at approximately 9 P.M., as that would be consistent according to the call log between Howell and Flowers. This is important, because in her statement to police, Howell states that on the night that she picked up Mr. Flowers, she left her daughter sleeping at home alone. McLean needs to recreate the drive to lock down the time it would have taken Brenda Howell to drive to pick up Mr. Flowers and then return to her apartment. So far, the shortest time round trip has been thirty-four minutes.

In McLean's passenger seat is one of his partners, Rachael O'Toole. Rachael is a thirty-six-year-old Irish woman with long, red hair, and rosy, chubby cheeks with just the right amount of freckles. She dresses comfortably in loose denim jeans with a matching jacket, and white running shoes. Her masculinity almost overpowers her femininity, yet her smile gives away her softer, tender side. Her right arm is resting on the rolled-down passenger window as she holds a stopwatch in her hand. Her left hand holds a small handheld video camera, which is facing out toward the windshield, recording the actual route Brenda Howell told homicide detectives that she took on the night in question.

During their run through, McLean receives a call on his cell phone. He checks the caller ID. It is lead defense attorney Michael Petagnas.

McLean answers, "Hey Mike. How is it going?" He listens and then responds, "OK, wow. I didn't see that coming."

Rachel silently indicates to McLean, who seems a bit distracted, not to miss his upcoming turn. He picks up on her cue and makes a left turn onto a poorly lit residential street and continues his phone conversation with Petagnas.

"Are you serious?" asks McLean with a grin.

Petagnas' next statement causes McLean to burst out with sarcastic laughter. Rachael stares at McLean with a puzzled and inquisitive look.

McLean, still focused on his current mission, quickly ends his conversation, "OK, you got it. I will go out there tomorrow and chat with him. Take it easy."

"What was that all about?" Rachael grills him right away.

"You won't believe this one … Brenda Howell is pregnant!" replies McLean.

Rachael's jaw drops in disbelief. "No way! Who's the father?" she asks.

"Well as far as what we know at this point, it could be any of three men," McLean replies.

"Do you think it could be Algernon?" asks a stunned Rachael.

"That would make for a very interesting trial," McLean jokes. "I am not looking forward to breaking this news to him tomorrow when I visit him at the jail. I can't imagine how this will impact him."

As they approach the Flowers' residence, Rachael looks at her stopwatch.

"OK, here we are ... Nineteen minutes," Rachel reports verbally as she records the time into a log notebook that sits on her lap.

"OK, now for the drive back to Howell's apartment," McLean announces as he pulls slightly into the driveway in order to turn back around on the narrow street. As they make the turn and head in the other direction, Rachael continues to monitor the stopwatch while periodically checking her frame in the camera's display.

"Wow, you know what, Nick?" Rachael pauses in mid-thought as she ponders this assignment they are currently on, and shares her personal thoughts with her partner. "I don't have any kids, but I can't imagine a mother or any parent leaving their three-year-old child home alone for any period of time."

McLean nods in agreement as she continues.

"I mean, now if she said she went out to her car for a minute to get something important, or even next door for something ... but not for this length of time ... and for what, to pick up her boyfriend, or lover or whatever? Very shady, Nicholas," Rachael states playfully.

Once again, McLean nods in agreement, "Very shady, indeed," he adds as his eyes literally light up while slowing his vehicle to a stop. Rachel turns her attention away from McLean to see what is causing the flashing red light.

"Should I keep the clock running?" she asks.

"Oh yes, you better keep that clock running," McLean replies.

In front of them, two large railroad crossing signs blink as two remote-controlled gate arms with flashing red lights collapse, blocking the road completely. The loud blare of a train's horn sounds as the ground begins to rumble. Rachael and McLean share eye contact and a smile as a symbolic high five. Suddenly a large freight train barrels along the tracks in front of them. McLean has to yell over the deafening noise as train car after train car passes by.

"Rachael, remember to find out how often this train passes this route weekly ... even better, find out if this train passed this route on the night in question!"

Rachael gives a thumbs up as she yells back, "Will do!"

She makes a note to remind herself of this newly assigned task in the notebook on her lap. The duo sits watching as the extremely long train passes by. Rachael raises her eyebrows and smiles as she holds up the stopwatch to McLean. The clock is still rolling, and it has already exceeded their previously recorded high time.

CHAPTER 10

It is sometime between breakfast and lunch. It's hard to tell the exact hour while sitting in the lockdown confines of A-Block on unit three here at the Local County Jail. One thing is certain, every moment drags on and feels like an eternity, except the thirty minutes of out-of-cell time. That seems to never be long enough. Here in cell number six located on the lower tier, Algernon Flowers stands in his cell holding a short golf pencil in his left hand. There are several pencil marks on the green brick walls. Inmate Flowers notches another one, indicating yet another day he is spending in this tiny cell assigned to him. He has no clue how many of these he will need, or if he should even bother to count. He has had very limited contact with the outside world and only knows the little his lawyer was able to share with him. Michael Petagnas has promised to file for a speedy trial, which would get him in front of a judge and jury within six months. Even that seems unbearable. To go from having a minor speeding ticket as the only experienced run-in with the law, to now being propelled into the role of murder suspect is a bit much for anyone. For Algernon Flowers, this is breaking his spirit and he doesn't know how he is going to last another night, much less the six long months awaiting trial. He nervously paces back and forth in the tiny space. This actually causes him more anxiety so he abandons the exercise and plops himself down on the hard bed. Looking up at the cracked, chipping paint on the ceiling, with its various brown water stains caused by the faulty plumbing in the cell above his, he tries to free his mind of any negative thoughts, which seems almost impossible. Perhaps when his commissary clears and kicks in, he can buy a book or some writing material to assist him in allowing his mind to escape his present predicament, even if only temporarily. The sounds of keys and doors slamming seem to echo and resonate throughout the halls in periodic waves, followed by the eerie silence in between. The first time Mr. Flowers heard that heavy iron cell door slam shut is something that will haunt him forever. Even still, he cannot get used to hearing that sound. His entire body trembles every time it happens. Unlike any sound he has heard before. This is a sound that he feels a few seconds after he hears it.

While he's lying on the bed, the heavy iron door begins to roll open. Mr. Flowers wasn't expecting to get his thirty minutes of out-of-cell time this early. He jumps to his feet, slides his county-issued sandals on and exits his cell. His first thought is to call his mother, for she must be worried-sick after not hearing from him in a couple of days. However, waiting outside his cell is a corrections officer who informs him that he has a visitor. Pleasantly surprised by this news, he eagerly follows the officer out of the unit and down the long hallway to the visitor's area of the facility. It is not until they pass the family visitation area and head toward the interview rooms that Algernon Flowers realizes that he isn't seeing his family, but his attorney. Not as rewarding, but at least he can send word to his loved ones through his legal counsel.

Before he is escorted into the interview room, inmate Flowers is patted down and searched, as is the custom whenever there is any contact visitation. This deters the spread of drugs and any other paraphernalia from getting into the jail. Once in the room, the door is locked from the outside by a corrections officer who remains vigilant and on standby. Mr. Flowers is surprised to see that it is not his attorney, but a tall stranger who stands to greet him.

"Mr. Flowers, my name is Nick McLean. Mr. Petagnas hired me and my team to head the investigation in your defense," declares the towering figure of a man.

McLean stands on his side of the table with his long arm extended. Algernon Flowers is a little apprehensive given McLean's police-like haircut and stature. Recalling Mr. Petagnas promising to hire a private investigator during their last meeting, Mr. Flowers reluctantly shakes McLean's hand, and sits down on his side of the table. Just being out of that tiny cell and having another human being to talk to is enough to lift his spirits. McLean also sits, and opens his binder. The private investigator looks across the table at the man whose life he is working diligently to save. Algernon Flowers looks worn and seems fidgety. McLean has to ask him some difficult questions, but doesn't want to add much more stress on the already emotionally spent young man.

"Nice to finally meet you, Algernon," McLean says before he is interrupted.

"Please, call me Al," Mr. Flowers interjects. "Can you please tell my mom that I am OK, and that I couldn't call her because they moved me? It's because I wasn't eating the slop they call food here," adds Mr. Flowers as he tries to make light of the situation.

"Sure, no problem at all. How are you holding up in here, Al?" McLean asks.

"As best as could be expected, I guess," replies Algernon Flowers.

McLean prepares himself before breaking the news of Howell's pregnancy. There is just no easy way to say it, so he decides on going with the 'ripping off a Band-Aid' approach.

"Al, there's that something Mr. Petagnas thought you should know," McLean begins.

Algernon Flowers can sense by McLean's tone and energy that this is probably some more bad news. He clearly still has feelings for Brenda Howell. He is concerned for her in all of this drama.

Algernon interrupts McLean, "Is it about Brenda? Is she OK?"

McLean visibly grimaces before he continues speaking.

"It does involve Brenda Howell. A reliable source told us that she is pregnant," states McLean.

The news throws Algernon Flowers for a loop. He is not sure what emotions he is experiencing. Naturally Mr. Flowers, being unaware that he was not Brenda Howell's only lover, assumes the child she now carries is his.

He remembers the day that Howell's daughter was pronounced dead, and the weeks before his arrest when he and Mrs. Howell continued their romantic relationship. While the authorities investigated the suspicious death, Brenda Howell moved out of her apartment, AKA the suspected crime scene, and moved to a small town where her parents live, approximately sixty miles away. The couple was discouraged from contacting one another. However, through a mutual friend, Howell would arrange meetings at hotels near and around the midway point of her parent's home and ground zero in Rocky Beach. During those romantic encounters, the forbidden lovers engaged in sexual activity on multiple occasions. In fact, it was during his way back from their last rendezvous that Algernon Flowers got the phone call on his cell that there was a warrant issued for his arrest.

There is more news, however, that will change his assumptions. McLean continues, "Also, when she told you that she moved in with her parents ... Well, it turns out that wasn't entirely true. She actually moved back into her old place with her husband, Detective Howell."

Algernon Flowers clutches his chest as if the gut-wrenching news is physically and literally breaking his heart. After a few deep breaths, Flowers breaks down and bursts into tears right in front of Nicholas McLean, as a tsunami of emotions overtakes the now mentally fragile young man. His mind flashes back to the past few weeks, and he comes to the very sad conclusion that he had indeed been taken for a ride by the woman who used seduction and manipulation to weave her web, and he got caught up in it. Still in a bit of denial, Mr. Flowers asks McLean, "Can I talk to her?"

McLean, who has 'been there/done that' when it comes to falling for his share of dishonest women, sympathizes with the distraught young man. He tries to help Mr. Flowers with the reality of the truth by speaking in a very brotherly tone.

"Al, I don't think it's a good idea for you to try to reach out to her. The truth is … the autopsy shows that the child's death was a homicide, and the DA wants someone to pay for that," McLean states firmly, yet with compassion. "Obviously they aren't looking at Brenda Howell as a suspect anymore. If she is as smart as I think she is, she will distance herself from you as to take no responsibility or any involvement."

These words appear to pierce Algernon Flowers as he drops his head to the table, sobbing in agony. The correctional officer standing guard just outside the door taps the window with a large brass skeleton key to get McLean's attention. McLean makes eye contact with the officer and waves him off as to indicate the situation is under control. McLean then returns his focus and attention back to Algernon Flowers. The blow caused by the information he has just received makes it difficult for Mr. Flowers to even lift his head off of the cool metal table. As it begins to settle in—the thought that he has undoubtedly been set up and left to rot in prison—Flowers breaks into a profuse sweat. He tries to gather himself together. As he lifts his head, he is difficult to look at. Between the tears streaming down his face, and mucus leaking from his nostrils, McLean has to offer him the handkerchief from his rear pants pocket in order to continue the interview. Flowers cleans his face and then lets out a very deep breath, gathering himself. There is a brief moment of awkward silence before McLean breaks it.

"Well, we are all working very hard on your behalf out there," he offers.

This makes Mr. Flowers smile, or at least the closest thing to a smile that he can muster.

"Thank you so much," responds a very humble and broken Algernon Flowers.

The tone shifts back to business as McLean shuffles through several pages in his binder.

"So, I know you have already told your story in the statement given to the police, but I am going to need you to recap the outline for my records, and then fill in some blanks for me. Is that cool?" asks McLean.

"Where should I begin?" replies Algernon Flowers.

McLean places an audio tape recorder in the center of the table and hits the red record button. Both men can see the mini audio cassette tape turning, and can almost hear it in the stillness of the moment.

McLean gets the ball rolling. "Let's start by telling me how you came to meet Brenda Howell."

CHAPTER 11

The mini audio cassette tape is rolling inside of Nick McLean's voice recorder in the center of the large wooden conference table at the Law Offices of Petagnas & Didia. The lead council, Michael Petagnas, sits at the head, while seated around the table is the entire defense team, including Nicholas McLean and his partner Rachael O'Toole. Seated in her usual spot directly next to Petagnas is Sandy Ward. Her reading glasses are on as she holds a transcript of Algernon Flowers' original and only statement given to police investigators during his initial interview. The room is completely still and silent, as the hiss of normal ambient room noise is heard coming from the running audio. A slight shuffle resembling the subtle movement of iron chair legs along a concrete floor is also heard coming from the recorder. The tension in the conference room is as a thick, low fog. Perhaps more of anticipation combined with nervous energy than tension, but all gathered around can feel it. The next sound heard is that of the man they have all been assigned to defend. His voice, weak and breaking at times, yet sure, as he reflects on the events that have altered his life during the past few months. Algernon Flowers gives his account:

"Well it was toward the end of August. I recently completed the cover of my CD. I had a few copies and was still awaiting the bulk order to be pressed. I gave a handful of them to some friends who participated and helped me with extra editing and vocals in the studio. One of those people was a friend from high school, Larry Thomas. Larry was also proud of the album since he did lead vocals on one of the songs. I guess he was letting some people listen to it. One of those people was his god-sister Brenda Howell. During their listening session, Brenda saw my photo on the album cover and inquired about me. Larry told her that I was single and on a sure path to becoming a legend in the music business. He approached me about her interest and we set up a date."

There is a slight pause in the recording before he corrects himself.

"Well not really, because it was the three of us—Larry, Brenda and I. We met at the twenty-four hour diner near the studio where I was working on packaging the CDs. I would say the 'date' went well, because there was a mutual attraction and we both seemed interested in seeing each other again. I mean, she was five years older than me, but didn't look a day over twenty-one. I thought she was pretty hot, and she made me feel like I was to her as well. So we went out a second time, but this time just the two of us. Again we hit it off and ended the night making out on the beach. I wasn't planning on things moving too fast, and not even sure where it was going to head, but at the time, it was a good and very welcomed distraction from all the hours I was putting in on the music project. Brenda was fun and knew how to use her sensuality ... it was her gift."

The memory is still fresh to Algernon, still palpable. The defense team hears it in his voice.

"At the end of our fourth or fifth date, as we were making out in the back of her car in the rain, she abruptly stopped everything and said she needed to tell me something. That was the first time she mentioned that she recently got divorced and that she had a three-year-old daughter. I'm not sure why she waited so long to bring that up. Perhaps she thought it would be a turn off for me, being a younger man. The truth is, I didn't care about any of that—especially not in the heat of that sexy, passionate moment.

"Anyway, the very next date was when she brought little Deja to meet me. We went to a family-style restaurant where they give the children coloring books and crayons and everything is family-friendly and bright. Such a cute little girl … and like Brenda, Deja and I hit it off great from day one."

A moment of silence plays on the recording, and the conference room fills with only the faint, static sound of the tape recorder's reels turning. The defense team waits silently for Algernon to continue.

"Eventually Brenda and I started seeing each other every day. Meeting for dinner in the evenings. Always out, never at her place. I wasn't sure why until one day she and her ex-husband got into a big fight. I mean things got pretty heated between them, according to Brenda. I suppose they were still living in the same apartment." He stops and corrects himself. "Well, let me rephrase that; she TOLD me that the reason they were still living together was because neither one of them wanted to move out and was trying to wait out the other. She said that argument was the last straw. She got a two-bedroom apartment in the city of South Rocky, and called me to help her move her things. So the next day I got my cousin Dwight to help, and we met her at the address she gave me. One of her girlfriends was also there to help with the moving. Her ex took Deja out of town to visit his family, so Brenda's thinking was that this was probably a good time to move without having a confrontation with him. About two days after she moved into her new place, she asked me if I wanted to spend the night there. I accepted the offer and before long I was sleeping over whenever I was not out of town promoting my album. We weren't officially living together, but I had a drawer and a nightstand. She eventually made a copy of house keys for me as well.

"After knowing her for two months and sleeping at her place for almost one of those months, things were moving pretty fast between the two of us. I would usually only go traveling during the weekends up until that point, but now at the end of October there was a big music conference in Nashville, Tennessee. I got an excellent opportunity to set up a table at this music event to sell my CDs and promote myself. It was where I could meet the right people that would invite my singers and me to travel all over the country doing what we loved. However, this would mean me going away for over a week. For the first time, Brenda would get a taste of what things would be like if I made it big. I would be traveling for various lengths of time, while she would be home alone. She was also a talented singer, so I think that's one thing we had in common, and at the same time, also something we couldn't really share. She was a school teacher and mother of a small child with shared custody. She couldn't just pick up and go on tour with a musical group.

"The deacon and pastor of a church I attended with my family were also going to this particular conference. They were driving and offered for me to ride with them. This was perfect for me because I wouldn't have to purchase a plane ticket and also pay to ship my merchandise. It all fit in their van.

"During that entire week when I was away, I got lots of calls and text messages from Brenda. It didn't seem excessive at the time. It felt like new relationship energy and excitement. That energy shifted into something else, though. I wasn't always able to answer her calls since I was working on my business. She became quite accusatory and would say she thinks I'm with other women. It just got weird. At first I thought the jealousy was, you know … cute. She must really like me, I thought."

Algernon halts. Ambient noise plays over the tape recorder. The defense team senses this is the turning point of his story.

"What made matters worse is that we were originally supposed to leave Nashville on Friday night, but the pastor received a last-minute invitation so we ended up staying later than expected. When I told Brenda that I would not be home by Saturday night, she hit the roof! She didn't believe my explanation for the change in schedule. The deacon ... Deacon George thought about us staying even one more day because he was too tired to drive. I knew this wouldn't go over too well with Brenda, so I volunteered to do all the driving. Although I was also pretty exhausted from the busy week I had, I drove the entire way from Tennessee to Rocky Beach. During the very lengthy trip I was getting many text messages from Brenda, as she grew more and more agitated. She kept questioning me as to where along the drive we were, and what time do I think I would arrive. The thing that really seemed to tick her off was when I gave her an ETA and then had to tell her that we stopped in Jacksonville to eat. She got really angry and accused me of lying about who I was with and what I was doing. She kept calling while we were at dinner and I wouldn't answer because I really didn't want to make a scene. That enraged her even more.

"After a long day on the road we finally made it back safely to Rocky Beach. I drove us to my mom's house, which is my actual address, and I saw that my car wasn't in the driveway. I then remembered that my sister asked to borrow my car since I was going to be away. So I got out of the pastor's van with my suitcase and the only box of CDs I had left. Deacon George took over behind the wheel. We said our goodbyes and they pulled off. I took my things to my room and I called Brenda and told her that I didn't have a ride to get over to her house until my sister returns, but I would have to call her to see how late she will be. Brenda told me not to worry about calling my sister, and that she is on her way to come and pick me up.

"I heard the shower running in my mom's bathroom and I wanted to leave before she got out and started asking me about my trip because she hadn't met Brenda yet. I don't think my mom would have approved of me dating an older woman who was divorced. My mom is really religious and into the beliefs of the church. In order to avoid the awkward introduction, I actually waited out at the side of the garage for Brenda to arrive.

"When Brenda arrived to pick me up, I got in her car and leaned in to greet her with a kiss, but she didn't really lean back in. Instead she began to reverse her car out of the driveway and started driving. I believe her exact words were, 'We have to hurry—I left her home in bed.' I remember turning around and seeing Deja's car seat empty. I don't recall my exact response but I basically asked her why she didn't bring her. She told me that Deja had not been feeling well and that she didn't want to wake her. So we drove back to her apartment. I don't think Brenda said anything else the entire drive back. I was doing all of the talking about the productive week I had and how many CDs I sold. I was happy to keep talking and avoiding an argument about the texts back and forth between us. It was like ignoring both the elephant in the room ... and the toddler that's not in the car."

Algernon's voice is near breaking. The defense team hears the raw emotion, the betrayal. And something else. Pain that is still fresh and raw, like a bleeding wound.

"Upon our arrival at her place, Brenda parked her car and we walked up the flight of stairs to the second floor landing. As soon as she opened the door and we stepped inside, she attacked me ... not like a fight, but passionately ... sexually. She pulled me quickly down the hall to her bedroom. I recall passing Deja's room. The door was cracked open slightly and I could see that the night light was on. When we got into Brenda's room, she closed the door and undressed me by the bed. Then she undressed herself and we fell onto the bed.

"After making love, we lay together for a brief moment to catch our breath and to enjoy the pulchritude of simultaneous mutual climax. Brenda got up and told me she has a surprise. On our first official date, I decided to try a mango and coconut frozen drink that our waiter suggested. It was delicious, but when we went back to that restaurant we found out that they only make it on certain days of the month. Her surprise was that she got the recipe online and wanted to make me one of the frozen drinks at home. She told me to go shower and relax. So I did. When I got out of the shower, she was standing right outside the bathroom door fully naked, holding this colorful frozen drink. She offered it to me, and as I stood there sipping it she pulled the towel from around my waist and … well, she went down … you know, orally. So that led to us getting back in bed and having sex again. After the second time, she handed me the glass with the leftover drink and told me to chug it and she will make me another one. So I did. She left with the empty glass to go to the kitchen and I got up to put on a pair of boxers and a T-shirt.

"After getting dressed I decided to peek in on Deja. As I began to step into her room, I got close enough to see the back of her head as her face was toward the wall. As I got closer to where I could see the side of her face, I noticed something. On her pillow, coming out of her mouth was a little pool or puddle … like she threw up some dark-brown stuff. Before I could take another step closer, Brenda came up behind me and said 'Hey, don't disturb her.' I informed her that it looks like Deja threw up. Brenda replied saying, 'Oh yeah she was sick all weekend. I fed her Salisbury steak and she threw it up earlier also.' She then handed me another full glass of the frozen drink and told me to go to bed and relax, and that she will clean Deja up.

"So I left Deja's room and went back into Brenda's room. I was on the bed … well more like sitting up in the bed drinking the frozen drink. I think I must have fallen asleep because the next thing that I remember, I woke up to shuffling noises. I turned over and Brenda was already dressed for work. She was pulling up her stockings and putting her shoes on. It was still pretty dark outside, as the sun didn't even rise yet. I don't always sleep in at her place on weekdays, but I know it seemed rather unusual for her to leave that early for work. So I asked her, why was she up so early? She told me that she forget to do some things in her classroom so she needed to go in early before her first class. With that said, she hustled out and closed the bedroom door. I went back to sleep.

"About an hour and a half later she called me and said that she was downstairs in the parking lot and wanted me to wake Deja up and bring her down to the car. This was when I first realized that she didn't take Deja with her like she would normally do. I was surprised. I asked her, 'Is Deja still here?' Brenda responded and said that she didn't want to wake her too early since she had not been feeling well the past few days.

"When I went into Deja's room to wake her, she was cold to the touch … and her … her skin was pale … and her lips were blue. I knew something was wrong and my first instinct was to pick her up, but then I thought it best to call 9-1-1. So I grabbed the cordless phone and ran outside to the top of the landing and called out for Brenda. I said, 'I think there is something wrong with Deja.' Brenda exited her car and came upstairs."

CHAPTER 12

Nick McLean presses the STOP button on the recorder. He ejects the mini audio cassette tape, and replaces it with another similar one. As McLean prepares to play the rest of Algernon Flowers' account, Sandy Ward speaks up from her seat next to lead council Michael Petagnas.

"So far his statement is pretty much word for word the same as the one that he gave to police," she says as she flips through the transcript of Flowers' original interview with police.

Michael Petagnas nods in agreement and replies, "He is very consistent, and also very articulate. He will make an excellent witness in his own defense at trial if necessary."

Petagnas sees that McLean has the next audio cassette ready and instructs him to continue, "All right, go ahead Nick."

Off of Petagnas' cue, McLean presses play and the entire defense team that is gathered around the conference table listens closely to the rest of Algernon Flowers' account:

.   .   .

"When Brenda entered Deja's bedroom, she scooped her up and carried her into the living room and kitchen area, where she then placed her onto the floor. Brenda was crying and Deja was limp and lifeless. At this point I'm already on the phone with 9-1-1. The dispatcher was talking me through performing CPR on Deja as we waited for the ambulance to arrive. Brenda stood by watching as I tried my best to do exactly what the dispatcher instructed me to do. It seemed like an eternity passed before the ambulance finally arrived. When they got there, they took over and I stood by Brenda. The paramedics then asked Brenda what happened, and she replied that Deja had been sick all weekend. They eventually placed Deja on a stretcher and carried her down to the ambulance. A female South Rocky Police officer showed up also. Brenda and I rode with the officer to the hospital behind the ambulance.

"When we arrived at the hospital, we were not permitted to go into the room where they were treating Deja. We were in a waiting area and some of Brenda's coworkers started showing up in support. It wasn't very long before a doctor came out of the room. It was a familiar face, too. Doctor Richard Mason is a friend of my mom. He happened to be filling in for another doctor in the emergency room that morning. He came out and approached Brenda and the rest of us standing around waiting. He gave us all the bad news that Deja was ... That they could not save her."

A pause and complete silence.

"We were all in disbelief. It was very hard to swallow those words. Everyone was crying. Doctor Mason saw me and asked me if I knew what happened to Deja. I told him that her mom said she was sick for a couple of days. He then asked me if I knew anything about the bruising on her lower abdomen. I had no idea what he was talking about. He went on to inform me that right below her belly button, Deja had some bruising. They didn't see them until they removed her toddler pull-up underwear, which sits high above the belly button. I told him that I didn't know anything about it ... I didn't even think about this at the time, but the last time I actually saw Deja was before I left to go to Tennessee. She was asleep the night I got in, and then the next morning ... Well, she just never woke up.

"After Dr. Mason mentioned the bruises to me, he excused himself and left the waiting area. Brenda asked me to go in with her to see Deja. It was not easy to see her little body just lying there ... Very sad." The defense team hears Algernon swallow hard. "The worst thing I ever had to witness.

"Upon returning to the waiting area, the crowd of supporters had grown significantly. Among them was the Rocky Beach Police chaplain. Since Deja's father is a police officer in his department, he got the call to come out to the hospital. He hugged Brenda and told her that Officer or Detective Howell was about three hours away on assignment, and that he will break the news to him as soon as possible.

"Brenda and I got a ride back to her apartment with one of her coworkers. Some of them stayed over at the apartment for support. Brenda kept telling everyone that Deja had been really sick. At one point Brenda went to go to the bathroom. I finally had her alone so I followed her and let her know that Dr. Mason asked me about bruises on Deja. Brenda said that they were probably from the EMTs doing CPR incorrectly on such a frail young child. She just sort of brushed it off, so I didn't think about it until later that afternoon when two investigators came to the apartment. They wanted Brenda to go with them to give a statement. She asked them if I could accompany her for support. They didn't have a problem with that.

"We rode along with the two investigators to a building near the pier. They took Brenda to a back room and had me wait in the lobby. After about an hour or so, they came out and asked me to come to the back. They put me in a different room and let me know that the building we were in was for a special task force of investigators. They went on to inform me that this was officially considered a homicide investigation. That was the first time I realized that this death was actually a murder."

The last word hangs in the air for a moment.

"Their questions were basic at first. Asking me about my relationship with Brenda, and Deja. They also wanted to know what time I got in the night prior, and did I actually see Deja move on her own when Brenda cleaned her up. They even asked me if I ever saw Brenda punish or abuse Deja. I totally defended her because the truth is I hadn't witnessed more than a little spanking on the buttocks or legs ... nothing too drastic, so I didn't mention it. They asked me if I knew how Brenda broke her fingernail and if she always wears her large rings.

"After a few questions of that nature they left, I assume to return to question Brenda further. They asked me to wait in that interview room. They later returned to ask me more questions, but this time the tone and energy shifted. They seemed to be suggesting that I knew more than I was saying. Asking me if I was protecting Brenda. Then they got personal and began to ask if I knew that her husband is a detective, and what do I think he is going to say about my relationship with his wife. I guess they were trying to intimidate me. They asked me if I knew that she was arrested for domestic violence against her husband. I didn't know if they were making it all up. I was offended when they kept asking very personal questions about our sex life. One of them said that she was probably just using me. They even went on to suggest that either I was covering for Brenda out of love, or maybe I had something to do with it. That was when I ended the interview. They wouldn't allow me to see Brenda. They kept her there. I had to call for a ride home.

"It wasn't until later that night that I was able to get in touch with Brenda on her cell phone. She actually appeared frustrated with the police saying it was an entire mess—suggesting that if the paramedics performed improper techniques and caused injuries to Deja, then they are responsible for her death. This would result in a major lawsuit, so they have to cast the blame elsewhere. She also said that the detectives, her ex-husband's buddies, were trying to make her look like a bad parent. She said she was going to stay with her parents out of town to get away for a while."

Algernon's tone shifts on this last sentence. The defense team knows this is because he is revealing one of Brenda's deceitful lies.

"The next time I heard from her was through a mutual friend, Larry, saying it's probably not a good idea for me to attend Deja's funeral because her ex and his family think that I had something to do with what happened. I couldn't believe it. I couldn't understand how I got caught up in this. It was a painful feeling ... people thinking you are even capable of such a horrendous thing. In fact, there was an article about Deja in the newspaper the day after she was pronounced deceased, and they were suggesting that both Brenda and I were suspects. I was floored. They were using terms like 'child abuse' and 'beating death.' All the while Brenda is telling me that it's not true, and that it's just her ex trying to ruin her.

"Over the following weeks, it was as if we were forbidden to see each other or be seen together. The rumors started swirling around that either one or both of us had some involvement in hurting Deja. I would say that depending on whom you talk to, initially a majority of the rumors were about Brenda having a hand in her own daughter's death. Basically I couldn't be seen meeting with Brenda because they would think that we were conspiring and comparing notes to cover our tracks. She said that she couldn't call me because the police have her phone bugged, and her fear was that they would twist anything she says to use against her.

"She would send messages through our mutual contact, the man who introduced us in the first place, Larry Thomas. As her god-brother, he would go see her without arousing suspicion, and then come back to me with a neutral meeting place.

Usually a hotel halfway between her parents hometown and Rocky Beach.

"Every time we would meet up, I asked her about what is going on and she would always assure me that once they investigate thoroughly and objectively, then they will know that we had nothing to do with it. That was it ... she never said much else about it. If I brought it up, she would change the subject. Almost as if she thought I was wearing a wire. Actually she would prefer that we both strip naked and take a shower together. The shower was the place she felt was the safest to talk. Most of the time she would just want to talk about how much she missed me and then we would make love.

"After a couple of hours of love making, we would have to both go our separate ways. It was like something out of a spy movie ... talk of being bugged and watched, and we couldn't even be seen leaving together. Registering rooms under aliases or her god-brother's name. How long was this expected to go on? Well after our last tryst, which was actually an overnighter, as I was on my way back to Rocky Beach, I received a phone call saying that there was a warrant out for my arrest. So I turned myself in to the South Rocky Police, and now here I am."

. . .

Nicholas McLean stops the audio recorder. The silence in the conference room begins to give in to light chatter amongst colleagues comparing notes and opinions. The room is soon brought back to order by Steven Didia, who is seated across from Sandy Ward, on the other side of Michael Petagnas.

"OK folks, let's call it lunch," he says as he looks at the clock on the wall.

With that order he stands and buttons his suit jacket. The rest of the team around the table also begins to leave as they continue to talk among themselves. Nick McLean and his partner Rachael O'Toole meet Michael Petagnas and Steven Didia by the conference room door.

"I hear you guys have been quite busy," Petagnas says with a smile.

McLean and Rachael reply, using only their confident smiles in return.

"Well I'm starving, let's talk about it over lunch," concludes Petagnas as they all exit the completely vacated conference room.

CHAPTER 13

It has been over two weeks since the arrest of Algernon Flowers, and here at the Law Offices of Petagnas & Didia his defense team works around the clock on what is, by the second, becoming a more intriguing case. Only two days until Christmas but not even the festive decorations, eggnog or holiday music can distract those who hold the task of defending a man accused and charged with the murder of a child. Needless to say this isn't the most popular case, but possibly one of the most challenging in the firm's history. Even with the order of all hands on deck for this case, the workload is exhausting. Among the greatest of challenges is finding valuable witnesses. As Michael Petagnas goes through the notes of his lead private investigator, he has mixed feelings and some concerns.

As a former prosecutor, Petagnas recalls his time with the district attorney's office. He has seen many witness lists and discovery, and he's always understood how any prosecutor worth his or her weight in gold would approach each scenario by using whatever angle possible. During his tenure at the Local County DA's office, Michael Petagnas was heralded as one of the greatest trial attorneys to ever go before a judge. After retiring with a one-hundred percent conviction rate, he left very little doubt that he was a force to be reckoned with. Being so respected in the legal community, he trained and mentored so many. It is this fact that can actually work to his disadvantage. For now the man whom he will face across the aisle is one of his former subordinates—one he himself trained and mentored. Mr. Petagnas was notorious for making any defendant look like the most heinous monster to ever breathe, and it has been said that during his opening statement to begin a trial, some defendants wave the white flag and beg for a plea deal. Petagnas has no doubt that this litigation prowess has rubbed off on his successor. It is already an uphill battle to present a man that is charged in the killing of a child before a jury without them viewing him as anything but a monster. The only thing more difficult would be suggesting that the actual monster is the child's biological mother, but that is what the initial report of investigator Nick McLean supports so far. Petagnas would rather have any other alternate theory.

Although Mr. Petagnas is well respected in the district attorney's office, he is not as equally admired. From those he passed over for promotions back when he was their boss, to the prosecutors he embarrassed and exposed for their unpreparedness during trials since becoming a defense attorney, there are many that have an axe to grind with Mr. Michael Petagnas.

Among the top of his list of concerns, Michael Petagnas is not getting much cooperation from the police or prosecution as it relates to obtaining evidence in a timely manner. Mr. Algernon Flowers begged his attorney to file for a speedy trial, however one of the very tricks used by Petagnas himself as a prosecutor was to play the "keep away up until the last possible moment" game. The last thing that he wants to do is fall into the prosecutor's trap of filing the motion for speedy trial and then get ambushed with truck loads of witness lists, transcripts and discovery to sort through with little time to prepare. So against his client's request, Petagnas finds it in Mr. Flowers' best interest to wave his right to a speedy trial.

Another of Petagnas' concerns would be the threatening phone calls and death threats he is receiving. On the afternoon that Mr. Flowers turned himself in to authorities, he was placed in a cell at the station where they held him until 6 P.M. so that the most-watched news segment would be on live as they paraded the handcuffed, frightened young man in front of the cameras. This is a good story for the South Rocky police chief who is up for re-election to be seen as responsible for the apprehension of an alleged child murderer. Even one of the chief's close associates, a local news reporter, was given a promotion for breaking the story. Recently here in Local County, less than a month before this case, there was a special task force put together. This task force consisted of investigators from over fifteen local, state and federal agencies. The purpose was to assist in investigations of major crimes and some cold cases. The indictment against Algernon Flowers is the very first the investigation unit has brought to the grand jury. They are going to want this to stick. Due to the heavy political implications and media surrounding this case, Petagnas is concerned for the safety of his family and those of his staff.

As Michael Petagnas sits in his office, he gets a visit from Steven Didia. Although Didia usually always carries his 'down to business' demeanor, Petagnas can tell that he didn't come bearing glad tidings of great joy for the holidays. Steven Didia leans up against Petagnas' desk and folds his arms as he addresses his partner.

"So the two witnesses that Nick spoke with, well now they're not speaking. In fact, Deborah Long lawyered up!" exclaims a frustrated Didia.

"What? How about the woman at the school office?" asks Petagnas.

"Audrey Richardson? Well something or someone spooked her really well ... poor girl quit her job, disconnected her cellphone and moved out of town. No one even knows how to reach her," Didia replies.

This is exactly the other thing on the top of Michael Petagnas' list of concerns ... not only valuable witnesses, but valuable *cooperating* witnesses. Didia and Petagnas can only look at each other and share a smile—one of dual meaning. This smile represents both frustration and acceptance of the challenge.

Didia turns and walks to the door. "Well, happy holidays!" he yells as he exits.

CHAPTER 14

Every year for as long as he can remember, Algernon Flowers has spent Christmas Eve trimming the tree with his family as his mother serves warm, homemade bread. After the ceremonial crowning of the tree with the bright star, Algernon plays carols on the piano. He is spending this Christmas Eve locked inside a tiny jail cell. In an attempt to boost his spirits and exercise his creativity, he is decorating by making his own tree made of empty silver candy wrapping paper and a cardboard spool from a roll of toilet paper. There is no piano for carols—none of mom's warm, fresh homemade bread—no family, and no holiday cheer. Perhaps this tree, though pitiful as it may be, is the only family tradition he can maintain this year. That is enough to motivate Algernon to complete his small but sentimental task. With several holiday cards laid out and open all around him, he sits on the floor of his cell concentrating on his masterpiece. However, just like the cards and letters from family and friends around him, the tree only creates more of a depressed feeling within him. Correspondence is said to be a good thing for inmates as contact with the outside world, but for Algernon Flowers they only serve as torment and a representation of the life he may never know again.

Beyond the stigma that a murder charge carries, the feeling of being falsely accused and having everything—life, family and career—stripped away, far surpasses in a way that only few can understand.

After doing the best he can to transform the limited objects he has to work with into a makeshift Christmas tree, Algernon uses dabs of toothpaste as an adhesive to stick the holiday greeting cards and family photos against the back of the iron cell door. By placing them on the door, when he looks at the thing binding him to this cell, he can see the people and things that are keeping him grounded and strong. It is also the best position to remain in eyeshot from the bed. As he lies down and stares interchangeably between the tiny silver paper tree in the corner by the door and the family photos, the lights go out for lockdown. He continues to hold his gaze in hopes that his eyes will adjust to the darkness, and he can fall asleep on Christmas Eve to the images of his family.

Christmas Eve at Hazel Flowers' home isn't the same, either. She couldn't even put up a tree this year. Even as her other children come to visit and bring her grandchildren; there is lots of love surrounding her. However this only makes her wish her youngest son Algernon were home to share some of the abundance. She knows that her homemade bread is his favorite, so she baked a loaf and cut an extra think slice, which she places in a small plate and sets on the top of the maple upright piano that her son plays every year on this usually joyous night.

In the home of Michael Petagnas, he and his wife Shelly sit on a couch in their living room wrapping gifts for their two young children. As the children sleep in their bedrooms, the sound of a crackling fire can be heard coming from the fireplace in the den. Mr. and Mrs. Petagnas exchange playful banter and joke about family and the stress that comes with the holiday season. One thing they do not talk about is Mr. Petagnas' current case, as he is hoping this short break can be the much-needed distraction from one of his biggest cases on the defense side of the aisle. He tries not to get too emotionally attached to clients, but there is something about this case that just pulls him in. He would almost rather prosecute a guilty man and lose, than to defend an innocent man and lose.

This Christmas Eve private investigator Nicholas McLean is sitting at the international airport. The place is crowded and a bit hectic as many last-minute travelers try to visit loved ones for the holidays. There are holiday decorations, music and even a Santa for the children at this terminal. Some stranded passengers sleep in chairs and on the floor. As for McLean, he missed his flight to Chicago and now has to fly standby. He has one more chance to get a seat assignment on the final outbound flight of the evening. McLean has been so busy this year that he has yet to visit his only sister and her husband. There are only two seats remaining on this next flight but he is next on the list. In his hand he holds a green gift bag, containing something he more than likely picked up at a gift shop here at the airport ... On his shoulder, a navy blue duffle bag, and on the floor between his feet, a small rolling suitcase. There is an announcement for general boarding and those with seat assignments. At the ticket counter, McLean overhears a couple pleading with the gate attendant. They are trying to get home to Chicago for Christmas but there is only room on the plane for one of them. The couple is told they will have to wait for the first flight out in the morning if they wish to travel together. The attendant then calls for Nick McLean to get his seat assignment so he can begin boarding. He gathers his luggage and walks eagerly toward the gate, while looking at the disappointed faces of the traveling couple.

.   .   .

After ringing the doorbell, McLean stands at the beige and brown door and waits. When it opens, Hazel Flowers is surprised to see the tall man standing in her doorway offering a green gift bag. She welcomes him in to meet Algernon's siblings, nieces and nephews. Nick McLean can feel the strong bond and family connection they all share with Algernon. He also gets lots of eggnog and fresh, hot homemade bread.

CHAPTER 15

With the start of a calendar year comes the positive expectation, and great anticipation as business gets back into full swing following the holiday break. Schools and businesses reopen, gyms and fitness facilities see spikes in membership, and CPAs prepare for another busy tax season. A time when diet and workout goals are still on track, and people have not yet gotten accustomed to writing the new year in their checkbooks. The adjustment into newness brings on the excitement of change and self-improvement. Here in Rocky Beach, this New Year brings the best and worst out of political candidates seeking to run for office or re-election. For Local County District Prosecutor David Edwards, who has been in office for less than one full term, his goal for the New Year is to maintain his position by being re-elected over his opponent Nancy Groover. Prosecutor Edwards took over for the former Prosecutor Rodney Briggs, after Briggs' failing health forced his early retirement. As Briggs' second in command, David Edwards by default stepped into the very powerful position. During his time as interim district attorney, Prosecutor Edwards has won many trials but hasn't come across any high-profile cases. When the case of Algernon Flowers came across his desk, Edwards knew right away that this was going to make his career. The child of a Rocky Beach police detective and an elementary school teacher being the victim of a vicious beating, and the accused murderer was involved in a romantic relationship with the mother of the victim. This had everything a big, high-profile case should: sex, violence, and an innocent life being taken way too soon. This was a formula for automatic re-election. By bringing the accused killer of this innocent child to justice, Edwards would be viewed as the face of justice by the voters in the Local County jurisdiction. In the same vein, failure to bring justice in this very sensitive case would almost guarantee his defeat in the coming election. The case should be a slam dunk, since any jury will want to see someone pay for what happened to the young victim. One concern for Edwards, however, is the person who held the office before Prosecutor Briggs. That person is Michael Petagnas.

As Prosecutor David Edwards walks into the Local County Prosecutor's Office building, he uses his ID card to buzz himself through the turnstile next to the security post. His polished leather dress shoes have wooden soles that echo through the marble corridor with each step he takes toward the elevator. His navy suit is accented with silver threads outlining the lapel of the single-breasted jacket. He carries a leather briefcase that is worn out by its heavy usage. His face is clean-shaven and his fingers freshly manicured. Now in his late forties, his once full, thick hair has fallen victim to male pattern baldness. However, he still maintains the lining of his sideburns and the back of his neck.

Prosecutor Edwards exits the elevator on the fourth floor and walks to his large corner office with a spectacular view of the harbor. He places his briefcase on the glass top of his desk, and unbuttons his jacket for comfort before sitting in his high-back leather chair. He logs on to his desktop computer and checks his schedule. He has depositions scheduled in the morning, followed by a lunch meeting with State Attorney Prosecutor Ramon Henderson. Henderson will serve as co-council during the Algernon Flowers murder trial since it is a capital first-degree felony, in which both the state and county are involved.

First on the agenda, a deposition with Earl Wallace, the first emergency medical technician to arrive on the scene on the morning that little Deja Howell was found unresponsive. His testimony is crucial and Prosecutor Edwards knows that his former boss—the man who taught him everything he knows, will be present and looking for holes in this witness' testimony. Edwards has to tread carefully as not to expose any weaknesses in his case. Edwards reads his files on Earl Wallace to go over what he initially told police. Any inconsistencies will create areas that the very skillful trial attorney Michael Petagnas can attack.

As Prosecutor Edwards works at his desk, he gets a visit from one of his paralegals, Jennifer Forde. Jennifer is a young, attractive blonde and recent law school graduate. Landing a job here at the district prosecutor's office is a great way to jump-start her career in law. She works full time while studying for the state bar exam. The Algernon Flowers murder case is not only her first, but also one that will most certainly be influential throughout her legal career. She will be sitting in on the deposition with Earl Wallace. As she enters the room, her confidence exudes from her like the fragrance of her perfume. Her extreme intelligence and breathtaking good looks force her to 'dumb it down' a notch at times in order to not further intimidate the older men she works for. Often afraid to give her opinion for fear that it will create tension and produce problems for her, she would rather just go with the flow and fly under the radar. However, as a part of her new year's resolution, she intends to speak up without fear. As she approaches her boss, her nerves cannot be hidden even beneath her extremely confident nature.

Jennifer Forde opens with a greeting. "Happy new year, Mr. Edwards."

Prosecutor Edwards doesn't even give her the courtesy of looking up from his work while responding.

"Thanks, same to you," he replies.

Jennifer continues to attempt small talk to both win over her boss, and buy herself more time to work up the courage to address something on her mind.

"How was your holiday? Do anything fun?" asks Jennifer with more humility than sincerity.

Still not looking up from his work, Prosecutor Edwards keeps his interaction with his young paralegal strictly business-related.

"Are you prepared for the deposition with the EMT?" he asks.

A little insulted, but maintaining her humility, she responds respectfully, "Yes, sir."

Edwards says nothing further. He keeps working at his desk, almost ignoring her presence. Picking up on his vibe, she holds her ground. She clearly has something on her mind and refuses to be ignored, even if it costs her this job.

"Mr. Edwards, you know I spent my entire break reviewing some of the evidence and statements in this case and I have to say ..."

Prosecutor Edwards cuts her off in mid-sentence.

"Jessica, I'm glad that you have the work ethic to do homework during your break, but as you can see I have a lot of work to do here."

His dismissive tone offends her.

"It's Jennifer," she corrects him boldly yet respectfully.

She turns to exit but then has second thoughts. She is not leaving without expressing her opinion and thoughts that she feels should be valued, no matter her age, gender or experience. The young paralegal turns back to face Edwards with even more boldness.

"Look, sir, I don't mean to come off as disrespectful. That is not my intention, but I will like to be heard."

Prosecutor Edwards stops what he is working on, sits back in his chair with a frustrated look on his face. He challenges her with obnoxious sarcasm.

"Well, go on. What is it that you feel is more important than this case we're working on … this case where a little girl was beaten to death? Go ahead, what have you been thinking with your what—a whole entire eight months out of law school?" he spits rudely.

Jennifer feels deflated and a bit belittled, but wants to speak her mind.

"Well sir, that's just it. I don't think this case is that open and shut. I mean …"

Edwards cuts her off again. "Listen, how long have you been trying murder cases?"

Getting the point, Jennifer doesn't answer as she absorbs the low blow from the seasoned prosecutor.

"Exactly. That's what I thought." Edwards continues, "It's not always about what you think, it's about what you can prove."

Jennifer is taken aback. "So are you saying …"

Edwards cut her off again.

"Do you think my job is easy?" asks Edwards as he stands and offers her his seat. "Do you think you can do it better?"

Jennifer doesn't respond. Realizing how much she has agitated her boss, she decides to let it go. However, Edwards isn't ready to end this conversation without resolve.

"Do you think I have any say in what cases come through my office? I don't get to choose the evidence, the suspects, or the victims. I have to go on what I'm given. Do you know what I'm given here?" he barks.

Jennifer knows that question is just rhetorical so she doesn't respond.

Edwards continues his rant. "Well, I will tell you what I am given here … a dead three-year-old girl, and my only choice of potential suspects is A–the little girl's mother who just so happens to be an elementary school teacher and the wife of a local police detective, or B–some guy that the mother was screwing for a couple of months who has no ties to the community or the child. This office I hold is responsible for bringing criminals to justice ... the people expect justice ... that little girl deserves justice. What are you suggesting, that I bring this grieving mother to trial and ask a jury of her peers to convict her—a mother—of such an unspeakable act? Now you tell me, what is it about the evidence here that you don't like? Or perhaps you have some evidence that makes my job any easier?"

Jennifer gives up. There is no breaking through to this stubborn man who is clearly unraveling beneath the pressure of this case. With only circumstantial evidence at best, anything contrary she offers at the moment will only fuel his rage further. She wisely lets it go.

"No, sir, not at all. I will meet you downstairs for the deposition," she concludes as she exits quickly.

A frustrated David Edwards plops back into his chair and throws his pen across the room in anger. He's not even completely sure why he is this upset.

CHAPTER 16

Private investigator Nicholas McLean leaves the Hot Shot shooting range and gets into his SUV. He tucks his small, concealed handgun into his waistband. This is the first time in years that he has fired his gun. In fact, this is the first time in years he even feels the need to carry his firearm. However, after potentially being followed on several occasions over the past month, he feels it is in his best interest to get reacquainted with carrying again. It is better to have and not need, than to need and not have.

This being the first day of the new school semester, McLean is heading out to the Richard M. Weinstein Elementary School where Brenda Howell worked. After losing a potentially good witness in Audrey Richardson, who seemed to vanish into thin air, McLean is planning to speak with the school deputy, Ronald Garzero. Hopefully he can shed some more light on the state of mind or intentions of Mrs. Brenda Howell. Any insight into her complex personal life would help steer him in the right direction. On his way to the school, McLean stops at a coffee shop nearby. After all, he is going to try to get some information from a law enforcement officer, and the best way to a cop's heart is with donuts.

Upon arriving at the school, McLean learns that Deputy Garzero requested to be reassigned to another school district in the county. Also, like Deborah Long, the handsome deputy retained a lawyer and refuses to cooperate without a court order. McLean and his investigative team have been running into roadblock after roadblock from day one. He decides to call a meeting with his team to discuss strategy.

. . .

In the private investigative office of McLean & Partners, Nick McLean sits with Rachael O'Toole, and two other investigators, Helena Wang and Brent Patterson. Helena Wang is a twenty-nine-year-old Asian female who specializes in computer science and technology. She also speaks four different languages. Brent Patterson is a thirty-six-year-old African-American male who is a former Navy SEAL and holds a degree in psychology. They share intelligence, and strategize over coffee and breakfast muffins.

Rachael O'Toole opens the dialogue. "Well, according to the train schedule, there was definitely a freight train that passed along the route that Howell claims she took to pick up Algernon on the night in question. This would push the time that she left Deja alone upwards of fifty minutes to an hour, easily."

Helena Wang adds, "When I checked the cell records, her phone was pinging from the South Rocky tower during that last call between her and Algernon Flowers. So she probably wasn't expecting him to need a ride, she was definitely at or near her apartment during that 8:58 P.M. call. There was also another call made from her phone to an office line at the Rocky Beach Police Department."

McLean makes a note of this as Helena continues.

"So if her husband was three hours away like the chaplain said, who was she calling at the station and why? If she's rushing to pick up Mr. Flowers, and get back to her sick sleeping child, what could that call be about?"

McLean questions, "How long was that call, Helena?"

Helena looks at her records, "Only a few seconds ... probably got the voicemail or answering service," she replies.

Brent Patterson interjects, "Well studies show that usually when cheating husbands or wives are going *to*, or leaving *from* being with their lover, they tend to call home to speak to their children or spouse. It's like some sort of coping mechanism to deal with the guilt, usually subconsciously."

McLean thinks they are on to something and makes some notation as he interjects his own take.

"Exactly, and he doesn't answer his phone at work where she expects him to be, so maybe in her mind she translates that to: perhaps he's out having his own affair as well," McLean adds.

"Very possible. This helps her justify her affair or relationship with Mr. Flowers," Brent concludes.

McLean ponders over several theories, and then addresses his team.

"Well, this drive to pick up Algernon while leaving her sick child all alone is a key to unlock this whole thing. We need to establish the moments prior to this. What was Howell doing that day? Did anyone see her and Deja out at the mall or grocery? Algernon said she made him a special drink, where did she get the ingredients? If we can find out where she shopped, perhaps there is surveillance footage that shows her either with or without Deja."

Everyone in the room seems to think this is a step in the right direction.

"I will look into that," offers Rachael as she makes a note of it in her notepad.

"Very good," replies McLean before moving on to the next thought.

"There is the matter of Brenda Howell's debit card statement. Have we filed to get that subpoenaed?" he asks generally.

Rachael responds, "Yes, we are waiting to get that from her bank."

McLean is satisfied with this.

Rachael adds, "Also, we are trying to get surveillance video from the hotels where Brenda Howell and Algernon met before his arrest."

"Awesome," McLean replies.

Brent Patterson raises his hand. He has something to say but he first needs to swallow the bite of muffin he's chewing. He quickly swallows and then speaks.

"My contact at the lab says the tests that forensics ran were sent to the DA's office, and then sent back for re-evaluation."

McLean finds this both unusual and very important.

"So they may have come back with results that weren't favorable to the case they're trying to build against Algernon," McLean speculates.

Helena interjects, "They really need to lock Deja's injuries into that small two-hour window that Howell was out of the apartment in order to eliminate her from the equation, leaving Algernon as the only probable suspect. We need to get those initial results."

McLean agrees, "Brent, can you look into getting more info from your guy at the lab?" he asks.

"I'm on it," Brent replies as he makes a note to himself.

McLean moves on. "So as you all know, both Deborah Long and Deputy Garzero have lawyered up and are refusing to cooperate with our investigation. Michael Petagnas cannot use any statements or facts about them without their documented testimonies and cooperation, otherwise it's just hearsay. We need to dig deeper."

The entire investigative team is writing notes while brainstorming. Helena reminds Rachael of a lead.

"Rachael, what about that lady that Brenda Howell made that comment to?"

McLean inquires about it. "What lady?" he asks.

"Oh, that's dead in the water," Rachael replies.

Off of McLean's puzzled look, Rachael continues to elaborate further.

"Apparently since they separated, there was an argument between Brenda and her husband in which he threatened to take custody of Deja, and since she has a prior arrest for domestic violence, the family courts would rule in his favor. Allegedly, to this she replied: *if she couldn't have Deja, no one would.*"

McLean wonders why Rachael isn't pursuing this lead. By his glare, Rachael can tell he is questioning this so she continues.

"However ... the woman who heard that story heard it from Ms. Audrey Richardson—the witness that has mysteriously disappeared."

The entire group is now looking at McLean. They know exactly what he's thinking and they all say it out loud at the same time, like a singing barbershop quartette:

"Let's find Audrey Richardson!"

CHAPTER 17

The deposition of emergency medical technician Earl Wallace is about to get underway. Present for the prosecution is David Edwards, State Attorney Ramon Henderson, and paralegal Jennifer Forde. For the defense, Michael Petagnas, Steven Didia, and Sandy Ward. A court-appointed reporter is also present to keep an official record. The prosecution asks Mr. Wallace to list some of his certifications, experience and training qualifications. Earl Wallace gives some of his background and then the questions begin about what he remembers on the morning he was called to the apartment of Brenda Howell. Both the prosecution and defense take notes as Wallace gives his testimony. Lead defense attorney Michael Petagnas is not sure just yet whether this witness can help, or hurt, his case.

As Earl Wallace gives his statement, both sides interrupt him on occasion as they seek clarity on various points. As far as depositions go, this is pretty average and nothing out of the ordinary. As a first responder, Wallace can only offer what he observed upon his arrival, and testify as to anything strange or out of the ordinary. Basically his testimony is that when he arrived at the apartment, he saw two adults, one male and one female. The male was down on the floor performing CPR on an unresponsive young female child, as the adult female stood in the other room a short distance away. When Wallace asked the female adult what happened to the child, the adult female, who identified herself as the child's mother, stated the child had been ill and threw up a couple of times the day and night before.

Mr. Wallace is also asked about the steps and measures he took, and whatever treatment he administered to the child prior to transporting her to the local hospital. Something mentioned in this portion of his statement sparks the interest of Michael Petagnas. Wallace states that while preparing to transport the young child, a standard procedure when a person is not breathing on his or her own is to provide artificial breathing. This is normally done by placing a tube down into the person's throat, which is then used to pump oxygen in and out of his or her lungs manually. While performing this action on the young child, Earl Wallace recalls it being very difficult to even open the jaw, and even more difficult to get the tube into the throat. This interests Michael Petagnas because during his extensive experience with cases involving death, the internal stiffening of the trachea is a sign that rigor mortis has begun to set in. At the time of death, a condition called primary flaccidity occurs. Following this, the muscles stiffen in rigor mortis. All muscles in the body are affected. Starting between three to six hours following death, rigor mortis begins with the eyelids, neck, and jaw. This translates well for the defense, because Brenda Howell left and returned in a little less than two hours. This would suggest then that as soon as she stepped out the door, Mr. Flowers ran into the Deja's room, and for some reason beat her, and then she bled out internally within seconds. This is the only way that by the time Brenda Howell returned Deja could have been in the state and condition in which she was when the emergency medical technicians arrived on the scene. Even that small window is highly unlikely, as four hours is the average for rigor mortis to begin.

At the conclusion of Earl Wallace's deposition, the next and only other deposition scheduled for today is that of Doctor Richard Mason. He was the resident physician on duty the morning that Deja Howell was brought to the emergency room. It was Dr. Mason who pronounced the official death.

Like the witness before him, Dr. Mason is asked to state his background, experience and training before getting into his recollection of events on the same morning. Also as with Earl Wallace, Dr. Mason is asked general follow-up questions from both sides for clarity. Another similarity with this deposition and the one prior, something mentioned grabs the attention of Michael Petagnas. Dr. Mason recounts when the call came into the emergency room. The term that the EMT used prompts Petagnas to question further. Petagnas asks for the meaning of the term. The term used was 'full load,' which is code for a deceased body. Michael Petagnas asks for an exact quote from the doctor's recollection. Dr. Mason repeats the exact words used by the EMT calling it in.

"We have a bus with a full load," Dr. Mason restates.

Petagnas and his team are satisfied, and have no further questions for this witness. The prosecution is also done with the witness so he is excused.

Before both parties dismiss, they schedule the next series of depositions that works with the schedules for all involved. Once this is established, they dismiss. Everyone exits the room with the exception of one—paralegal for the prosecution, Jennifer Forde. She reads over her notes from the two witnesses that were deposed earlier. She is growing increasingly uncomfortable with the feeling she has that perhaps she is on a prosecution team that is potentially going to send an innocent man to prison or death. Her feelings for the victim outweigh everything else, but she is uneasy with the facts and evidence in this case. She dare not voice her opinion or concerns again. She is in conflict with herself. Her career and conscious battle within her as she collects her things and exits the room.

CHAPTER 18

It has been almost three months since the funeral service for little Deja Howell was held at the Booker Lake Baptist church, located in the heart of Booker Lake County. This is the hometown of Brenda Howell's parents, and the small town she grew up in. Today there is another big event at the church. In the same spot where funeral services for their daughter were held less than ninety days ago, the Howells will be renewing their vows. The couple that very recently had secret martial problems is now showing a public sign of solidarity and recommitment to one another.

Brenda Howell walks down the long center aisle of the church with her father as the bridal processional song plays from an old style house organ. Family and friends stand and snap photos as the proud father walks his daughter down the aisle as if for the first time. Brenda smiles and blushes as she makes her way to the altar. The ivory gown cascading her hourglass figure rivals the most stunning of dresses in the entire world, yet still pales in comparison to her natural beauty. She caresses her baby bump, causing many to tear up with emotion. Her flawless skin and well-balanced features are perfectly framed by her long, flowing black hair. She steps forward to where her groom awaits her arrival. He is Detective Frank Howell. Good-looking, clean-cut, and in immaculate physical shape. He is sporting a navy blue tuxedo and has a best man at his side. The church is full of Frank's family, friends and several other police men and women who drove from Rocky Beach to support their fellow officer. Brenda also has family present, along with some old friends. A handful of her co-workers showed up as well. Also blended into the crowd is a member of Nick McLean's investigative team, Brent Patterson. He is also snapping photos of the lovely couple and their guests, however not for precious memories, but documentation. Among the invited guests, select members of the Rocky Beach media. For what can best be described as a lavish publicity stunt, this display of rekindled love comes off as either very sweet, or extremely classless—depending on whom you ask.

After the ceremony, the couple is flocked by several guests for photo opportunities. The Howells make the perfect couple. They smile, embrace, and kiss for the cameras. If there were any doubt that Detective Howell suspected his wife of harming their daughter, this eliminates that doubt. They appear to be truly in love.

Supporters cheer and throw confetti while following the couple as they exit the church. Patterson stays close by while still blending in with the crowd. He continues to snap photos as the couple gets into the back seat of a waiting car ... a silver sedan with dark tinted windows.

The newly remarried couple is chauffeured away to the cheers of their supporters. Brent Patterson observes one of the news reporters standing off in a distant corner with the South Rocky police chief. They appear to be engaging in a very fiery moment, similar to a pair of bickering lovers. He cannot hear what is being said, but he captures a few photos of them before retreating back to his car.

.   .   .

About thirty miles away, basically the halfway point between Booker Lake and Rocky Beach, investigator Rachel O'Toole enters the back office of a hotel where Algernon Flowers and Brenda Howell stayed after the death of Brenda's daughter. The hotel manager leads Rachael to the back office, and into the surveillance room, where several cameras capture and record video footage around the clock. Rachael's request is to pull up footage from a certain night matching a payment on Brenda Howell's credit card statement.

As Rachael and the hotel manager scroll through the footage, she notices Brenda Howell entering the lobby and stopping at the front desk. Mrs. Howell gets a key from the attendant, and then walks to the elevator. She exits on the third floor and enters a room. Shortly after Brenda's arrival, Algernon Flowers enters the lobby. However he doesn't stop at the front desk, he goes straight to the elevator and up to the third floor. He knocks on the door of the room Brenda entered and the door is opened. He then enters the room and the door closes. Rachael concludes that Howell registered the room, and then called Flowers to tell him the room number after she checked in.

The video is then fast-forwarded to when the door reopens. Rachael watches the video closely to see who emerges. It is Algernon Flowers exiting alone. He enters the elevator and then another camera picks him up exiting through the lobby. An outside camera facing the parking lot shows Algernon Flowers walking to his car and then driving off. Rachael is about to switch back to the interior cameras, but something grabs her attention. She pauses and rewinds the tape. As Mr. Flowers pulls off in his car, the headlights of a car parked nearby come on and the car appears to follow Mr. Flowers. The silver sedan with dark tinted windows slowly exits the video frame.

.   .   .

At the Mandarin Street locksmith in Rocky Beach, investigator Helena Wang is waiting in line to be assisted. There is a man in front of her who is waiting on getting a broken key fixed. The elderly gentleman who owns the shop keeps customers returning because of his sweet personality, definitely not because of his speedy service. After what seems like decades, it is finally Helena's turn to be helped. She only has a question.

"How much does it cost to get a set of keys copied?" she asks.

"Two dollars per key, so that will be a total of four dollars," replies the old man.

She has a follow-up question. "So if I were to get two copies made, that would bring my total to eight dollars?" asks Helena.

The old man appears confused as he repeats her question before answering. "If you were to get two sets made? If you were to get two sets of two keys at two dollars per key, then yes, that would be eight dollars total."

Helena looks at something in her hand. It is a copy of Brenda Howell's debit card purchases. She made a purchase here at the Mandarin Street locksmith for eight dollars. In her statement to police Brenda said she made a copy of the apartment keys for Algernon Flowers the day after she moved in. However the price she paid is for two copies. Helena concludes that someone else has a copy of the apartment keys ... but who? Investigator Wang thanks the old man for his help and then leaves the store.

"Wait, if you get two sets I can throw in a free clip-on key ring!" the old man offers as she exits.

CHAPTER 19

At the Local County Prosecutor's Office, District Prosecutor David Edwards gets into the elevator at the end of another full workday. There is one other person already standing in the elevator. It is Nancy Groover, who just so happens to be going after Edwards' job during this year's upcoming election. The two are amicable as professionals, but there is obviously both mutual respect and disdain between them.

"Prosecutor Edwards!" acknowledges Nancy Groover while keeping her head and eyes straight ahead.

David Edwards replies in the same dry tone, with a fake smile and similar body language, "Groover!"

There is a brief moment of silence that is suddenly disrupted by Nancy Groover.

"So I hear your big case is going well," she offers as an opening to strike up a conversation. Prosecutor Edwards reads more sarcasm than may have actually been intended.

"Really, what have you heard, Nancy?" he replies almost rhetorically, not expecting an answer.

Groover is clearly trying to ruffle Edwards' feathers a bit.

"Oh, I just hear that your investigators may have rushed to judgment and some of your evidence is more suitably labeled as perhaps defense-friendly. Word is that you have no real evidence tying your suspect to this crime ... other than the word of the cheating wife of a police detective, who claims the victim was alive and well when she last saw her. Doesn't sound like you have much of a case at all," spews Nancy Groover as she feels her words dig deep into a very sensitive area.

Edwards takes offense to this and scoffs back, "Never mind what I don't have ... you know what I DO have? A perfect conviction rate! I have not lost a trial in my career."

Nancy Groover chuckles at his arrogance and quickly snaps, "True, you've never lost a trial ... but neither has Michael Petagnas."

The elevator doors open and a few other people enter. The rest of the ride down is silent. As the elevator reaches the lobby, and the occupants file out, Groover takes one last stab at Edwards.

"Maybe they will take that plea deal and you can save face," she whispers loud enough for him to hear as she walks away.

Edwards doesn't feel that warrants a response and only shakes his head in disgust as the two go their separate ways.

Once in his car, Prosecutor Edwards makes a call on his cell phone.

"So where are we with the medical examiner's full report?" he asks and then waits for a response from the other end. He clearly does not like what he hears. He pulls the phone away, squeezing it in frustration. He regains his composure and then returns the phone to his ear.

"Listen, I don't care, we've got to make this stick! The defense doesn't get a copy of anything until I approve it! The judge can say whatever he wants, if it's not available it's just not available. Do you copy? It is NOT available!"

He hangs up, starts his car, and then drives off.

.   .   .

As Michael Petagnas wraps up his work for the evening, Sandy Ward enters his office.

"Michael, the lab just called back and said they are having delays getting the full medical examiner's report," she informs her boss.

Petagnas smiles at that news, as if he expected it.

"Well, did you tell them that we have our own expert that will evaluate the evidence as well?" he asks.

"I did, and I was told that due to improper preservation of the evidence, our expert will be limited to viewing slides only. No physical tissue or samples," Sandy replies.

Petagnas didn't expect the prosecution to play this dirty.

"So are they saying that they have enough 'probable cause' to arrest our client, but they can't provide the evidence that supports anything? I find that hard to believe." Petagnas pauses for a moment and then continues to vent. "How do you not preserve the only physical evidence that you have? Unreal. Tell you what, Sandy, schedule a discovery hearing with the judge as soon as possible," orders Petagnas.

Sandy nods affirmatively. "Will do," she replies and then exits.

Michael Petagnas is all too familiar with the tricks and schemes of the Local County Prosecutor's Office. He taught most of them. He is almost offended that they would even attempt to pull this on him. He dials a number on his phone and waits for the other end to pick up before speaking.

"Nick, it's me. So Sandy is having a little trouble obtaining some evidence from the lab. I'm not about to be held hostage by frivolous hearings and weeks of unnecessary paperwork. I'm just not going to play their game ... I need you to get me more."

.   .   .

Private investigator Nick McLean is on his cell phone while driving his SUV. He wraps up is conversation.

"You got it, Mike. I'm working a lead as we speak. I will call you back."

He hangs up and then looks for a house in a neighborhood several miles away from Rocky Beach. He is not exactly sure of the house he's looking for, but he will know it when he sees it. According to a source close to one of McLean's investigative team members, they received a tip as to where he can find a potential witness. However, this source only knows the general neighborhood so McLean must patrol the entire area and hope to get lucky. After hours of driving up and down the streets, his work finally pays off. He sees what he has been looking for. Parked in an open garage is a white, late-model coupe belonging to former Richard M. Weinstein Elementary School employee, Ms. Audrey Richardson.

CHAPTER 20

Algernon Flowers marks another notch on the green brick wall of his tiny cell. The notches are adding up and becoming numerous. With each notch representing a day he woke up here at the Local County Jail, Algernon Flowers begins to wonder which will he possibly run out of first: space on the wall ... or hope. His very appearance has changed. The bags under his puffy eyes make him look as though he has aged ten years, while the inactivity and lack of exercise have added fifteen pounds to his body. His unshaven face almost makes him unrecognizable. At this stage of his incarceration, he has adjusted to life here and is nearly able to sleep through the slamming of cell doors throughout the night. The visits from his family seem more draining than anything else as each visit forces him to pretend he is doing well. Although he is struggling in his mind, he doesn't want his family to worry about him, so he tries to mask his fear and pain with a forced smile and bad jokes. Upon returning to his cell after the half hour visits, he collapses to his knees from the exhaustion of pulling energy from a place that is only filled with darkness.

Once every thirty days, a team of staff psychologists from the jail visit with some of the lock down custody inmates for a routine check of their mental wellbeing, and to follow up on their status. This monthly visit comes around and there are new questions for Algernon Flowers from the team of doctors. They are familiar with his case and decide to question him about how he feels about the birth of Brenda Howell's new baby—a little boy. This is news to inmate Flowers. As he hears it for the first time, he knows that he cannot allow any emotion to show, in fear that they will read into it and label him unstable, and order him to be moved to another unit. Algernon pretends to have already heard of this news through his family. He expresses his blessings to her and her husband, and wishes the best for them. Satisfied with his coping and understanding of the situation, they leave, concluding their monthly evaluation. The truth is, this was a major emotional blow to Mr. Flowers— the heartbreak of feeling betrayed by his former lover, and the added insult of realizing that not only did she set him up and destroy his life, but to top it all off, there she is enjoying her life and restarting her family. This weighs heavily on him. He needs an outlet. He decides that in order to maintain his sanity, he needs to turn to creativity. Before his incarceration, writing songs that encouraged others to be strong in times of crisis was what he enjoyed doing, so he turns to that now. However, this proves easier said than done. It's much easier to stand on top of the mountain and yell down to others to keep climbing. It's not so easy when you're at the bottom and need to cheer yourself to the top.

As Algernon Flowers tries to distract himself from the nagging anguish he feels in his heart, he seeks inspiration from somewhere—anywhere—in order to begin writing a song. On top of a stack of greeting cards he received in the mail is one from his mother. It is very simple illustration of a cartoon character holding onto a tree as a gusty wind blows. Next to the character, two simple words: HOLD ON.

.   .   .

"Hold on," says Hazel Flowers into the cordless phone as she turns the television down in her living room. She then returns the phone to her ear. "Yes, sorry I had trouble hearing you over the television. This is Hazel." After a pause, her countenance changes. She is getting some bad news. The call is from the nursing home where her aunt Myra is. Ms. Flowers learns that her aunt passed away a half hour ago.

Aunt Myra was the great-aunt of Algernon Flowers, and one of his biggest supporters. She was suffering from complications due to her age and failing liver. When she was still living at the Flowers' home, if ever she was in pain, the elderly woman would ask Algernon to play music on the piano. This would seem to soothe her entire body. It got to the point that whenever Algernon would hear his great-aunt moaning in pain, he would just start playing the piano, and like magic the notes would become a pain-relieving drug. After Algernon's arrest, Aunt Myra's health took a turn for the worse and she needed twenty-four-hour nursing care. She finally succumbed to her illness. Naturally Algernon Flowers will blame himself for not being there to provide Aunt Myra with her dose of musical medicine.

CHAPTER
21

As Michael Petagnas works on his defense strategy, he is still awaiting some tests results to return from the lab. Although she is not charged in this case, Brenda Howell, at the urging of her family, has hired a lawyer to protect her rights. Michael Petagnas has been trying to schedule a deposition with Mrs. Howell, but wants to save her for last. He wants to have all the lab tests in his possession before his confrontation with her. The only request made by her lawyer is that the deposition not be done during her pregnancy to avoid adding stress to upset her, which may create complications with the baby. Now that her second child is born, Howell's lawyer has let Petagnas know that she will be available for her deposition as early as next week.

As for progress in the case, Michael Petagnas won his client a small victory this morning during a discovery hearing in front of the presiding judge, the Honorable Judge Warren

Jackson. Judge Jackson ruled in favor of the defense, stating that the prosecution must turn over all evidence by the end of the week. Although the date for Petagnas to file for a speedy trial has expired, getting the full medical examiner's report and all physical evidence will get the ball rolling.

Not wanting to delay meeting with his medical expert, Petagnas brings Dr. Harvey Walters in to meet with him at his office. Dr. Walters is very experienced and well respected in the medical and science community. He has an extensive background as a retired medical examiner and pathologist. He is meeting with Michael Petagnas, Steven Didia, Sandy Ward, and a few other members of the Algernon Flowers defense team. Dr. Walters uses a dry erase board as he explains to the team the twelve stages of death and what usually happens to the body.

"Moment of Death:

1) The heart stops.

2) The skin gets tight and grey in color.

3) All of the muscles relax.

4) The bladder and bowels empty."

As Dr. Walters speaks and writes on the board, everyone in the room takes notes like anxious medical students preparing for a big exam. Dr. Harvey Walters continues:

"After 30 minutes:

5) The skin gets purple and waxy.

6) The lips, fingernails, and toenails fade to a pale color or turn white as the blood leaves.

7) Blood pools at the lowest parts of the body leaving a dark purple-black stain called lividity.

8) The hands and feet turn blue.

9) The eyes start to sink into the skull.

After four hours:

10) Rigor mortis starts to set in.

11) The purpling of the skin and pooling of blood continue.

12) Rigor mortis begins to tighten the muscles for up to another 24 hours, then will reverse and the body will return to a limp state."

After concluding his presentation, Dr. Walters gets a question from Petagnas.

"So, Doctor Walters, would this be consistent with the EMT and ER physician's testimonies that I sent you?" asks Michael Petagnas.

"It would actually. This all depends on locking down an exact time of death, and I am not prepared to do anything further until I can examine some tissue and blood samples," Dr. Walters replies.

Petagnas asks another question. "What if the victim sustained an initial beating approximately twelve hours prior to the EMTs having trouble with the tube and the condition of the body? Could the victim have bled internally after sustaining the initial injuries, but death not occur for several hours afterward?"

Dr. Walters answers right away. "Very good, Michael. That is most likely what occurred here and would therefore make sense as to what the EMT and treating physician testified to ... But again, I cannot say anything with certainty until I have those samples."

Michael Petagnas and his team feel Dr. Walters' expert testimony can really help their case. Now it is up to the prosecution to play fair and deliver the physical evidence so that Dr. Walters can get to work. With so much riding on the physical evidence in this case, the fact that it is taking this long for the medical examiner to release it gives Petagnas and his team both anxiety and hope.

CHAPTER 22

Private investigator Nicholas McLean sits at his desk mulling over his notes on the Algernon Flowers case. Also present in his office is the team of investigators: Rachael O'Toole, Helena Wang, and Brent Patterson. They review and discuss their progress thus far. McLean is trying to put together a timeline to help them figure out where to look next for a key witness or key piece of evidence that helps the defense. As the team brainstorms, Rachael O'Toole writes on a large three-foot-tall oak tag paper that is held up by metal pushpins against a corkboard wall. Periodically the group disagrees on a specific order or definitive time table, but after a couple of hours, they all seem to have reached a map of events that makes the most sense according to the corroborated statements and evidence they have gathered. Lead investigator Nick McLean then gives the list one last talk through before approving it to go the Michael Petagnas.

"OK, so let's start with what we know," McLean begins, checking items off the carefully compiled list. "Back in January of last year, according to Deborah Long, Brenda Howell has to be physically restrained from disciplining her daughter, Deja.

"At some point during the school year, Brenda Howell gets flirty and very friendly with the school deputy, Ron Garzero. At some point soon thereafter, detective Frank Howell walks in on his wife and Deputy Garzero a little too close for his comfort. Detective Howell then threatens to create some sort of 'trouble' for Brenda if she doesn't stop hanging out with Garzero. During or around this time, an argument between Brenda and Detective Howell escalates to violence and Brenda is arrested and charged with domestic assault.

"By early summer, the Howells separate—divorce papers are filed.

"In August, Brenda Howell and Algernon Flowers meet and begin dating. Brenda Howell moves into the two-bedroom apartment in the middle of September, on or around the fifteenth. Within the next couple of days she goes to the Mandarin Street locksmith, and for some reason makes two copies of the apartment keys.

"The following day she gives Algernon Flowers one copy. Other copy … unknown???

"Algernon Flowers is away the last week in October. Travels back from TN. After making the long drive back to Florida, he calls Brenda Howell to inform her that he doesn't have his car. At approximately 9 P.M. Brenda Howell leaves three-year-old Deja at the apartment alone, and possibly injured. She drives at least twenty minutes each way from South Rocky to Rocky Beach to pick up Algernon Flowers and bring him back to her apartment. While driving she makes a call to the Rocky Beach Police Station.

"At some point during the evening Brenda Howell makes frozen drinks, and Algernon Flowers makes the discovery of Deja lying in a pool of brown vomit of some sort in her room. After pointing this out to Brenda, Algernon returns to Brenda's room while Brenda stays behind to clean and tend to the child. Algernon doesn't see if Deja actually ever moved on her own.

"The next morning Brenda Howell makes a hurried exit from the apartment to head to work earlier than usual. Upon her arrival she parks in an unusual spot, in an unusual way. She then proceeds to ask several coworkers for time confirmation— possibly establishing an alibi.

"Less than or about an hour later, she remembers that she doesn't have an early class so she returns back to her apartment in South Rocky.

"Upon arriving back home she doesn't exit her vehicle. She remains parked downstairs and calls Algernon Flowers on the phone and asks him to wake Deja and bring her downstairs. As Algernon Flowers discovers Deja unresponsive, he alerts Brenda Howell and calls 9-1-1. While on the phone with the 9-1-1 dispatcher only Algernon Flowers makes an attempt to resuscitate Deja as Brenda Howell watches.

"Paramedics arrive on the scene. Brenda Howell tells them Deja has been ill.

"After the death is ruled a homicide, Rocky Beach detectives interview Brenda Howell and decide to take photos of her hands due to the pattern of a specific broken fingernail and her large, oval-shaped diamond rings—consistent with the shapes of bruising on the victim's lower abdomen.

"At some point during the interview, the investigation shifts from Brenda Howell to both Howell and Mr. Flowers

"After they are released, the investigation continues, during which time Brenda Howell and Algernon Flowers meet at an out-of-town location. We know that at least on one occasion an unmarked silver sedan, registered to the Rocky Beach police department, was trailing Mr. Flowers at a hotel. The same silver sedan that we have reason to believe is keeping close surveillance on this investigative team—perhaps to dampen any leads and intimidate any potential defense witnesses, the likes of Audrey Richardson, who now refuses to return to Rocky Beach to testify.

"Other witnesses seem to be afraid or unwilling to get involved.

"Deputy Ron Garzero requests a transfer and has retained a lawyer.

"Brenda and Frank Howell renew their vows in what appears to be a publicity stunt, and where the Rocky Beach police chief and a key member of the local media (that tend to keep being seen together) get into some sort of quarrel.

"Initial lab results either inclusive or not 'prosecution friendly.'"

McLean concludes, "I think that's about right."

His team agrees, and they begin to shuffle their papers, packing items up to call it a night.

"Oh yeah, so about what we discussed earlier ... Is everyone in agreement?" asks McLean.

All three investigators raise their hands confidently in a unanimous vote.

CHAPTER 23

Bright and early, Michael Petagnas walks into the coffee shop near the courthouse. He is meeting with the judge and prosecutor to review the status of discovery and the surrender of all prosecution evidence. As he places his order and reaches for his wallet to pay, an arm extends from behind and hands the cashier a bill.

A male voice says, "I got it, Michael."

Petagnas turns around and sees Prosecutor David Edwards.

As the two men wait for their specialty drinks to be prepared, Prosecutor Edwards engages Petagnas in small talk. It seems innocent at first, asking about Mrs. Petagnas and the children, when was his last golf game. It all appears to sound like two old chums catching up. That changes when the drinks arrive and the two lawyers exit the coffee shop to take the walk over to the county courthouse. David Edwards sees this as a closing opportunity to speak with his former boss before entering the courtroom. Once in the courtroom, Michael Peta-gnas becomes a raging lion, taking no prisoners. Edwards hopes that while still outside the realm of the legal battlefield, he can get some desired information from his opponent. David Edwards appears semi-bashful, like an adolescent boy wanting to ask a girl to the school prom. There is clearly something he wants to talk about, but is trying to tread carefully.

"Mike, so people in my office want to know ... I mean, your services are pretty expensive, and I hear you've also got an entire investigative team on staff. Not to mention the renowned Dr. Harvey Walters as your medical expert?"

David Edwards continues to beat around the bush, but Petagnas can tell where he's heading with this. Although Peta-gnas enjoys watching the nervous prosecutor squirm, he decides to let him off the hook.

"Let me guess, you—or 'people in your office'—want to know, how is Algernon Flowers paying for his defense?" asks Petagnas.

Uncomfortable but satisfied as to the truth within Peta-gnas' keen observation, Edwards responds, "Well yeah, I mean this is a kid just out of college, gigging as a musician in small towns. How can he afford someone of your caliber?"

The two men reach the large revolving glass door that leads into the courthouse lobby. This moment is almost sym-bolic of two gladiators entering an arena. Any personal and cordial talk ends here, and business begins. Michael Petagnas doesn't offer Edwards any satisfaction with his answer.

"Attorney-client privilege, David ... you remember that, right?" replies Petagnas as he pushes the revolving door, leaving Prosecutor Edwards behind.

"Touché, Mr. Petagnas," mumbles Edwards as he, too, en-ters the revolving door.

·   ·   ·

In courtroom number nine the Honorable Judge Warren Jack-son exits his chambers and takes his seat on the bench. Known for his notorious Southern-style, military background and no-nonsense policies, he is both revered and feared by prosecutors and defense attorneys alike. Though fair and knowledgeable of the law, he has been given the nickname 'Hangman Jackson' for his harsh sentencing and stern punishment of offenders. As the tall sixty-one-year-old judge takes his place on the bench, he zips up his long black robe and looks over his glasses, quickly surveying the now-standing parties assembled in his courtroom. As the judge sits, his bailiff instructs the entire room to take their seats. Present for the prosecution are David Edwards and Ramon Henderson. Paralegal Jennifer Forde is also present and seated in the back row of the courtroom gallery, on the side behind the prosecution table. Present at the defense table is Michael Petagnas and the defendant, Algernon Flowers. Some family members and friends are seated in the gallery behind the defense table in show of support for Mr. Flowers. Since this is an official pretrial hearing, it is required for the defendant to be present.

Seated next to his attorney, Algernon Flowers is dressed in the standard county-issued orange jumpsuit, and brown sandals. His hands are cuffed in front of him and his ankles are shackled together. The clanging of chain links tying his feet together can be heard throughout the entire courtroom as the young defendant trembles in fear, looking almost as an animal that has grown accustomed to the confinement of his cage. The large, open space of courtroom number nine now creates anxiety. Algernon Flowers would much rather be back in the safety of his tiny cell at the Local County Jail than stand before the notorious Hangman Jackson.

Judge Warren Jackson begins the hearing by making record of all the parties present. To ensure that all goes smoothly and that there are no errors that can create a mistrial or grounds for a later issue in the court of appeals, the experienced judge makes certain all the necessary parties are present and accounted for. Once this is established and to the judge's satisfaction, he opens the floor to the prosecution to offer where they stand in regards to discovery and sharing of evidence. Both Prosecutor Edwards and Prosecutor Henderson report that the medical examiner's full report is in. However, as for the defense receiving tissue and blood samples? That is out of the question, claiming that due to mishandling, there was a failure to properly preserve that physical evidence. An outraged Michael Petagnas stands and states his argument for allowing his expert, Dr. Walters, the opportunity to view exactly what the Local County medical examiner had in order to determine an approximate time of death, including all samples to determine when the victim sustained the fatal injuries.

After several back-and-forth arguments between the prosecution and defense, Judge Jackson is ready to rule on the matter. After scolding the prosecution for failure to preserve valuable evidence, he sides with neither the prosecution nor defense directly, stating that if there is corrupt preservation of that particular evidence, the defense will have to use the only available evidence, which is that of the county medical examiner's report, photos and microscopic slides all taken during the initial autopsy. This ruling does, in some way, favor the prosecution. Now the medical expert for the defense is limited to only what was actually handled correctly and properly preserved. Not exactly a great win for the prosecution, as the window of time of death and time of initial injury is still up in the air and open for debate. However, if they were hiding something that wasn't favorable to their case, today's ruling has helped bury it.

Before ending the hearing, the judge confers with the lawyers from both sides to lock down a date for the next pretrial hearing. Once both sides agree to a date and time, Judge Jackson strikes his gavel, all rise, and he returns to his chambers.

Michael Petagnas briefly informs his client of what the ruling means and lets him know that he is going to have his expert, Dr. Walters, view the photos and slides, give his opinion, and then take it from there. He makes sure that Mr. Flowers understands that with the limited information they have to work with, they are facing a tough battle ahead. Michael

Petagnas then stops to chat with Algernon's family before he exits the courtroom. Algernon Flowers looks back at his family and offers a nod of his head, acknowledging their presence and symbolizing his appreciation for their support. He is then transferred to the holding cell where he will await transportation back to the county jail.

CHAPTER 24

Steven Didia Jr. has recently graduated from Walton Law School in California. This is his first day of work at the law firm of Petagnas & Didia, which his father, Steven Didia Sr., co-founded. Steven Jr. has gotten his height and good looks from his mother, yet has his father's thick, full head of black hair. Also unlike his father, Steven Jr.'s suits actually look like those of an attorney and not a New York City mobster. Very proud that his son not only followed his career path, but also came on to join his firm and work side by side, Steven Didia Sr. introduces his boy to the rest of the staff.

Steven Jr. has been thrown right into the mix of possibly the biggest case this firm has taken on. Now with very little physical evidence for their medical expert to review, the defense of Algernon Flowers is under pressure. Steven Didia Jr. will not jump into the trenches just yet. For it is customary that every staff member, on his or her first day, to take coffee orders for the entire office staff prior to starting the day. It is a ritual that doesn't even exclude the son of one of the firm's co-founders. So before he sits in on any depositions or looks up any case law, Steven Jr. takes coffee orders. Some simple: like black, or light and sweet. Others not so simple: like triple mocha frappe, with caramel drizzle, two percent soy, et cetera. Once the good-looking young Steven Jr. has collected everyone's order, he heads out to the Cup O'Joe coffee house a few minutes away from the office.

Steven Didia Jr. arrives in his brand-new white Mercedes Benz—a graduation present from his parents. He places his many different orders and then waits at a near by table as they are being prepared.

"Wow, you must really need a morning pick-me-up … that's a lot of coffee," says a very attractive female seated at the table.

Steven Jr. didn't realize the table was taken. He apologizes and stands to get up.

"Oh, I'm sorry, I didn't realize you were sitting here," offers Steven Jr.

He is almost rendered speechless by the gorgeous, blonde young woman with the prettiest smile he has ever seen. Her soft eyes melt him instantly.

"No worries, that seat is actually not taken … neither is this table. I'm actually just waiting on my order also," replies the beautiful young woman as she looks back down to her phone to continue checking her work emails. "I was just saying that you ordered a whole lot of coffee," she continues as she multi-tasks.

Steven Jr. is more than happy to sit back down. He doesn't feel the compulsion to explain his large coffee order, but doing so will offer him an opportunity to engage this beautiful woman further.

"Well, they're not all for me. Today is my first day at a law firm here in Rocky Beach, and it's like a ritual for the new guy to do a coffee run on his first day ... like a rite of passage," Steven Jr. explains.

The pretty young blonde looks up from her phone with a smile.

"That's cute ... I wish we did fun things like that at my office. Unfortunately, I work in a pretty uptight environment," she says with a chuckle.

Her drink order is called and she excuses herself.

"Well, that's me. Nice sharing a table with you," she concludes.

The attractive young woman walks to the counter to get her drink. Steven Jr. fears that he may never see this lovely creature again. As she walks away from the counter to exit, he decides to make his move. He steps in front of her to block her path, and they almost collide as she walks while looking down at her phone. When she realizes that the handsome, well-dressed young man is now directly in front of her, she smiles curiously.

"Maybe we can share a table again sometime?" Steven Jr. suggests with a big smile of his own.

The pretty blonde extends her hand and replies, "That sounds good to me. My name is Jennifer."

.   .   .

Steven Didia Jr. walks back into the law office of Petagnas & Didia with a new confidence that radiates from him as brightly as the Florida morning sun. Young Steven is all smiles as he delivers every staff member their drink. Usually on someone's first day he or she tends to get one or two drink orders wrong, but not Steven Jr. He carries several drinks in a torn cardboard box. His new co-workers are all very impressed. His morning is off to a great start. First day in his dad's law firm, AND he meets the woman of his dreams ... or at least he can say that about her good looks. He will get to learn more about her this evening, as he and Jennifer have made plans to meet for a drink after work. Steven Jr. seems to almost walk on air as he delivers his last coffee. It is to Steven Sr. After handing his father the last cup from the makeshift cardboard box carrier, the young Didia turns the empty box upside down as a symbol of a completed mission, and then takes an exaggerated performance bow. The entire office offers applause and cheers as a welcome to the team.

.   .   .

It is early in the afternoon when private investigator Nicholas McLean arrives at the Law Office of Petagnas & Didia. He is bringing his redacted and latest findings for Michael Petagnas to review in preparation for his case. As McLean enters the office, he is told that Michael Petagnas has called an impromptu meeting with the entire staff as now all are involved in the Algernon Flowers case. McLean enters the conference room as the meeting is already underway. Petagnas sees him and pauses to invite him into the discussion.

"Good, Nick is here also ... Nick come on in, this involves you and your team also," says Petagnas.

McLean steps in and takes the closest available seat as Petagnas continues to address his staff.

"So as I was saying, the prosecution is trying to wait out Algernon's retainer. They know that he can't afford to pay for an entire trial, a lengthy investigation, and expert witnesses. They figure if they stall long enough, he will run out of resources and take a plea. I guess they think that everyone in this room and in Nick's office that have worked so diligently to help in Algernon's defense will all disappear when the retainer runs out. You see, we that are assembled around this table decided to do criminal defense not for the money, but for justice in cases like this. Sure, Algernon Flowers can get an overworked public defender, but that person is not going to work for him as much as I will, or Steven, or Sandy, or Nick McLean. You see, anywhere else Algernon Flowers isn't a person, but a number. In jail, he's just an inmate identified by a number ... in the court system he is just a case number, and to the prosecution he's not an innocent man, he's a potential notch on prosecutor Edwards' belt … But not here. No, here at Petagnas & Didia he is more than just a number, more than just a paycheck, more than just another high-profile case. My friends, here, Algernon Flowers is more than just another innocent life. He represents the reason we do what we do. Now I can't force you, and I won't ask any of you to work a pro bono case if it comes to it … but I, for one, will not stand by and allow this young man to become a second victim in this case. I can't do it without you, but if I have to I will fight to the end, even if it's just Algernon Flowers and me standing alone when the dust settles."

Michael Petagnas brings tears to the eyes of some in the room with his stirring speech that resembles that of a fired-up coach at halftime. It is very evident why he is so influential in his arguments at trial. One by one all around the room, hands go up as people respond with the words, "I'm in!" Soon every hand in the room is raised, even that of Didia Jr., who is having an eventful first day. Nick McLean raises his hand and asks to be heard.

"Michael, my team and I discussed this already last night. We took a vote that if the Flowers' family could no longer pay for our services, we would still work for justice in this case. We are ALL in," McLean concludes much to the delight of all-present.

The energy in the room is electric and erupts into cheers and applause as Michael Petagnas yells a battle cry of sorts:

"Well then let's fight for this man as if he were our own flesh and blood!"

CHAPTER 25

At the end of the first day on his new job, Steven Didia Jr. walks into the Trinidadian restaurant and makes his way to the bar. He spots the beautiful young woman he met at the coffee house this morning. She waves him over to a corner seat at the end of the bar that she has saved for him. The gorgeous blonde, or 'Jennifer from the coffee shop,' as she is saved in his phone, looks even more beautiful than Steven Jr. remembers. Perhaps it's her after-work glow. He walks to her and offers a handshake, but to his surprise Jennifer welcomes him in for a hug and also offers him a kiss on the cheek. Steven is all smiles. He can see that she is really interested in him and she is not afraid to show it. Her confidence makes her even more attractive, if that were even possible. The plan for this evening is simple—have a drink, and if that goes well, move to a table for dinner. As the young couple share laughs and swap law school stories, their natural chemistry is obvious. After two drinks they decide to get a table and have dinner together. After sitting and placing their orders, Jennifer gets a text from her boss. As she checks it, Steven Jr. can see that her countenance is affected by something work-related. She knows that he can tell she is a little stressed, so she decides to share.

"I know we future lawyers aren't supposed to share private confidential things about work, but this case I'm working on right now has me very conflicted," says Jennifer as she puts her phone away as to not allow it to further get in the way of the wonderful time she is having. She continues to share: "I think that there are times when we get it wrong. My gut is telling me this and I want to speak up but I don't think anyone wants to hear it. I guess they figure that being fresh out of law school, we're robots programmed to go straight by the book and to not feel."

Steven Jr. can relate to what she is feeling and shows his support.

"Well my dad always told me that there comes a case in every lawyer's career that hits them in the gut. It is these cases that create passion within. I guess you are just having your 'gut moment' early in your career," he says with a charming smile.

Jennifer smiles back and thanks Steven Jr. for the words of support and encouragement. Not wanting 'work talk' to overtake the evening, they decide to change the subject and not discuss their careers any further. Their food arrives and they enjoy a delicious meal and light, non-work conversation.

.   .   .

It is late in the evening and the last few guests leave the home of Hazel Flowers. After the funeral service of her aunt, many family members and friends stopped by to pay their respects, offer condolences, and show support. Among the guests is private investigator Nick McLean. He wanted to represent Algernon Flowers, who due to his lockdown status was not allowed to attend the funeral of his great-aunt. McLean is about to make his exit when Algernon's sister, Natasha Flowers, stops him. Natasha recently changed her college major from social science to criminal justice. This change is no doubt directly related to what she feels is the wrongful and unjust incarceration and prosecution of her brother. She asks McLean if he has gotten enough to eat, and thanks him for coming to show support for her family. She then inquires of much more personal matters.

"Nick, can you tell me how my brother is 'really' doing? My mom tries to wear that forced smile all the time, but I can see right through it. I asked her to put me on the visitation list so that I can go visit him from time to time in her place ... that never happened. How is he doing ... truthfully?"

"Well, I know he is being strong and he knows all the love and support he has here at home," McLean replies.

Natasha isn't at all interested in this generic response that McLean is offering so she asks another question. "Do you think she did it?"

McLean pauses, as he is not sure how to answer that question.

Picking up on his hesitation, Natasha continues to elaborate. "I mean, I know it's an ongoing investigation and all, and more than likely Brenda knows more than she is saying, but do you think, in your opinion—based on your all your leads, do you think she intentionally set my brother up for murder?"

Before Nick McLean can respond, Hazel Flowers interrupts to introduce McLean to some of her out-of-town family that travelled for the funeral. They all have questions for the lead investigator. McLean tries to give everyone a satisfactory answer without revealing too much of his findings during this very sensitive ongoing investigation. His concern is that the more people talk, the more covering up he will have to deal with. So, while keeping most of his information close to his belt, he gets through the barrage of questions like a skillful media relations specialist. Natasha Flowers, who is still standing nearby, looks at McLean and nods with a smile. She doesn't need him to directly answer her question anymore. She can tell that her brother Algernon is in good hands.

.   .   .

As Nick McLean exits the Flowers' residence, he must walk a few houses down to where he parked his SUV. Due to the large number of visitors attending the Flowers' home, some guests were forced to park along the residential street, while still not blocking any of the neighbors' driveways. On his way to his car, another vehicle catches McLean's eye. It is a silver sedan with dark tinted windows. The mysterious car is parked across the street, one house up from McLean's SUV. This means that he has to walk past it in order to get to his vehicle. McLean can feel the acceleration of his heart rate as he approaches the vehicle. The engine of the silver sedan is cranked on and the gas pedal is revved up as if partaking in a street drag race. Nick McLean reaches his right hand behind him and feels for the handle of his concealed firearm located in the small of his back. Again the engine of the silver sedan revs up. McLean grows more nervous with each step he takes in the direction of this mysterious vehicle. Trying to walk as close to his side of the street as possible, McLean attempts to catch a glimpse of the occupants inside the silver sedan, however the illegally dark tints make it impossible, especially at night. McLean slides his weapon out a little, readying himself for a possible physical confrontation. As McLean gets within a few yards from the silver sedan, the mysterious car spins out and speeds away down the street. McLean watches as the car disappears around the corner of the next intersection. With his hand still on his weapon, McLean turns back to his SUV. He tries to figure out if the occupants of that vehicle are following him, or just so happened to be watching the Flowers' home. He soon rules out the latter, since the police shouldn't be keeping surveillance on a residence that is not currently occupied by a potential suspect—in this case, Algernon Flowers, who is currently in the Local County Jail. He surmises that they are tailing him, and that awkward display he just encountered was a lame attempt to intimidate him ... but why? What is he getting too close to that they are afraid of?

McLean looks around, carefully checking his surroundings before removing his hand from his firearm. He then gets into his vehicle, locks the doors and drives away.

CHAPTER 26

Early in the morning after head count at the Local County Jail, Algernon Flowers' cell door is rolled open. During a previous conversation, a correctional officer mentioned he went to school with Detective Frank Howell. Ever since then, Algernon has not quite trusted this particular chubby officer. On this day, the officer confronts him—informing him that due to a problem with the plumbing in the cell located on the tier directly above his, they will have to relocate him to another cell on the other side of the unit. Algernon is watched closely as he packs up his bed linens and towel. He also packs his cards, letters and photos to carry to his new temporary cell. Once in his new cell, the door rolls closed behind him. Algernon unpacks his things and tries to recreate the feel of the cell he had gotten accustomed to since the day of his arrival.

Shortly after breakfast is served, there is an announcement of a 'shakedown' to take place immediately. All the cell doors roll open simultaneously as a slew of officers, one for each cell, enters the unit. Each officer is wearing blue rubber gloves and carrying a large, clear garbage bag to collect any and all contraband. Each inmate is ordered to stand directly outside of his assigned cell while the officers enter the cells to search. An officer, whom Algernon has not noticed before in the months that he has been here, is assigned to search his cell. The 'new' officer goes directly to the toilet-sink combo and reaches his hand underneath the narrow space between the floor and bottom of the sink portion. This area is approximately two inches in height. He pulls out a white, number ten mailing envelope that was stuck to the underside of the sink, held in place with toothpaste. The 'new' officer then opens the envelope and dumps out its contents. About twenty small, white round pills fall to the ground.

·   ·   ·

By noon Algernon Flowers is brought before a hearing committee consisting of various ranking officers at the jail. Also present is the 'new' officer to provide details to the committee as to what he discovered. Mr. Flowers is given an opportunity to speak. He pleads his case, stating that he was relocated to that cell moments earlier, and that he has never seen those pills before. He explains that he gets no contact visitation and therefore could in no way obtain the pills. He dare not accuse the 'new' officer of planting the envelope ... or at least not to his face, anyway. Either way, the defense of 'it was planted there' and 'I never saw those drugs before' usually doesn't work well. After allowing Mr. Flowers his two minutes to plead his case, the committee is ready to make its ruling. The decision is unanimous, 'GUILTY' of illegal contraband. Algernon is then given his punishment, which goes into effect immediately: Fifteen days in solitary! What this means for an already special custody inmate is no out-of-cell time, no phone calls, no mail, and no snacks. Full twenty-four hour, constant lockdown for half of the month, with a five-minute shower once per week. This is sort of a 'jail within the jail' scenario.

Upon entering the solitary confinement cell to begin his fifteen-day sentence, Algernon Flowers can only think of two things. First, what is his mom going to think when she comes to visit him and is then told that he has been placed in solitary for drug possession? Secondly, if this is how this jailhouse committee hearing went, how is he going to fare in the big courthouse during a murder trial before Judge Hangman Jackson?

.   .   .

After about four days in solitary confinement, a deflated and mentally exhausted Algernon Flowers sits on the hard concrete floor in the tiny cell. He tries to keep his mind full of positive thoughts but he is in pure emotional anguish. Unable to contact his family to let them know that he is all right, his mind only wanders to dark places and worst-case scenarios. He wonders if the stunt with the pills was intended to break him down mentally and try to make him go insane so that a jury would believe that possibly this crazy man would actually hurt an innocent child. He has seen other inmates mentally snap from the heavy mental strain of lockdown status, and he witnessed them being carried out in chains. His other thought is that the stunt with the pills could be a way to suggest that his attorney gave them to him, since that is the only sort of contact visitation he has. Could this be their plan, to get his attorney disbarred and unable to defend him in court? How could the jail officials think he could have gotten those pills past the officers who search him before and after each visit? As these thoughts race through his head, his attention is diverted by a tray of food sliding in through the rectangular cutout in the iron door. Algernon Flowers is starving. Without his snack privileges, his family cannot purchase him any snacks, therefore his nutrition relies solely on the three daily county jail meals that are just enough to keep an inmate alive. Algernon devours the tiny meal and licks the tray clean.

"Eleven more days to go," he sobs in a whisper.

CHAPTER 27

On their way to the Local County Courthouse, Steven Didia and his son Steven Jr. ride together in Jr.'s car. Today Steven Jr. is sitting in with his father and Michael Petagnas on a deposition of a woman who lived in the apartment directly below Brenda Howell's. During the drive, the men talk about the new young lady Steven Jr. is going out on date number two with later tonight.

"She is absolutely gorgeous, Dad," proclaims an excited Steven Jr. "She is also preparing to take the bar exam this fall, so we can study together," he adds to assure his father that his priorities are still in order, and if anything, this woman will be more of an accountability partner than a distraction. Steven Sr. is glad to see his son has his head on straight, and he is happy that his boy met a nice Local County girl.

As the father and son duo arrive at the courthouse, they meet Michael Petagnas and Sandy Ward in the lobby. They all immediately begin preparing to depose the woman that the prosecution is considering '*an ear witness*'. Petagnas and his defense team review the woman's original statement to the police on the day the ambulance and South Rocky police were called out to Brenda Howell's apartment. Steven Sr. realizes that he left a folder in the back seat of his son's car. He asks Steven Jr. to go out and retrieve it for him. Michael Petagnas, Steven Sr., and Sandy Ward continue with their preparation. Prosecutor David Edwards' paralegal Jennifer Forde approaches the defense team to inform them that all involved parties are in place, and ready to begin whenever they are ready. She then heads back up to the room where the deposition will be held.

In the deposition room, Prosecutor Edwards and Prosecutor Henderson also review the original statement of the woman who lived downstairs from Brenda Howell. The woman—Patricia Gaddis—is also present and seated in her chair awaiting the arrival of the defense team. Jennifer Forde returns to the room and takes her seat next to Prosecutor Edwards. After several moments pass by, those present make small talk as they continue to await the arrival of the defense. Prosecutor Edwards offers the woman a drink of water. She declines but requests a cup of hot tea for her throat instead. Prosecutor Edwards sends his paralegal Jennifer down to the lobby to get a cup of tea for what he hopes is an excellent prosecution witness.

.   .   .

At the arrival of Michael Petagnas and his team to the deposition room, both prosecutors stand and greet them, before all take their seats and prepare to get underway. The prosecution is prepared to begin when Jennifer returns with a cup of hot tea for the witness.

"Sorry for the delay, but the hot water kettle downstairs is out of order so I had to run over to the coffee shop across the street," says a winded Jennifer as she quickly walks the cup over to Patricia Gaddis.

As Jennifer looks up, her eyes land on something that distracts her and she almost burns Ms. Gaddis by spilling some of the hot liquid drink in front of her.

"I'm so sorry, are you all right?" offers Jennifer as she wipes the liquid off the table with a napkin.

Ms. Gaddis is in good spirits about the mishap and assures her that all is well. Jennifer appears as though she has seen a ghost as she walks to her seat next to Prosecutor Edwards. She is staring at the familiar face of Steven Didia Jr., who is preoccupied with reading Patricia Gaddis' police statement. He is so focused on his reading that he doesn't see Jennifer, who is now seated directly across from him. She tries to get his attention somehow telepathically by staring directly into him as Prosecutor Edwards officially begins the deposition.

Edwards asks the witness to introduce herself, briefly describe what she does for a living, how long she has lived at her current address, and share basic general background information. Jennifer cannot seem to get Steven Jr.'s attention without creating a scene or drawing too much attention to herself. She decides to send him a text message. Steven Jr.'s phone makes an audible alert sound, which causes his father and Prosecutor Edwards to look at him. Realizing that he forgot to place his phone on vibrate, and too embarrassed to even look up as he can almost feel the eyes of his father piercing the side of his skull, the younger Didia quickly slides the button that places his phone into silent mode. He looks at the phone and sees that he has a text message–the sender–'Jennifer from the coffee shop.' This makes him smile. The text reads: *Hey!* Steven Jr. decides to text right back, smiling the entire time: *Hey you! What's up?* Jennifer closes her eyes and shakes her head in disbelief. She reads his text message and responds: *In a deposition!* Steven Jr. is now completely disengaged from the rest of the room as all of his attention is solely on his phone. He reads her message and replies: *Me too … Snoozer.* Jennifer cannot believe this man has not looked up and noticed her sitting only a few feet from him. She sends one more text: *Look up!!!*

Steven Jr. finds this to be a strange message. Maybe she sent him a text intended for someone else ... or perhaps she meant it metaphorically—as in staying positive. However he does look up and is mortified to see his date for tonight sitting next to the prosecutor on the case he is working on. They both give each other the 'What are you doing here?' look, followed by the 'We need to talk' look.

After stating her background information, Patricia Gaddis then goes on to give her statement. She states that on the morning in question she heard a 'thump' followed by running footsteps coming from the apartment above her. She soon after saw the ambulance and police arrive on the scene. The prosecution is considering Ms. Gaddis to be *an ear witness* suggesting that what she heard was the beating of the young victim. Michael Petagnas can see flaws in this prosecution witness' story but he decides to wait to confront her during the trial. The defense has no additional questions for this witness, and she is dismissed.

There is one more prosecution witness that is scheduled to do his deposition today—Homicide Detective Rodney Hunter. It is Detective Hunter who was directly assigned to this case. As the lead investigator, he oversees all of the interviews and collection of evidence. Detective Hunter is a middle-aged man with pale skin and an average build. He enters the deposition room wearing a tan suit and a royal blue dress shirt. His badge is proudly displayed on the front left breast of his suit jacket. He shakes hands with both prosecutors before taking his seat.

Like the witness before him, Detective Hunter is asked by the prosecution to give his background. He also states his credentials and experience within the homicide division. The prosecution then asks him to go back over the events and steps he took during his investigation in this case. Detective Hunter gives his statement.

"After getting word of a suspicious death of a toddler, I went to the Rocky Beach Memorial hospital. There I met with the treating physician, Doctor Richard Mason. He didn't have an exact cause of death but he mentioned bruising located on the lower abdomen. I proceeded to take photos of the bruising for my records. I was told that when the child was discovered unresponsive, both Detective Howell's wife and ..."

Prosecutor Edwards interrupts his witness, "Detective, sorry for interrupting but let's refrain from using inferences as to any relationship with the Rocky Beach P.D. as not to give the impression of any bias," he cautions.

Detective Hunter nods in agreement and continues on with his statement.

"Yes, sir. So after being told that when the child was discovered unresponsive, both the child's mother and the mother's boyfriend were the only adults present, I decided to speak with them ... Well, we wanted to speak with the mother first because my experience, with cases like these, is that there is usually some history of abuse or neglect involved.

"After presenting the child's mother with photos of the bruising, she said that her boyfriend noticed them, but that was the first time she was seeing them. I asked her directly if she beat her daughter. She said no, and that her boyfriend informed her over the phone that the child was unresponsive. After speaking with the mother, I went to speak with her boyfriend. He also denied any involvement. He said that he found the child unresponsive. My partner and I decided to continue to grill him because he seemed arrogant in his demeanor. Upon further questioning, the boyfriend stated that he was terminating the interview. We didn't have enough to charge him with anything, and he had no outstanding warrants on which we could hold him, so he was released and we continued to speak with the mother. She too was later released and we continued to look for witnesses and await the medical examiner to determine time of death. Over the next few weeks, the case was taken to a grand jury and an indictment was signed charging the boyfriend, Algernon Flowers."

Detective Rodney Hunter concludes his statement. Michael Petagnas has some questions for this witness.

"Detective, so the child's mother, Brenda Howell, told you that her boyfriend, Algernon Flowers, saw the bruises and brought it to her attention?" asks Petagnas.

"That is correct," Detective Hunter replies.

Petagnas inquires further. "How, if at all, did that affect your opinion of Mr. Flowers?"

"Well, naturally, it made me feel as though he must have information as to what happened to the little girl. That's why we wanted to talk to him," replies Hunter.

Petagnas looks at the notes he took while Detective Hunter was giving his statement. He has another question. "You didn't mention this, but who took the photos of Brenda Howell's hand?"

Detective Hunter, without even thinking, looks directly toward the two prosecutors before answering. Petagnas and Didia both pick up on his slight, yet significant, hesitation.

"That would've been me," Detective Hunter replies.

"Nothing further from the defense," Petagnas concludes.

What he really means is: 'Nothing further until I have you in front of a jury.'

Detective Hunter is released, which concludes the depositions for the day. Both sides briefly discuss scheduling any future depositions before dismissing for the day. While exiting the deposition room, Jennifer Forde and Steven Didia Jr. exit a little slower than the others. As the prosecution and defense teams walk ahead and are distracted in their conversations, the young couple quietly engages one another as not to be noticed by the others.

"You work for THEM?" Jennifer asks.

"You work for THEM?" Steven Jr. replies with the same question and exact tone. They look at each other, puzzled as they follow their respective parties in opposite directions.

CHAPTER 28

As far as cases go, for private investigator Nicholas McLean and his team this is among the most frustrating. It feels as though they are battling against a corrupt police investigation with tainted evidence, and far too many uncooperative witnesses to be coincidence. If he is going to get down to the meat and heart of this case, Nick McLean knows that he has got to dig deep within the hierarchy of the Rocky Beach Police Department. The safest way to kill a snake without getting bitten is to chop off its head.

·   ·   ·

Police Chief Donald Nelson comes from a long bloodline of police officers. His father was a police officer—his father's father was a police officer—and his father before that. Chief Nelson's son is also following in the family occupation, as he too is a young detective with the Rocky Beach Police Department. Chief

Nelson prides himself on having a department that is both respected and feared. With close ties to the local media, he tries to present his officers to the public as the best and brightest. Today the chief is having lunch at the Tavern Bay Restaurant with news reporter Heather Hoffman. Since she was a child, Heather Hoffman always dreamed of anchoring the evening news. Growing up she would see the sophisticated, well-dressed women reporting the breaking news with such grace and eloquence. Practicing in her mirror as a little girl, she knew that she wanted to be among the great news anchors. She studied journalism at the Local University, and then landed her first gig as a field reporter at Channel Thirteen News. Her goal is to get promoted to evening anchor, and then use that experience to one day anchor a national news broadcast in New York City or Los Angeles. However, it is hard for a young girl from Local County, Florida, to gain national attention covering silly stories about alligators found in residential backyards, or the local minor league baseball team getting a new stadium. Heather Hoffman understands that in order for her to be taken seriously, get promoted and move up in this industry, she needs to first report big news-worthy stories, and here in Local County, the big story right now is the upcoming murder trial of Algernon Flowers. It was Heather who got the exclusive footage of Algernon Flowers being taken in handcuffs from the South Rocky Police Station to the Local County Jail. None of the other stations had word of the indictment, or where Algernon Flowers was being held before being transferred to the jail. Only Heather Hoffman had that information. Using her inside information, she showed up with her cameraman and got to report the big story to open the 6 o'clock news.

As Police Chief Nelson and Heather Hoffman sit and enjoy lunch together, Nick McLean observes them from a booth nearby. McLean suspects it was Chief Nelson that gave the order for Algernon Flowers to be held in the South Rocky Police station holding cell. Algernon turned himself in shortly after noon on the day of his arrest, however he was held until 6

P.M. before being cuffed and taken to the county jail. McLean feels that by developing an inappropriate relationship with the much older, married chief of police, Heather Hoffman has gained herself exclusive rights to the breaking news surrounding the case. As the news becomes available, Chief Nelson calls his young mistress, who then reports it first, increasing her airtime and improving her chances of making evening anchor. It is a win-win for them both, as Chief Nelson gets to have media coverage spun in the best, most favorable light when it comes to his department and the handling of major cases ... not to mention he gets a sexy young lover in the process. McLean tries to process the events from the perspective of the police chief. If, in fact, when the wife of a police officer murders their daughter and uncovers a history of domestic violence and abuse within the life of one of his detectives, that will reflect on his entire department poorly and ultimately affect his bid for re-election. The question Nick McLean needs to have answered: Is there a cover up, and does the chief know about it? That is what McLean, the very resourceful investigator, is here to find out.

From his vantage point, Nick McLean can see there may be trouble in paradise between the chief and his young mistress. He cannot clearly make out what the couple is talking about, but their body language suggests it is more of a quarrel than blissful banter. The background noise in the restaurant makes it difficult for McLean to hear, but he can make out a few phrases. He catches a very clear line from the young news reporter. She mentions something about a much bigger story. Unsure of what that means, McLean writes it down in his notepad and underlines it. He figures it must be extremely important because of the chief's response to it. He turns bright red with anger and points at her in a threatening manner. Soon thereafter, Heather Hoffman throws down her fork and napkin, grabs her purse and casually storms away. McLean can't fully make out what she said, but he writes down what he thinks he heard: *Oh yeah, watch me!* McLean underlines these words in his notepad as to remind him later of their significance. He continues to keep an eye on the chief of police, who is now seated alone.

Chief Nelson looks around, hoping no one witnessed the minor scene that his young mistress just performed like a spoiled brat. McLean quickly buries his face in the menu as to not arouse the chief's suspicion. Chief Nelson makes a phone call on his cell. McLean cannot actually hear him. It seems that the chief, unlike Ms. Hoffman, is much more discreet and secretive. The call lasts only a few seconds and then the chief finishes his meal, leaves a tip and walks to the counter to pay his tab.

.   .   .

As Heather Hoffman storms off to her car, Nick McLean's partner, Rachael O'Toole, follows her. Rachael gets in her car and trails the young reporter. Heather Hoffman drives toward the beach and pulls into a beachside motel. Rachael watches from a safe distance as Ms. Hoffman parks her vehicle. Rachael finds a distant parking spot where she can maintain a clear visual of Hoffman's car. Several moments go by before there is any activity. Rachael then notices Ms. Hoffman exit her vehicle, but there is something very different about her. The pretty brunette is now disguised in a blonde wig and large sunglasses. Rachael's initial thought is, perhaps she is doing some undercover news report and is attempting to conceal her true identity. Rachael continues to observe Hoffman as she walks to a door on the second floor landing. After knocking on the door, Hoffman looks around, as she clearly doesn't want to be seen. The room door soon opens and Hoffman quickly disappears into the room as the door closes. Rachael exits her car and walks to the motel office. After bribing the young man behind the glass counter, she gets the name of the person renting the room that the shady news reporter just entered. It is an alias: John Doe. The person used cash to rent the room and didn't show ID. One piece of good information that Rachael's fifty dollars bought her from the young motel employee is that whoever rented the room parked his or her car around the back of the building away from the street, with each room having an assigned parking spot. Using this information, Rachael knows she is looking for parking spot number forty-six. Heather Hoffman's car is in a visitor's parking spot, so Rachael walks around toward the back of the building. She looks at the parking spot numbers, painted in white. She gets to the one she is looking for, number forty-six. Parked in the space is a familiar silver sedan with dark tinted windows.

CHAPTER 29

Steven Didia Jr. and Jennifer Forde decided it would be best to meet and talk immediately after work, rather than waiting for a dinner date later. They are meeting at the same coffee shop where they first met. Huddled at a corner table, they speak as if they are two spies possibly being watched.

"Why didn't you mention that you work for the DA?" a frantic Steven Jr. asks the pretty blonde.

"Me? You never mentioned that your father works with the most popular defense attorney in all of Rocky Beach?" Jennifer replies.

She grabs her head with her hands.

"Ugh, I should have asked for your last name! This is bad. This is really, really bad," says a stressed-out Jennifer.

Steven Jr. takes her hand, but Jennifer pulls away by natural instinct and out of pure nervousness.

"It's not the end of the world," Steven Jr. states calmly.

"Not the end of the world but the end of my career! I mean … I told you how I felt about the case I'm working on and that I think we've got it all wrong, and it just so happens that your father, and the firm that YOU now work for, is defending the guy in a first-degree murder trial! I'd say it's the end all right!" exclaims Jennifer in a panic.

The young couple frantically deliberate back and forth as they mull over the events of the day, wondering how this happened. Things were going so well between them, but the decision to not talk about work has gotten them in quite the bind. How can Steven now tell his father that the woman he said would not become a distraction to him is now possibly going to cause problems in the biggest case in their firm's history? Didia Sr. is going to want to grill Jr. about everything he discussed with Jennifer. Jennifer is probably going to have to expect the same from Prosecutor Edwards, except in her case she has already disclosed her controversial personal feelings to her boss, and now with the son of one of the men defending the man he is prosecuting. David Edwards is not going to like this one bit.

After weighing their options, Steven Jr. and Jennifer both agree that their best and only option is to be upfront and open about it all. Jennifer will tell her boss that she has be seeing a member of Algernon Flowers' defense team on a personal level, and Steven Jr. will inform his father and Michael Petagnas that he has been personally involved with a member of the prosecution team, also known as 'the enemy.'

.   .   .

Hazel Flowers goes to visit her son Algernon at the Local County Jail. She hasn't heard from him in a few days now and has grown very concerned about his health and welfare. She endures another drive out along the winding and poorly lit roads that lead to the desolate, wooded area where the county jail is located. She goes through the scrutiny of another security check and pat down. After enduring another crowded, malodorous jailhouse waiting room, she is finally informed that her son's visiting privileges have been revoked due to his new solitary confinement status. When she hears this news she becomes agitated and makes a request to speak with the supervising officer. When the on-duty supervisor comes out to meet with Ms. Flowers, things become clear to her that her son is being mistreated. She doesn't understand how he could be found guilty of drug possession. How could he get drugs? Ms. Flowers has many questions, but the very rude and dismissive tone she receives from the shift supervisor lets her know that she wouldn't get the answers here. She takes the long drive back home and plans to meet with her son's attorney as soon as possible.

.   .   .

As Algernon Flowers sits in his tiny, empty cell, he tries to keep his mind on anything positive. However, the upcoming murder trial and his growling stomach seem to be the only things that consume his thoughts. He is looking forward to the weekend, when he can get to finally take a shower. Even though all he seems to do is sleep all day, his body odor is up to 'major funk' level. Feeling dirty, hungry and afraid is not how this young man envisioned his life just a few months after recording his first CD. The connections he made during his trip to Nashville, Tennessee, were very encouraging and promising. He figured that by this time he would've been touring the nation and sharing his music with the world. This is a far cry from the fame and fortune he saw when he imagined what his life would be like.

Not even sure what day it is, Algernon Flowers pretends it is his last day living in the county jail. He fantasizes about someone coming forth with some evidence that vindicates him, or that Brenda Howell would become so overwhelmed with guilt that she confesses, and lets the police know that he had nothing to do with the death of little Deja. The feeling of injustice is extremely difficult to let go of. It consumes his mind every waking moment. Even the way he ended up in solitary confinement on a bogus drug charge gives him little hope that he would ever get a fair trial, as he stands accused of an unthinkable crime. Algernon can only hope that somewhere out there, Michael Petagnas and his skillful private investigator Nick McLean are fighting hard for him.

·　　　·　　　·

Rachael O'Toole has been sitting in her car watching the same motel room door since late afternoon. It is now late in the evening and still there has been no activity. Her partner Nick McLean now joins her on the stakeout. McLean is parked in the rear of the building in his SUV, keeping an eye on the silver sedan. The two communicate using their cell phones. McLean is waiting for a cue from Rachael as to when either Heather Hoffman or the driver of the silver sedan emerges from the room.

Another vehicle arrives carrying the other half of the McLean investigative foursome, Helena Wang and Brent Patterson. They are here to relieve their partners for bathroom breaks and to provide fresh coffee and food. Helena gets into Rachael's car so that Rachael can go to the restroom in the motel lobby. Brent Patterson drives around to bring McLean a fresh cup of coffee and a sandwich. McLean refuses to take a bathroom break. He is not going to miss an opportunity to see who the driver of the mysterious silver sedan is—who has been following him and trying to intimidate him for weeks now—and also the person who was following Algernon Flowers when he met with Brenda Howell. If McLean can figure out the 'WHO,' then maybe he can figure out the 'WHY.'

·　　　·　　　·

Several hours pass by with no activity at the motel room door. Finally the door opens, and Channel Thirteen News reporter Heather Hoffman emerges and looks around suspiciously as she quickly walks down to her car, still sporting the blonde wig and large sunglasses, even under the dark cover of night.

The suspicious-looking reporter gets into her vehicle and drives away. Rachael calls McLean to alert him of this recent activity. She lets him know she is trailing Ms. Hoffman and that he should be expecting the driver of the silver sedan shortly.

Every moment feels like an eternity as Nick McLean awaits the driver of the silver sedan to return to his vehicle. Finally after about twenty minutes from the time he received Rachael's call, McLean gets his first glimpse of the driver: the man that may hold the key to unlock a door of many skeletons, lies, and cover-ups. He is an average height male, with a slim yet muscular build. He is dressed in jeans and a slim-fitting, short-sleeve shirt. He has medium-length hair and chiseled facial features. On his waist, a badge and a gun. The man looks around before getting into his vehicle. Nick McLean waits for the best opportunity to snap a digital photo of the man. He gets it—a perfect front profile shot. The man doesn't see McLean parked in a dark area with very little light. McLean readies his hand to start his engine as he sees the brake lights illuminate on the silver sedan. As the sedan backs out of the parking space and pulls around to the front of the motel, McLean starts his engine and pursues the mystery lawman.

Rachael calls to report that she followed Heather Hoffman to the address that is listed as her permanent residence. When she got out of her car, she no longer wore the blonde wig or large sunglasses. She entered her home, took out her trash and then it was lights out. McLean informs Rachael that he is tailing the silver sedan and that she should go home to get some sleep.

. . .

Nick McLean carefully trails the silver sedan from a safe distance. He is certain the law enforcement officer will know how to detect when he's being followed, especially if he has something to hide. At one point McLean thinks he loses sight of the vehicle, but then he relocates it up ahead. The sedan turns into a gated residential area. The driver's window rolls down—the driver enters a code on the keypad—the large gate slides open and the silver sedan enters. McLean tries to speed up to the gate before it rolls shut but he doesn't make it. He makes a few attempted guesses as to a correct code, but none of them work. It appears as though McLean has lost the mysterious and elusive silver sedan. At least for now.

CHAPTER 30

As the Florida sun rises, suburban life comes alive with the activation of automatic sprinklers on the cultivated landscaping, dog walkers, and early-morning joggers. Minivans and school buses carry children to schools, and recycling trucks make their rounds collecting spent household items from green and blue plastic bins. Just another average weekday here in the private community that Hazel Flowers calls home. As she exits her garage, she stops at the mailbox at the end of her curved driveway. She places a letter addressed to her son Algernon at the Local County Jail. She is not even sure her if son is allowed to receive mail while in solitary confinement, but she closes the mailbox, raises the red flag to alert her postman to pick up when he makes his rounds later this morning. Ms. Flowers is usually still at home when the postman arrives, but this morning, before heading to her daycare center, she is paying a visit to her son's defense lawyer, Michael Petagnas.

When Hazel Flowers arrives at the Law Office of Petagnas & Didia she is greeted by Sandy Ward, who is expecting her. Ms. Flowers and Sandy Ward have developed a bond as mothers. It is Sandy Ward who usually receives all the calls from Ms. Flowers and takes the lead in communicating with the Flowers family, as Michael Petagnas is mostly busy with all of the pretrial legal action. The two women share a cup of coffee in the small break room area and partake in some small talk as they await the arrival of Michael Petagnas.

When Michael Petagnas arrives, he invites both Sandy Ward and Hazel Flowers into his office. Petagnas expresses his devotion and dedication to her son's defense, and assures her that he and his entire team are fighting vigorously for Algernon. Ms. Flowers appreciates this and needs that boost of confidence. However, she has concerns about her son's mental and emotional state.

"I think they are trying to break him mentally," explains a distraught Hazel Flowers.

She goes on to explain what she has learned during her last visit. She cannot understand how he could have gotten drugs. She feels that by placing him in solitary confinement, the once- happy, always smiling, and very social young man she once knew will become anti-social and develop emotional problems.

"This cannot be good for his mental state, to be isolated to that extreme," Ms. Flowers continues.

Michael Petagnas and Sandy Ward are learning this for the first time. Not only of this incident, but the previous incident in which Algernon was placed in the suicide unit. Ms. Flowers wants her son to be taken out of the special lockdown status and placed among others so that he isn't affected with long-term social issues. However Michael Petagnas disagrees with this suggestion. As a former prosecutor, Petagnas would use jailhouse informants to help level cases in his favor. The idea is basically offering a dropped or reduced sentence to an inmate in exchange for testimony that incriminates another inmate.

Petagnas explains, "If Algernon is taken out of his special lock down status, the first thing they will do is place him with a cellmate who is facing a potentially lengthy prison sentence, and who is desperate. That cellmate will then get on the witness stand at trial and tell the jury that Algernon confessed to him that he was involved in this murder. It's called jailhouse snitching. I've used them in the past, and I am sure Prosecutor Edwards would use one in this case if he had the opportunity. He needs something like that to boost his case. I think this solitary confinement is a stunt to break Algernon down to want to request going into general population. Trust me, it's a bad idea."

Michael Petagnas asks Ms. Flowers to encourage her son that no matter what, he needs to remain in protective custody as a high-profile inmate. She doesn't like the idea, but agrees that it is probably in his best interests. Before ending the meeting, Sandy Ward and Michael Petagnas give Ms. Flowers some information they have discovered in her son's favor, however they keep much of it to themselves as to not risk showing their hand too soon. They tell her not to mention any of it to anyone, not even Algernon Flowers.

A few doors down the hall from Michael Petagnas' office is the office of his partner, Steven Didia Sr. There is another meeting currently taking place in Didia's office as Steven Jr. has just informed his father that the new girl he is dating is the paralegal for Prosecutor David Edwards. Steven Sr. does not take this news well. This is his son's first week with his firm, and he has already managed to potentially jeopardize their biggest case.

"Well how much of the case have you discussed with this girl?" asks a frustrated Steven Sr.

Michael Petagnas enters Didia's office after his meeting with Ms. Flowers.

"What is it, Steve? You said it was urgent," asks Petagnas upon his arrival.

Didia Sr. commences to deliver the terrible news. Steven Jr. interjects in an attempt to minimize his role in this.

"I didn't say anything about the case, she was the one that mentioned feelings she had about the case she was working on!" he exclaims.

Steven Sr. only rebukes him and offers his own theory. "This girl played you. She used her good looks to get you to talk about what we have so far in this case ... and you fell for it!" he spews.

That suggestion offends Steven Jr. and he defends Jennifer.

"I don't think so ... she didn't even know my last name or what firm I'm working with," he explains.

"Steven, tell us everything that was discussed so that we can access what's been compromised," interjects Michael Petagnas.

The three men discuss and evaluate their options before deciding that someone needs to put a call in to the prosecutor's office.

.   .   .

Jennifer Forde packs the personal items from her desk into a box. She has dried-up tears on her cheeks and her nose is bright red. When she informed Prosecutor Edwards and Prosecutor Henderson of the possible scandal she might have exposed their already-fragile case to, she was terminated on the spot. Her honesty in also sharing the fact that she expressed her opinion about the prosecution having the case all wrong to a member of the defense team really didn't help her plea. After clearing her desk and saying her goodbyes to some coworkers, Jennifer takes the elevator ride of shame down to the lobby, holding her things in the small box. She is totally embarrassed. She is also afraid this may ruin her career and blacklist her in the legal community.

When the elevator opens in the lobby, Jennifer feels like every eye is on her in judgment. She cannot escape fast enough as her heels echo throughout the marble halls. Even before she reaches the parking lot, her emotions cannot wait until she is in the privacy of her vehicle. She breaks down in a flood of tears right outside the large glass door, beneath the sign that reads: Office of the Local County District Attorney.

CHAPTER 31

Nicholas McLean sits in his office with his team of investigators. They sift through online photos of the various members of the Rocky Beach Police Department, specifically in the detectives division. The plan for the morning, and only item on the agenda, is to use the photo taken by McLean at the motel to identify the man in the silver sedan. This proves rather difficult, even for this veteran team of crafty investigators, because for the safety of the officers, no undercover detective's photos are listed on public record. Investigator Brent Patterson recalls the familiar face of the mystery man. He also has a photo of the man taken at the vow renewal ceremony of the Howells. He was Detective Frank Howell's best man. McLean concludes that this search may need to physically go into the Rocky Beach Police Station. Helena Wang, who finds the mystery man to be rather sexy, volunteers to take this particular man hunt on personally.

"Hey, maybe if I find him I can get him to take me out on a date," jokes Helena.

After a brief chuckle from the group, McLean replies. "Actually, that's not a bad idea," he says, as he appears to have a brilliant plan up his sleeve.

McLean figures any detective that is brazen enough to have an affair with the mistress of the chief of police either has a death wish, or an uncontrollable weakness for the ladies. As he shares his plan with the team, everyone seems to be on board with it—even Helena Wang, who was merely joking about a date with the guy.

"Let's just hope he's into Asian women," states a playful yet determined Helena.

.   .   .

Hazel Flowers usually drives past the Rocky Beach Police Department during her daily commute from her home to the daycare center. Lately she detours out of her way, which adds an additional fifteen minutes to her drive. However, she would much rather endure the added travel time than drive by the place that she now views as symbolic to the corruption and misappropriation that has spiraled into a first-degree murder charge for her son, Algernon. She can't stomach the idea of seeing that place every day. Even the sight of Rocky Beach police cars patrolling the streets gives Ms. Flowers the chills. The shield that once held a place of respect and honor in her mind now exemplifies mistrust in her heart and represents oppression in her life.

On this particular morning there are road closures on her newer route, so she is forced to take the drive past the Rocky Beach Police Station. She tries not to look over as she passes the station on her right. Then something deep within her—the strongest desire she's had for confrontation in a while—just simply takes over and she turns to pull into the visitor's parking lot of the station. Not really sure why she's there, or even what she will say, or whom she will say it to, this woman is raging with passion and hostility and needs to vent. Without even thinking about it, Hazel Flowers finds a parking spot, exits her vehicle and is now walking toward the entrance of the Rocky Beach Police Station. She passes a sign that reads: Rocky Beach Police–Protect, Respect, & Serve–Chief Donald Nelson. She would love nothing more than to rip that sign off the brick wall as she views it as false advertisement. When she reaches the door and puts her hand on the handle, she can feel her heart beating rapidly as she almost tears the door from its hinges upon opening it. Her aggressive walk down the hall toward the reception desk gives the impression that this woman has something to say and will not be stopped. When she reaches the desk, a female officer greets her. This young and friendly officer welcomes Ms. Flowers with such courtesy and respect that almost instantaneously, the enraged mother has an epiphany of sorts. She realizes that although there are some within the department that may be lacking morality and integrity, there is still hope for the future of this department in young officers, such as the one smiling before her.

"Good morning ma'am, how may I help you today?" asks the charming and polite young officer.

Ms. Flowers cannot possibly take out her rage on this lovely young woman, and she dare not ask to speak directly with Chief Nelson. She decides to maintain her composure and bow out gracefully. Noticing pamphlets for police recruitment on the counter, Ms. Flowers quickly diverts her focus elsewhere.

"Taking one of these for my nephew. He is thinking about getting into law enforcement," explains Ms. Flowers as she reaches for one of the pamphlets.

She thanks the officer and exits. She almost has a smile on her face as she pushes past the exit door ... drama and disaster averted.

A well-dressed woman who is entering the station passes Ms. Flowers. The woman walks confidently down the hall as her high heels gently and gracefully caress the floor with each step. The woman is Channel Thirteen News reporter Heather

Hoffman. She approaches the young female officer at the reception desk and states her business.

"Yes, I'm here to see Chief Nelson ... Heather Hoffman, he's expecting me," exclaims a cocky Ms. Hoffman.

.   .   .

From his vantage point, private investigator Nick McLean can see the large front entrance of the gated community where he lost sight of the mysterious silver sedan. He can also see the shiny red sports car with the hood up and the woman underneath it. McLean keeps an eye on the gate while communicating to his partner Helena Wang through a Bluetooth earpiece connected to her cell phone. Helena, who is in full makeup and a long wig, pretends to have broken down right at the front entrance of the exclusive gated community. Wearing her short, tight dress and high heels, Helena has to ward off several other male motorists who seem extremely overeager to help the damsel in distress. In order to achieve this she simply tells them that her husband is just down the street on his way to assist her, when in fact she is waiting on a particular knight in shining armor ... silver armor ... with dark tinted windows.

As the silver sedan approaches the main entrance, the tall front gate slowly rolls open. Nick McLean calls in the activity to his partner Helena Wang.

"We're rolling, Helena," he exclaims anxiously.

"Showtime," replies Helena.

As the silver sedan exits the front gate, a bubbly and vivacious Helena jumps out in front of the slow-moving sedan while pointing over to her disabled vehicle off to the side a few yards away. The stunned driver pulls over behind the red car with the hood up, and exits his car. Helena has now repositioned herself to the front of her car, leaning under the hood and pretending to diagnose the problem. McLean can see the man as he walks from his silver sedan toward the front of Helena's car. The man is checking out Helena's long, shapely legs and well-rounded buttocks. As the mystery man slows down to enjoy the view, McLean reports into Helena's earpiece.

"You got 'em, girl," states McLean with a smirk.

When the man finally takes his eyes off of the baited eye-candy, he doesn't even attempt to look under the hood. He is more concerned with getting acquainted with the sexy woman and offering her a ride. After a little mutual flirting and a fake call to her 'mechanic' to tell him where to pick up her broken-down vehicle, Helena takes the man up on his offer to give her a ride to the nearest coffee shop. Mentioning that he is a police officer and flashing his badge was not only intended to make the distressed damsel comfortable enough to get in the car with a stranger, but also an attempt to turn her on, as he feels all women are attracted to power and authority. Once Helena gets in the silver sedan and they drive off, McLean tails them as another vehicle driven by another investigator, Brent Patterson, pulls up to the red car. Rachael O'Toole gets out of Patterson's vehicle, reconnects the battery on Helena's car, and closes the hood. She gets into the shiny red car and both cars drive away.

Helena Wang has successfully infiltrated the secret mystery man's sanctuary—the Holy Grail—the elusive silver sedan. It is almost surreal as she rides inside the darkened windows and is so close to the mysterious man. The handsome and very frisky man caresses Helena's arm and leg as he tries to seduce the sexy lady he believes he rescued. His forwardness is making Helena uncomfortable as he feels as though she now 'owes him.' She tries to play shy as not to turn him off or reject him just yet.

"Why don't we take the day off and just go hang out by the beach? I'm sure you can use a beach day after the morning you've had," suggests the mystery man as he places his hand on Helena's knee.

Helena wants to get information out of this guy quickly and make her exit … the sooner, the better.

"My brother is going to meet me at the coffee shop. He lives nearby … besides, an off day? How can you just take an off day, don't you have to fight crime and catch criminals?" replies a quick-thinking Helena.

The man grins and moves his hand higher up Helena's leg. She is cringing but tries to play it cool.

"I'm not like the other officers. I march to the beat of my own drum," says the cocky mystery man.

"Oh, how so, because you work undercover?" inquires Helena.

The man glances over at the attractive woman in his passenger seat and proudly reveals, "No, because the police chief is my dad!"

CHAPTER 32

Michael Petagnas and Steven Didia Sr., along with Prosecutors Edwards and Henderson, are assembled in the chambers of the Honorable Judge Warren Jackson. They are wrapping up an emergency meeting to discuss any conflicts of interest or any possible exchange of privileged information between Steven Didia Jr. and Prosecutor Edwards' now former paralegal, Jennifer Forde. The prosecution wants to ban Jennifer Forde as a potential defense witness.

"Her 'opinion' about our case, and whom we seek to indict and how we prosecute them, should not be called into account to a jury, or even hinted at by the defense," exclaims a rattled David Edwards to the annoyed judge.

Steven Didia Sr. apologizes again. "I personally apologize for my son unknowingly receiving any information that the prosecution feels may or may not jeopardize their case. However, your Honor, the circumstances surrounding our staff member hearing the 'opinion' of a former prosecution staff member have absolutely no bearing on this case whatsoever," argues Didia Sr.

After several back-and-forth arguments between the two opposing sides, the judge makes a decision. The defense cannot list Jennifer Forde as a defense witness, nor can they use any hearsay testimony relating to any information coming from within the county prosecutor's office due to the indiscretion of the former employee. However, he is not removing Petagnas & Didia from Algernon Flowers' defense, as was requested by the prosecution.

"I fail to see how this in any way inhibits due process in this case," states Judge Jackson.

With that ruling, he dismisses the gentlemen from his chambers until the next appointed pretrial hearing.

.   .   .

When Michael Petagnas and Steven Didia Sr. get into Petagnas' car to drive back to their office, they both agree that in order to avoid any potential legal or future appellate issues with their case, Steven Didia Jr. will be off the Algernon Flowers case. He will remain at the firm, and for now will handle other newer cases that come in.

"We totally dodged a major bullet with this, my friend," says Petagnas to his partner.

The two men share a laugh about it, but they both know how messy that could've gotten, and that they may have been forced off of the Flowers' case by the judge. They return to the office to continue working on this ever-evolving case.

.   .   .

While sitting on a bench overlooking the ocean, Jennifer Forde has a sense of relief as she thinks in retrospect. Her gut feeling about the Algernon Flowers murder case made her very un-comfortable and she was never at ease about it. She views the events of the past couple of days as a blessing in disguise. Not that she is happy to have lost her job, but now she can sleep better at night without the stress of working on a case that can potentially send an innocent man to prison. Also on the bright side, she can focus all of her efforts and energy on studying for the state bar examination ... that and the handsome young man that is sitting next to her here at the Rocky Beach shores. Steven Jr. puts his arm around Jennifer as they drink frozen smoothies and watch the waves beating against the soft sand beach. Now that neither of them is currently working on the demanding murder case, they can freely spend time together and help each other study and prepare for the upcoming bar exam. Brought together by fate—perhaps one day for these two future attorneys, their next case together, they will be playing on the same team.

. . .

Channel Thirteen News reporter Heather Hoffman exits the Rocky Beach Police station in a rage. Apparently her face-to-face with the chief didn't go so well. She mumbles to herself as she marches to her car in the parking lot. Her black sports car exits the lot and her tires screech as she peels off at a high rate of speed. Her cell phone rings in her opened purse. She glances down at the caller ID and sees that it is Chief Nelson. She ignores his call and continues to drive at an excessive speed. Again her phone rings, but she doesn't even bother to check who is calling. Her car races along the busy street, weaving in and out of the slower-moving traffic. She is in a rush to get somewhere. Again her cell phone rings and again Heather Hoffman ignores the call, yet grows more agitated with every ring. She finally slows down when she reaches the Channel Thirteen News building. Before her car can come to a complete stop, Ms. Hoffman has her door open and one foot already out of the car. She quickly puts the car in park, and turns the engine off. She closes her door and then remembers she left her purse on the front passenger seat. She turns back to retrieve the purse from her car, which, she finds, fell to the floor of the passenger side during her hasty driving and abrupt breaking. She reaches down to grab it and then quickly slams the car door. As she hustles toward the rear employee entrance of the Channel Thirteen News building, she looks around nervously. She reaches the door only to realize that it is locked. She hears the screech of tires and the roar of a powerful engine coming around toward the back of the building. She quickly fumbles through her purse, searching for her work keys. They aren't in her purse. They must have fallen out when her purse slid off the front seat and onto the floor. Heather Hoffman takes her heels off and carries them in her hands as she sprints back to her parked car. The roar of an approaching engine feels like it is getting closer, which creates an even greater panic within the nervous reporter. She is only a few feet away from her vehicle when her purse and heels fly into the air. One of her shoes lands on the hood of another vehicle … The infamous silver sedan with dark tinted windows—its engine still roaring.

CHAPTER 33

"His name is Detective Peter Nelson, the son of Chief Donald Nelson!" exclaims an amped-up Nicholas McLean.

The private investigator reports to Michael Petagnas as they meet at the office of Nick McLean & Associates. Also present are investigators Rachael O'Toole, Brent Patterson, and Helena Wang. When the team discovered who the driver of the silver sedan is and his ties to the police chief, they called Petagnas in immediately to discuss possible theories.

"The chief's son?" asks a shocked Michael Petagnas.

"Yup, and Helena got a date with him," jokes Rachael O'Toole.

That statement gets a dirty yet playful look from Helena Wang.

Nick McLean offers his theory. "Suppose this young field reporter, Heather Hoffman, figures that the fastest way to move up in her career is to report the big stories and report them first.

What better way to do that than to create a close relationship with the chief of police? Chief Nelson is approached by this young, attractive woman who needs his help—he plays a little 'I'll scratch your back if you scratch mine.' She agrees to sleep with him in exchange for exclusive access to all the big stories. That could be why they kept Algernon in a holding cell for all that time and then brought him out just in time for the 6 o'clock news ... Remember who reported that story?"

"Heather Hoffman," Michael Petagnas recalls verbally.

"Exactly!" replies McLean.

He pauses briefly to allow this all to digest before continuing to lay out his possible theories. Petagnas is definitely intrigued.

"Not sure how long it has been going on, but at some point either Ms. Hoffman falls for the chief's son, or the chief's son finds out his father has a young, hot mistress and he wants a piece of the action," states McLean.

"The latter sounds more like it to me. That guy is a major creep," adds Helena Wang.

"If that is the case, perhaps he threatened to expose Heather Hoffman for having an affair with the chief, which would ruin her image, career, and possible promotion. Perhaps he is black mailing her, or maybe she and the younger Nelson are genuinely in love. Whatever the case is, it makes for a crazy love triangle," suggests McLean.

"So what direct involvement do you think this has with our case?" inquires Petagnas.

"A lot!" McLean replies. "Let's just suppose the chief, in his haste to impress his young mistress, jumped the gun with the investigation into the death of Deja Howell. He gets her mouth watering with talk of a big story, however the direct evidence doesn't support his initial theory that Algernon is the killer. In fact, the evidence begins to point in the direction of the wife of one of his prized detectives. Doesn't look good for him and his bid for re-election. So perhaps he has his son, the one person he thinks he can trust to keep things under the table, to sort of 'work the evidence' and steer the prosecutors in the direction of Algernon Flowers and away from Detective Frank Howell's wife, Brenda."

Rachael interjects, "We know the silver sedan was following Algernon when he would meet with Brenda Howell during the homicide investigation, and everywhere that this car has been seen we end up with intimidated witnesses who are unwilling to talk or soon after recant their stories."

"Not to mention the Howells got into that silver sedan after their wedding vow renewal ceremony. As his best man, it's safe to say that Detectives Howell and Nelson are pretty tight," adds Brent Patterson.

McLean has another thought as well. "Perhaps there is even something more to that... Maybe Detective Frank Howell and Detective Peter Nelson have more in common than we think. Remember the call that Brenda Howell made to the Rocky Beach Police Station on her way to pick up Algernon? She should've known that her husband was three hours away out of town, so why call him at the office? Why not call his cell? Unless she wasn't calling her husband, but another lover ... Detective Nelson. Both he and Brenda seem to have their fair share of lovers."

Michael Petagnas and the team of investigators like the way McLean is thinking. Petagnas likes this theory and can see reasonable doubt written all over this case for his client, if they can prove any of it. He listens and takes notes as McLean continues.

"Now we have a whole new option as to who may have the second set of keys that Brenda Howell made for her apartment. Where was Detective Nelson when Brenda Howell took the long drive to the Flowers' home, leaving Deja all alone?"

"That's worth looking into," Rachael adds. She makes a note to herself as McLean continues.

"So now at some point, Heather Hoffman overhears something, or comes across something that points to another possible suspect in this murder, and it's not Algernon

Flowers. The story is now bigger and juicier, and something this promotion-hungry reporter cannot resist … She wants to go with the bigger story, but the chief is against it. Maybe Ms. Hoffman feels the case against Algernon Flowers isn't solid enough. She will not have her big story if they can't convict the man she paraded in front of her cameras. Suppose she thinks that someone else will get the 'bigger story' of corruption and cover ups within the police department, so she threatens to go forward with that story, which would ruin the chief, yet make her career soar. That could very well be what that blow up was about between Heather Hoffman and the chief at the diner," concludes McLean.

Michael Petagnas likes where this can potentially go.

"Great work, you guys! Now let's talk to Ms. Heather Hoffman, and see what she has to say," exclaims a motivated Petagnas.

CHAPTER 34

Algernon Flowers is finally getting out of his solitary confinement cell and permitted to take a shower. It has been several days since he has been able to take more than the few steps allowed in the tiny cell he has been occupying. Although the shower is only lukewarm and smells like dirty mop water, Algernon is thankful for the opportunity to bathe. Even with the correctional officer watching and telling him to 'hurry up' every thirty seconds, this is by far the best two and a half minutes he has experienced in the past several days.

Upon returning to the cell, he dries off and puts back on the orange department of corrections jumpsuit. Algernon Flowers has put on twenty-three more pounds due to a combination of the heavy starch jail diet and limited physical activity. He feels lethargic and sluggish, and tends to sleep often. The boredom and depressive thoughts make sleeping this inmate's best friend. While asleep, Algernon has pleasant thoughts and dreams of his family, the children at the daycare that know him as 'Uncle Al,' his music and friends. In fact, the only time that Algernon Flowers has pleasant thoughts is when he is asleep. Looking at photos sent by old girlfriends makes him miss the scent and kiss of a woman. The letters from friends, supporters and even a few new love interests seem to make him overanxious about his pending trial. Visits from his mother make him feel like he has to perform and pretend to be emotionless in order to not further upset her. The only refuge from the agonizing thoughts that bombard his mind—the only sanctuary from the mental and emotional turmoil—the only peace that Algernon Flowers can find is in the sweet state of slumber. So he closes his eyes and goes back to his happy place.

.   .   .

Some of the parents have yet to pick up their children from the Emmanuel Daycare Center. Hazel Flowers started keeping weekend hours to help supplement the financial burden placed on her by having to fund her son's legal bills, and deposit money into his commissary. She only closes on Sundays so that she doesn't miss her regular church services. While waiting for the last couple of parents to pick up their children, Ms. Flowers plays her son's CD. The music he recorded shortly before his arrest brings her mixed emotions. The music that was in his heart is so pure—full of hope and uplifting encouragement. She only wishes he could hear his own songs now. He is in a period of intense darkness, and the light in his musical message is illuminating so many lives as it is played on the local inspirational radio station. Hazel Flowers has written down the lyrics to the songs and mailed them to her son, but fears it may depress him further. She hopes that he is finding new inspiration to write new, fresh melodies and self-inspiring songs during this—the most difficult period of his life.

One parent, Destiny Dorsey, enters the daycare center to pick up her two young children, three-year-old Timmy and fourteen-month-old Lila. Several months ago when Ms. Dorsey came to the daycare center to pick up her children, she saw Algernon Flowers out on the lawn, sitting on a blanket with Lila.

She sat in her car and watched the gentle and loving interaction between this man and her infant daughter. It was pure love. She could see their mutual connection. On many other occasions she would observe how excited little Lila would get whenever 'Uncle Al' would enter the room. She found such delight and joy in his presence. It was these moments that prompted her to ask Algernon Flowers to be the godfather of baby Lila. Destiny Dorsey has been a fan and supporter of Mr. Flowers from day one, and the negative media has in no way altered her opinion of the man her children affectionately call 'Uncle Al.' Ms. Dorsey and all the other parents with children at the daycare center have seen the heart of Algernon Flowers, and completely believe in his innocence.

Destiny Dorsey always brings weekly photos of her children for Ms. Flowers to mail to Algernon. Her son Timmy likes to draw and color portraits of his beloved Uncle Al wearing his signature hat and big smile. However, Timmy adds a feature to his drawings: a cape. Perhaps that's how all the children saw the funny, smiling and gentle Algernon—as a super hero. This week, Destiny Dorsey brings great personal news. She has gotten engaged to a wonderful guy—an actor from New York City. She and the children will be relocating soon, but she promises to always stay in touch and to continue to send photos of the children that Uncle Al loves. Ms. Dorsey, like all of the other parents, is on Michael Petagnas' list of character witnesses—which will only be needed if Algernon Flowers is convicted of the first-degree murder charge. The character witnesses would be called to testify on his behalf in an attempt to spare Mr. Flowers from the death penalty. Ms. Dorsey is hoping that justice will prevail and therefore her testimony will not be needed.

"Hopefully I Will NOT see you in court," states Destiny Dorsey with a smile as she hugs Hazel Flowers. The bond of motherhood makes this hug last a little longer than usual.

. . .

After the last of the children have been picked up, Hazel Flowers goes outside and checks the mailbox. Normally, Saturday mail is regular junk coupons that clutter the box, but she is hoping for a letter from her son, Algernon. He has not been allowed to write or have visitation since he has been in solitary confinement, but she hopes that a letter he may have written prior has straggled late in the mail. She would really love to hear from him. She opens the mailbox to find nothing but junk mail. As she turns to walk away, a man's voice calls her name. A man in a black car pulls up to the curb and exits his vehicle and calls her name again.

"Hazel Flowers?" the man inquires.

Ms. Flowers confirms that she is indeed the person he is looking for and inquires as to his business. The man hands Ms. Flowers an envelope—it is a subpoena. The prosecution has listed Ms. Hazel Flowers as a prosecution witness. Although there is no possible information that she could offer to empower their case against her son, by being placed on the prosecution's witness list Ms. Flowers will not be permitted to sit in the courtroom to support her son Algernon during his murder trial. As a witness, she will have to remain outside until if and when she is called to take the stand. Ms. Flowers has no reason to believe they will actually call her to testify as to how amazing her son is with children. She sees this as a ploy to remove Algernon's major support system, and discourage him further. It can be very helpful when someone who is on trial for his or her life to look back and see family members seated behind him or her in court. Now both Algernon's mother and sister have been placed on the witness list for the prosecution. Who will be next?

Due to limited seating in the courtroom of Judge Warren Jackson, there is also a high demand from the local media for front-row seats to all the trial action. The prosecution is making sure to fill those seats with 'prosecution-friendly' reporters with whom they have a good rapport. It is important for Prosecutor David Edwards to come out of this thing looking his best, and he is relying on his friends in local media to make that happen. As for Michael Petagnas, his concern is not how the story is reported, but rather how it ends.

CHAPTER 35

After the weekend, Monday morning is not very welcomed for most. For private investigator Nicholas McLean, it is another opportunity to get back to work on his current case—a case that has become multidimensional, and has gotten more complex by the hour. It seems as though the more he discovers, the more there is to discover. Like the peeling of an onion with its many layers, this case is also causing a few tears ... in particular from the people who loved the victim, Deja Howell, and those who love the accused, Algernon Flowers—who McLean considers 'victim number two.' It has become abundantly clear to McLean and his team that Algernon Flowers is the victim of a cruel and shameful cover up ... just another innocent life sacrificed.

Nicholas McLean has been sitting outside of the Channel Thirteen News station building since 4 A.M.. The early-morning news crew and a few other station employees are the only ones to arrive since he's been staking out the place. McLean is hoping to catch field reporter Heather Hoffman leaving the station as she heads out to cover a story. He has a lot of questions for the attractive young reporter, who has been secretly seeing both the chief of police as well as the chief's son. Hopefully due to her intimate encounters on the inside, she has come across some information that can be useful to this investigation. McLean finishes a breakfast burrito as he sits in his vehicle that is now strategically parked in a spot that allows him to watch both the front and rear entrances of the news building. He doesn't want to miss an opportunity to question the shady news reporter. From his vantage point McLean can also partially see the tail end of Heather Hoffman's car. This tells him that either she is inside and heading out to the field, or is already out in the field with her camera truck, and will be returning back to the station. In the meantime, McLean will wait patiently for this very crucial piece of the puzzle that is the murder case of Algernon Flowers.

.   .   .

Monday mornings for Michael Petagnas are not always his favorite. After enjoying the weekend with his wife and children, he heads into the office early and returns late. When he gets home in the evenings, his children are usually already in bed. He enjoys the weekends as it affords him the opportunity to have breakfast, lunch, and dinner with his children, and can also tuck them in bed at night. Monday mornings do, however, mean he returns to beast mode as the no-nonsense trial attorney that has gained the respect of all in the legal community. It is the preparation for trial and the actual trial process that allow him to be his best. His greatest strength is finding weakness in the opposing lawyer's case, and Petagnas is taking *this* case very personally. Not only does he feel that an innocent man has been wrongfully accused, but there is a little girl whose killer thinks he or she has committed the perfect crime ... or at least the perfect cover up. Petagnas kisses the foreheads of his sleeping children, grabs his briefcase and keys, kisses his wife and heads out to the office.

.   .   .

Today Michael Petagnas is expecting a report from his medical expert, Dr. Harvey Walters, on his findings. Although Dr. Walters has been given limited evidence due to the improper preservation by the medical examiner, Petagnas is optimistic that this medical expert will have enough to work with in order to help his case. Dr. Walters' findings are crucial to this defense, because by the way this evidence has been handled and processed, it is clear that somebody has something to hide.

.   .   .

As morning turns to afternoon, Michael Petagnas is in meeting number twelve. He has met with several people from a list given to him by his private investigator, Nick McLean. Although each of these individuals has something positive to add to his defense of Algernon Flowers, Petagnas must narrow them down to the really exceptional and crucial witnesses to schedule for depositions. One thing becomes more and more evident to Petagnas as he meets with these potential defense witnesses—Algernon Flowers is NOT the murderer in this case. This only adds to the insurmountable pressure of clearing this innocent young man. Witness after witness confirms Petagnas' initial feeling about this case ... his client has been set up, and Petagnas has no idea how high up the ladder the cover up goes. Is Prosecutor Edwards aware of the lack of evidence and fabrications surrounding this case? Is he willfully prosecuting an innocent man because it is an easier win ... Or is he being fooled as well? How much does Police Chief Nelson know about the actual events surrounding this case? How involved is he really? Who else knows anything? Is this just a case of one very smart woman that has everyone thinking she is the grieving mother of a child that was taken away from her by an evil man? Has she really fooled her husband, the chief of police, and the prosecutors, or are there more parties involved in the cover up? How much of a coincidence is it that the physical evidence, the most important—especially in a case like this—is mishandled and not preserved? Who is hiding what, and how deep does this really go? These are the questions Michael Petagnas is hoping to have answered before he has to present Algernon Flowers to a jury of men and women that will decide his fate.

.   .   .

Private investigator Nicholas McLean sits in his SUV awaiting a visual of Channel Thirteen News reporter Heather Hoffman. He has a gut feeling that she is the key to unlocking something big in this case. There has been no activity with her vehicle, nor has she left or entered the building all day. McLean decides to exit his SUV and go take a closer look. He casually walks over toward the back of the building. He notices a security camera facing the rear of the building, so he must appear as though he belongs in the area, as to not draw suspicion. McLean makes his way over to Heather Hoffman's car. He pretends to be talking on his cell phone as he looks inside of the car. He notices that the driver's side door is unlocked. He also sees a set of keys on the passenger side floor mat. There is a woman's shoe partially sticking out from underneath the car. McLean wants to enter the vehicle but doesn't want to trigger the alarm. He knows the importance of talking to Ms. Hoffman, and from his experience, things go better for him when he catches people off guard, before they can think of lies to cover their tracks. He doesn't want to blow his cover too soon, but he needs to find this woman. He has a plan.

.   .   .

After lunch, Michael Petagnas gets the news he's been waiting for—the report from his medical expert, Dr. Harvey Walters. Petagnas and his partner, Steven Didia Sr., sit in Petagnas' office and review it. Dr. Walters' report places the time of the victim's injuries within a rather large eighteen-hour window. That is the narrowest he can determine with the limited evidence he has been given. Unlike the Local County medical examiner, Dr. Harvey Walters is internationally renowned and recognized for his work with NASA and airline companies during tragic accidents. It is Dr. Walters who was responsible for putting the victims' remains together after airline crashes and the shuttle explosion. So being no stranger to having very little to work with, Dr. Harvey Walters can vouch for what Michael Petagnas will tell the jury in Algernon Flowers' murder trial. Although he would love to have the opportunity to view and test actual tissue, Dr. Walters puts the case into a whole new light. This news of the time of injuries helps Michael Petagnas, but is not even the most defense-friendly part of Dr. Walters' report. When he looked at the vomit collected from the victim's dirty pillowcase, Dr. Walters discovered that it wasn't Salisbury steak gravy, but blood—blood with Salisbury steak gravy in it, to be exact.

"So Brenda Howell isn't a TOTAL liar ... she did feed her daughter Salisbury steak," Steven Didia Sr. says mockingly.

Michael Petagnas has been waiting for these lab and test results. He is now finally ready to schedule the deposition of Mrs. Brenda Howell.

·   ·   ·

Private investigator Nick McLean enters the lobby of the Channel Thirteen News building. He approaches the receptionist and offers his ID. He announces himself as an investigator for an insurance company. He states that he is following up on a claim that a car of one of their insurers' was hit while parked, and a note left on the vehicle matched the description and plate number of one of the cars parked in the rear of the building. He has written down Heather Hoffman's plate number and vehicle description. The receptionist asks McLean to wait as she goes to get a manager. She returns moments later with one of the station managers—Heather Hoffman's supervisor. The woman doesn't seem to be very pleased with Ms. Hoffman. The supervisor informs McLean that Heather Hoffman hasn't been seen since Friday afternoon. McLean also learns that there was an email from Ms. Hoffman stating she had a family emergency and needed to go out of town. The email also stated she is not sure when she will return to Rocky Beach. McLean finds this strange. Why would she leave her car parked at work and not at home, or drive her car out of town? Something is just not sitting right with him. Another potential witness and key to this case has just gone away. McLean thinks quickly and makes a request to see video footage from the surveillance camera facing the rear of the building. He states that it will be helpful to his investigation if he can see who was driving that car, and if it had any damage when it came in ... However that request is denied.

"The police had to take all the video footage from the cameras surrounding the building," the supervisor informs McLean.

"Why did the police confiscate the surveillance tapes?" asks McLean.

"Due to recent drug and gang activity, and a possible shooting Friday night. They were hoping to find some evidence caught on camera," explains the supervisor.

McLean inquires further as to a name of the officer she spoke with.

"Detective Nelson, I believe he said his name was," she replies.

McLean knows there is much more to this. He exits the news station building and runs to his car. He is heading to the Law Offices of Petagnas & Didia.

CHAPTER 36

"Anyone could've sent that email from Heather Hoffman's account. Perhaps even from her cell phone," exclaims Nick McLean as he is getting Michael Petagnas up to speed on the recent events. "Her supervisor said that a Detective Nelson needed to collect all of their surveillance tapes from Friday night. This thing is pretty intense, Mike."

Michael Petagnas doesn't need to prove any criminal wrongdoing by the chief of police or his son, but anything that has any bearing on this case that will help clear his client would be appreciated. Nick and his team will continue their hunt for the shady news reporter Heather Hoffman, while also keeping close tabs on the chief and his son. Petagnas is placing all of his focus and attention on the center of this murder trial, the woman who has a lot of difficult questions to answer: Mrs. Brenda Howell.

When he gets his opportunity to question Brenda Howell during her deposition, Michael Petagnas can go for the jugular.

He can be aggressive and get some of the answers he needs. He knows he would have to approach her differently during the trial. With the jury present during trial, by questioning Mrs. Howell aggressively, the jury may view that as the defense lawyer being a bully, or attacking the mother of the innocent child that was murdered. That tactic can backfire and cause the jury to dislike Petagnas ... and if the jury doesn't like the defense council, they won't like the defendant. Petagnas must employ a different strategy. By going after Mrs. Howell aggressively during her deposition, he can later be less aggressive in front of the jury, yet still have her transcribed deposition, which can be used when a witness is on the stand. Petagnas needs to rattle her cage just enough to get her to implicate herself or remove Algernon Flowers from the equation.

Over the next few days, Michael Petagnas will be reviewing hours of audio- and video-taped statements from countless witnesses, and boxes of documented testimony in preparation for the most important pretrial deposition of his career. During his illustrious career, Michael Petagnas has never backed down from a challenge. When he was a prosecutor, he didn't allow friends of drug dealers, or gang members to intimidate him while working a case, and he refuses to allow the police to intimidate him in this case, either. As a prosecutor, had this case come across his desk he would not have hesitated to charge Brenda Howell with the murder of her daughter. As difficult as it would be to get a Florida jury to convict a mother of murdering her child, Petagnas would always do the right thing and worry about the degree of difficulty as an afterthought. Now as a defense attorney, Petagnas views the choice to go after Algernon Flowers, or the lesser degree of difficulty, as a cowardice move on the part of the district attorney. Michael Petagnas has vowed to not let this case claim a second victim. He is going to war, and the key to winning a war—stock up on firepower—and know thy enemy.

.   .   .

As for private investigator Nick McLean, he and his team of investigators will be revisiting potential and promising witnesses, as well as looking into the lives of Chief Nelson and his son Detective Nelson. One other main focal point: Locate Heather Hoffman and find out exactly what she knows.

Defense investigator Rachael O'Toole visits the closest known relative of Heather Hoffman—a first cousin on her mother's side of the family, Emily Williams. Emily is just as good looking as her cousin Heather—thanks to the strong genes of their mothers, who were twins. Emily, who is a few years older than Heather, speaks openly with Rachael O'Toole, who introduced herself as an old college friend of Ms. Hoffman. The two ladies share a cup of coffee and some warm apple pie at a small outdoor cafe. Rachael learns that Heather Hoffman was quite the loner. She seldom visited or attended family functions, and didn't really socialize outside of work.

"Covering the news has been Heather's dream for as long as I can remember," recalls Emily of her bright and pretty cousin.

Investigator O'Toole also learns that there were rumors swirling around within the family about Heather dating an older, married man.

"We just figured it was a phase, like someone who could advance her career ... a lot of women sleep their way to the top, and Heather has all the right assets to do just that," Emily states without apology.

Rachael O'Toole leaves a number for Emily to call when she hears from her cousin. Before leaving, Rachael pays the tab. She then gets in her car, and enters the highway back to Rocky Beach.

. . .

Defense investigator Helena Wang, posing as an old friend from California, is meeting with Heather Hoffman's cameraman and driver, Scott Walton. Walton recalls the last time he saw or heard from Heather.

"It was Friday afternoon or early evening ... she told me to standby ... she might have a huge story," Walton claims.

He goes on to mention how Heather Hoffman gave him the impression that this story would catapult her career and go down into journalism history.

"Believe me, this is going to change everything, and I'm taking you with me, my friend," Walton recalls Hoffman saying during their last phone conversation.

The very cooperative cameraman claims he never heard from her again, except for the vague email sent out to several Channel Thirteen News staff members. Investigator Wang leaves a number for Walton to call if he hears from Heather Hoffman.

.   .   .

Defense investigator Brent Patterson is parked near Heather Hoffman's residence, keeping a watchful eye out for the pretty, yet shady, news reporter. The hope is that she will stop at home whenever she returns to Rocky Beach. Patterson reclines his driver's seat slightly, and turns on his car radio. He is prepared to be here for the long haul.

.   .   .

Lead defense investigator Nicholas McLean is looking around the parking lot at the rear of the Channel Thirteen News building. Under the clever ruse of collecting evidence in a potential accident with Hoffman's vehicle and a parked vehicle of one of his company's insured drivers, McLean bought himself time and liberty to look around and take photos without drawing suspicion. During his search of the area around Hoffman's car McLean sees a discarded woman's high heel shoe. It is partially sticking out from underneath the front driver's side tire. Upon closer inspection, two other items catch the investigator's eye. A small tube of lip-gloss seems to have rolled under the car. Also, thanks to the lip-gloss serving as a paperweight, a folded note. McLean reaches underneath the car and grabs the folded note. Understanding that all of these items could have been trash left prior to Heather Hoffman parking here, McLean doesn't get too excited ... that is until he reads what's written on the note: MAJOR STORY—'BABY BLANKET.'

CHAPTER 37

Week number two in solitary confinement has been really tough on Algernon Flowers. He has been sleeping approximately sixteen hours a day. His facial hair is out of control, and he appears to have put on another couple of pounds. The look in his eyes almost resembles that of a zombie. He maintains existence—but is not living.

Mr. Flowers has not served his full two-week sentence when officers take him out of the solitary confinement cell. He is informed that he must to go to see his lawyer. When he arrives at the interview room, a smiling Nicholas McLean greets him. After learning about the solitary confinement status from Algernon's mother, McLean came up with a plan to give the young, emotionally defeated man a break. Algernon is someone McLean has developed a bond with through the Flowers family. The plan is to bring some simple documents, and tell the jail officials that these are important court-related forms that

ALGERNON

Algernon's attorney needs him to sign immediately, knowing this would be reason for mandatory allowance of legal-counsel visitation. Algernon Flowers is unaware that the papers he is signing have nothing to do with his case, but more importantly, so is the corrections officer standing outside the door. McLean places a stack of forms in front of Mr. Flowers and has him sign a line at the bottom of each one. While doing this, McLean engages the depressed-looking young man in small talk. Noticing how much Algernon's hands are shaking involuntarily, McLean asks him how he's doing. He can tell that Algernon is in a very low place. McLean looks at the corrections officer standing outside before slipping Algernon a tissue. Wrapped inside the tissue is Algernon's favorite candy bar, a dark chocolate, coconut and almond bar. McLean winks and Algernon smiles for the first time in days. He holds the tissue as if wiping his nose every time he takes a bite of the best-tasting candy bar he has ever had. After the completion of the candy bar, and signing of a few more fake forms, Algernon extends a trembling hand to shake McLean's and listen to his words of support.

"Don't worry Al, we're going to get you back home soon," says a confident Nick McLean.

He then gathers his things and exits toward the visitor's reception desk. After McLean's departure, Algernon Flowers is strip-searched and then taken back to his solitary confinement cell to finish serving out his sentence. He has a slight smile and a sweet taste still in his mouth. He is grateful for Nick McLean getting him out of his current situation—even if it *was* only temporarily. That, along with the encouraging words, was the fuel Algernon needed to make it through this next week.

· · ·

"What do you do with a blanket?" asks Nick McLean rhetorically. "You cover things with it, that's what," he concludes as he answers his own question.

McLean is speaking with investigators Rachael O'Toole and Helena Wang about the note he found underneath Heather Hoffman's car.

176

"Baby blanket, sounds to me like some code or a story about the cover up of a child's death," adds McLean.

Helena Wang is searching for something on her tablet. She finds what she is looking for. During her ride in Detective Nelson's silver sedan, she left a small GPS tracking device underneath the passenger seat. She pulls up the history, which shows that Detective Nelson, or at least his custom sedan, was near the Channel Thirteen News building on Friday evening.

"Well, we already know he was there, because he collected the video tapes from the security cameras. We need to place him with Heather Hoffman at that time," says investigator Wang.

She checks the tracker's current location but it is now off line. The team of investigators figure that if Detective Nelson had his car cleaned, any decent car wash would have easily vacuumed up the tiny device.

"Perhaps he was getting rid of some 'evidence' and had his car cleaned out," suggests Rachael O'Toole.

McLean takes the suggestion even further.

"Or if he took someone against her will and there was a struggle—he later discovered the device, and he could have thought it was from the person he struggled with," he adds.

The entire team believes that Detective Nelson has something to do with the young missing reporter, but everything is just circumstantial. McLean wants more before he takes this to Michael Petagnas. If they have enough to tie Detective Nelson or Chief Nelson to any involvement of a cover up, it would be very helpful to Petagnas to have in his arsenal when questioning Mrs. Brenda Howell. Nick McLean has a plan. It may be dangerous, but this is part of the job and the risks that come with it. He looks directly at investigator Wang.

"Well Helena, we may need you to play dress up again," he says with a touch of humor.

Helena looks at Rachael O'Toole, who is about to comment, and cuts her off. "Whatever, Rachael," barks Helena playfully as she rolls her eyes.

McLean's plan is to have Helena set up a coffee date with Detective Nelson and try to get another tracking device installed. If they are going to locate Heather Hoffman, Detective Nelson is their chance to do so. They need to keep close tabs on him. Helena is up for it, so McLean implements the plan that is now the team's top and only priority.

·   ·   ·

In the district attorney's office, Prosecutor David Edwards and Prosecutor Ramon Henderson have just received a call from Brenda Howell's lawyer. Michael Petagnas has contacted them inquiring as to their availability for a deposition. The request was that it be done as soon as possible. This makes the prosecutors nervous, because if Petagnas is this eager to depose the only other person that was once considered a suspect, he must have something that he is keeping close to his vest. Prosecutor Henderson schedules a meeting with Brenda Howell and her lawyer to prep her for her deposition with the skillful Michael Petagnas. They want to coach her, since she *is* the prosecution's star witness. During this conversation with Howell's lawyer, a deal of total immunity was granted to Brenda Howell. This takes the pressure off of her to answer Petagnas' questions without worrying about incriminating herself. By granting her full immunity, the prosecution cannot use Brenda Howell's testimony in an attempt to convict Algernon Flowers, and then later turn around and charge her as well. Brenda Howell cannot ever be charged in the murder of her daughter. Much to her relief, she has eluded any criminal responsibility in the death of her daughter as far as the courts are concerned. Now if she performs well enough during the trial of Algernon Flowers, she can also win in the court of public opinion. She may not be the one sitting in jail facing murder charges, but there are those in and around Rocky Beach who think the baby-faced mother is not as innocent as she appears ... and that bothers Brenda Howell. Her main objective now is for her testimony to remove any and all doubt in the eye of the public that she harmed her own child.

CHAPTER 38

Algernon Flowers has just completed his fourteen-day sentence in solitary confinement, and is now being relocated back to his originally assigned cell. When he steps into the cell that he occupied previously, it feels like a mansion compared to the smaller cell in solitary. His markings are still intact on the wall. He uses his golf pencil to add fourteen more notches to the total count. The days are adding up. As the markings mount on the green brick wall, the stress mounts in his mind.

Not having much to be excited about lately, he is looking forward to a couple of things. His mail, visitation, and commissary privileges will be restored, and today, he will get thirty minutes to take a shower and call his mother. Things that he will never ever take for granted again.

·　　　·　　　·

Investigator Helena Wang enters the Rocky Beach Police station in a stunning black dress that hugs her slim, shapely body. She is in full makeup, and her perfume is so intoxicating that as she passes several officers, they linger in her fragrance. Her heels elevate and accent her buttocks, while also making her calves pop. The oversexed, creepy Detective Nelson doesn't stand a chance against McLean's sexy weapon of lethal femininity.

By telling the officer at the reception desk that she came by to thank Detective Nelson for helping her while being stranded on the side of the road, she is granted access to the back offices. She is escorted by an officer who seems very excited to present the chief's son with the gorgeous gift, packaged nicely in a tight, form-fitting black dress. Helena Wang carries in her hand a plate of homemade cookies, an offering of gratitude for Detective Nelson going out of his way to give her a ride.

Detective Nelson is seated at his desk when he first sets eyes on the very beautiful Helena. An officer leads her in, staring at her butt and legs as she approaches Nelson's desk.

"Hello again. I baked you a little something to say thank you for stopping and offering me a ride the other day ... maybe we should go somewhere to get a nice cup of coffee to wash these down with," offers Helena Wang seductively.

Detective Nelson is all smiles as he takes the bait.

·   ·   ·

On the way to the coffee shop, Helena Wang quickly completes her job and plants another tracking device in the detective's silver sedan. She leaves one under the seat, and a second one in the side pocket of the passenger door for good measure. The plan is to remove her from the danger of being alone with the unpredictable detective for any longer than need be. She sneaks a text message to McLean letting him know that her mission is accomplished.

·   ·   ·

Nick McLean receives a text message from investigator Helena Wang, which reads: '*Seeds planted.*' McLean, who is following behind the silver sedan in case anything goes wrong, calls Helena's phone. He pretends to be her mother's nurse, calling to alert her that she needs to get home immediately.

.   .   .

Helena Wang puts on the performance of her life when she gets the phone call from Nick McLean. With tears rolling down her face, the seemingly upset Helena tells her 'date' that she has to cut things short and take a rain check. Even this sleaze-ball detective is fooled by her award-winning act. He turns his siren on and speeds her back to her car that is parked at the police station. She thanks him and takes his cell phone number, but she hopes to never see him again.

Nick McLean and his team will be keeping a watchful eye on Detective 'Lover-Boy' Nelson, and his father Chief Nelson. Somewhere among them is the key to unlock this mysterious case that gets stranger by the day. The Nelson family of police will keep McLean and his team occupied, while Michael Petagnas and Steven Didia Sr. focus their attention to the other major piece to this puzzle.

.   .   .

Mrs. Brenda Howell walks into the district attorney's office with a small entourage. Her husband Detective Frank Howell, her mother and father, Police Chief Donald Nelson, and her lawyer Kelly Sloan. Brenda Howell carries her infant son as he sleeps on her chest, with her police officer husband walking with her hand in hand. This picture is a powerful statement, and most likely a display for the news reporter and cameraman that are accompanying them. Normally it would be news reporter Heather Hoffman that gets all the exclusive access in this case, but due to her absence, another pretty reporter from a rival network is now in the mix. With Chief Nelson acting almost as a film director, this group appears to be the perfect family.

The cameraman and reporter exit the elevator first to catch the group making its way down the hallway to the prosecutor's office in perfect synchronization. They march in formation as if this were previously rehearsed. Brenda Howell—grieving mother clutching her new child as if given a second chance by the fertility gods. This is the image that Police Chief Nelson and prosecutors want headlining tonight's primetime news. The young, pretty news reporter smiles at the chief of police, as she knows this will boost her value and stock price back at her network. Chief Nelson winks back flirtatiously.

·   ·   ·

As Brenda Howell signs her 'immunity from prosecution' agreement, her lawyer stands on one side of her, with Prosecutor Edwards on the other, while the camera man films as if a politician were signing a new law into effect. After Brenda Howell signs the agreement, Prosecutor Edwards takes the pen and also adds his signature. As the ink dries, the prosecutor and Howell's lawyer shake hands.

Within minutes of the signing, Howell's lawyer, Kelly Sloan, speaks to the camera. With the Howells, Brenda's parents and the police chief standing behind her, Ms. Sloan delivers her brief but powerful statement.

"In spite of the many rumors that my client, Brenda Howell, had something to do with causing the death of her daughter Deja Howell, today the district attorney and state attorney agreed and sided with the Howell family." She smiles and gestures to Brenda holding her infant son.

The pretty, young news reporter gives Chief Nelson a thumbs up and mouths the words: 'Thank you.'

Standing off to the side, completely out of the camera frame, is Prosecutor David Edwards. He doesn't appear too elated. For Brenda Howell this may be a personal victory, but as for Edwards, he has to face a courtroom gladiator in the person of Michael Petagnas. Prosecutor Edwards knows this is far from over. He secretly hopes that every Rocky Beach citizen

182

who will make up the potential jury pool sees this media stunt displayed, and forms his or her opinions before even hearing a shred of evidence. However, even if that happens, the skillful and crafty Michael Petagnas can swiftly turn the tables in a trial within his opening statement alone. David Edwards is not going to be lulled to sleep by thinking that Brenda Howell will now be seen in a more positive light. He must prepare her to hold her own on the witness stand during cross-examination. This must be done as soon as possible ... as her deposition is scheduled for next week.

CHAPTER 39

Defense Attorney Michael Petagnas is sitting on his couch after a great dinner prepared by his wife. He gets a call from his partner Steven Didia Sr. telling him to turn on Channel Eight News. Petagnas quickly grabs the remote control and turns the television on and to channel eight. He sees Kelly Sloan, Esquire, surrounded by the Howells and Police Chief Nelson. He turns up the volume to catch the end of Ms. Sloan's statement, after which the camera cuts to Brenda Howell and Prosecutor Edwards signing the immunity agreement.

Michael Petagnas is still on the phone with Steven Didia Sr. when the news segment ends. All they can do is chuckle at the display they just witnessed. The prosecution is overcompensating for their lack of any real solid evidence against their client. These seasoned trial attorneys know the jury in this case is going to want someone to pay for what happened to the innocent young victim. Now with Brenda Howell off the hook—with no chance of ever being charged in the case—the only person the jury can execute its rage toward is their client, Algernon Flowers. In the prosecution's attempt to play hardball, they've also painted themselves into a corner. Now they MUST get a conviction of Algernon Flowers because they've just eliminated their only other option. Michael Petagnas knows all too well that by putting that sort of pressure on a circumstantial and shaky case, this prosecution team is going to be very desperate.

.　　　　.　　　　.

Hazel Flowers cannot believe what she just saw on the news. How is the prosecution allowing Brenda Howell to walk free? Ms. Flowers is disgusted. The only consolation she has is in knowing that her son Algernon doesn't have a television to watch and witness what she has just seen. This is the first time Hazel Flowers actually hopes that her son is still in solitary confinement so he won't have to read about Brenda Howell's immunity in tomorrow morning's newspaper.

.　　　　.　　　　.

When the correctional officer working the night shift informs Algernon Flowers of Brenda Howell receiving full immunity, he is devastated. He has been through much in the past few weeks and this only adds to his pain. In the back of his mind he was hoping that Brenda's guilt would get the best of her and she would confess to any knowledge of what happened to her daughter. However, this granting of immunity throws out any hope of that ever happening, as it appears she has committed the perfect crime, and found the perfect scapegoat. As for his current incarceration, Algernon Flowers was hoping this was all an elaborate stunt to scare him into telling what he knew about any wrongdoing committed by Brenda. This latest news puts all doubt to rest ... he has been set up and left to fight for his life. Even if it weren't time for lights out at the Local

County Jail, Algernon Flowers is going to bed. The emotional pain tends to go away when he is asleep.

.   .   .

At Jennifer Forde's apartment, she is studying with her new boyfriend, Steven Didia Jr. As they prepare for the upcoming state bar exam, several cases come up in case law that strike a nerve with Jennifer. She tries to keep her mind from wandering back to the Algernon Flowers case, but she can't seem to let it go.

"He's innocent, you know?" says Jennifer to a preoccupied Steven Jr. "I know we shouldn't discuss it, but neither one of us is actively working on that case anymore," she adds.

Steven Jr. changes the subject and decides to order take out for a late, study-night dinner. Jennifer goes along with his unwillingness to talk about that particular subject. However, when Steven Jr. goes into her kitchen to hunt for take-out menus, she looks under her textbook where she has written down several points of weakness in the prosecution's case against Algernon Flowers.

"How about Indian food?" yells Steven Jr. from the kitchen.

"Fine with me," Jennifer replies.

Jennifer then quickly grabs the page upon which she has written down all the flaws in the prosecution's case, and slips it in the middle of Steven Jr.'s textbook just as he is returning to the room.

"What's this?" he asks, referring to the page she just tried to sneak into his book.

Jennifer doesn't respond. There is no need to respond because Steven Jr. is now holding the page and reading what she has written down.

"I know what you're going to say, but just leave it around your dad's office and let someone find it," explains Jennifer.

Steven Jr. doesn't think it is a good idea.

"Look, I understand you feel like there is need for justice here, and I totally agree. However, my dad and Mr. Petagnas have been doing this for quite some time now. They don't need your information or inside knowledge from when you worked for the prosecutor. Trust me, Algernon Flowers is in the best legal hands possible," Steven Jr. says with a smile as he attempts to relax his anxious girlfriend.

He rips the paper and crumples the pieces into a ball, which he then throws in the trash. Jennifer is still troubled by this particular case.

"They gave her immunity ... can you believe that?" asks a frustrated Jennifer.

Steven Jr. looks at her and takes her by the hand. The fact that she has taken time to review evidence, form an opinion, and stick with her gut feeling makes Jennifer even more attractive to him.

"Let's stay focused ... tonight, we study and then eat. No time to worry about something we can't control," says Steven Jr. lovingly.

Finally, a smile from Jennifer as she appears to let it go ... for now.

"Now, what do you want from the Indian restaurant?" asks Steven Jr. as he opens the menu.

. . .

Private investigator Nicholas McLean walks through the twenty-four hour pharmacy looking for skin ointment. When he first heard that the district attorney offered Brenda Howell full immunity from prosecution, he burned his hand by being distracted while pouring hot water to make a cup of tea. He could not believe that she will not be charged after all the evidence he dug up in just his first three days on the case alone. Surely the homicide detectives could have found something tying her to this crime. The physical evidence and all the strange events surrounding this murder all point in her direction, however she was smart enough to leave the house with someone there to take the blame. It could have been a young babysitter, a next-door neighbor, or any guy she was sleeping with ... anyone trusting enough to assume little Deja was just asleep when Brenda Howell left to establish an alibi ... but it was Algernon Flowers who happened to be available, and trusting. Now he is being labeled as a killer, and she is granted full immunity. Before heading to the counter to pay for the ointment for his hand, McLean stops in the book and magazine aisle to purchase some to mail to Algernon. McLean is all too familiar with how long the pretrial process can drag out, so he knows Algernon will appreciate lots of good reading material to occupy his mind while awaiting trial. As Nick McLean exits the twenty-four hour pharmacy, the newspaper truck is dropping off tomorrow morning's edition. There is a small headline on the front left corner that reads: 'Toddler's mom will not be charged in slaying.' Nick McLean shakes his head in disgust. All he can do at this point is keep searching for anything or anyone that can clear Algernon Flowers in this case.

CHAPTER 40

The Tuesday morning news is on but Hazel Flowers cannot watch. There was a time when she would watch the local news while having her morning coffee. That has changed since last December when she saw her son, Algernon, handcuffed and being taken off to the Local County Jail. Ever since then, any news about this case upsets her stomach and gives her awful headaches. Today Ms. Flowers is taking the day off from the daycare center. Her sister is covering for her to give her a break. After last night's news, Hazel Flowers can't seem to stop worrying. She has exhausted all of her resources on her son's legal expenses. She was hoping things would not have gotten this far. Her hope was that after further investigating by defense investigators, some evidence or solid witness would have surfaced to end her family's ordeal. Now that the district attorney has given Brenda Howell full immunity from prosecution, Ms. Flowers knows that her son is in it for the long haul. Unfortunately, they don't have long-haul money. The district attorney's office has unlimited resources. They can fight forever.

Instead of watching the depressing morning news, Hazel Flowers turns to her faith and reads her Bible while having her morning coffee. Appropriately, this morning's Biblical passage, as outlined in her weekly Bible study group, is first Samuel, chapter seventeen—the story of the giant Goliath versus the boy David. This fascinating story tells of a young boy named David who goes up to battle against the mighty giant known as Goliath in a fight to the death. With the odds completely against him, little David defeats the giant and he only required a rock and a slingshot. This gives Hazel Flowers the courage she needs. She sees David in her son Algernon. She wants him to be strong and fearless when going up against the mighty, giant district attorney—AKA Goliath. Algernon Flowers has a rock in Michael Petagnas and a slingshot in Nicholas McLean. McLean's investigation can catapult Michael Petagnas' case into the skull of the giant they are facing.

· · ·

Michael Petagnas doesn't watch the morning news, either. He doesn't care for the media and spotlight. He doesn't want to be distracted from the task at hand. He is preparing to face off in a very important deposition in less than a week. Petagnas is not in the least worried about the tactics and media circus displayed by the prosecutor and police. In fact, he and his partner Steven Didia Sr. literally laughed out loud when they saw the news last night. This all actually works in Petagnas' favor. Because Brenda Howell has been given full immunity from prosecution, she will be a little more liberal and free with her tongue. Now that she knows she won't be locked up and thrown directly into jail for saying the wrong thing, she will be more relaxed ... and that's just what Petagnas wants ... to catch her relaxed and off guard.

Michael Petagnas drives to his office by taking the same route every morning, but the last couple of weeks he has been changing up his routine, and mixing up his activity. He has been getting threatening phone calls from a blocked number. The male caller only says, 'Get off this case, or else' and then hangs up. Those calls went on for a while. However, recently the caller mentioned something about putting a bullet through Petagnas' windshield when he passes the gas station on Seventh Street. That's when Petagnas got the feeling he was being followed. He is no stranger to threats and people wanting to intimidate him, but that was usually by criminals and gang members back when he was the district attorney. It is quite disturbing to experience the same thug-like behavior from police officers. Petagnas knows that at least one caller was a police officer, because he heard a police car radio call coming in right before the caller hung up. All of this is still not going to stop Michael Petagnas from providing Algernon Flowers with the best defense possible. The threats don't mean he is going to stop fighting for the young man he believes in. It doesn't mean he is going to allow the threats to distract him from being well prepared for trial. The threats only mean that Petagnas is going to slightly duck his head down whenever he passes the gas station on Seventh Street.

.   .   .

Hazel Flowers gets a wonderful and unexpected surprise when private investigator Nicholas McLean pays her an early-morning visit. He brings cupcakes and conversation ... exactly what she needs to brighten her day. McLean also brings reading material for her to mail to her son, Algernon. Over cupcakes and coffee, Ms. Flowers and Nick McLean talk about the status of Algernon's first-degree murder case. McLean shares some of the information he and his investigative team uncovered. He also encourages Ms. Flowers to let her son know that he has a lot of amazing people working their fingers to the bone in his defense. He reminds her to try to keep his focus off of any negative media, and to not sweat what the police-friendly reporters say.

"Michael Petagnas and his legal team fight their battles in the courtroom, not in the local news," states Nick McLean.

At the end of McLean's visit, Hazel Flowers feels much better. She also learned that her son is out of solitary confinement and can now receive visitation again. She looks forward to seeing him soon.

.   .   .

Michael Petagnas, Steven Didia Sr., and Sandy Ward are in Petagnas' office working on the Brenda Howell deposition. This needs to be handled delicately, and with much care, since the prosecution has thrown all of their eggs into one basket and is banking on presenting Mrs. Howell as a grieving mother. If the jury buys that argument, then Petagnas and his team will be strategizing for Algernon Flowers' sentencing. The defense would love more concrete evidence from Nick McLean and his team, but they don't have time to wait. They must prepare to face Brenda Howell with what they currently have, yet not give away too much of their trial strategy this early. Michael Petagnas and Steven Didia Sr. take turns presenting questions to each other, and then discuss how each question will go over in the Brenda Howell deposition. Sandy Ward takes thorough notes of the entire preparation process. By noon they break for lunch and plan to get back to it later in the afternoon.

.   .   .

Private investigator Nicholas McLean has lunch with his team as they strategize their campaign to locate Heather Hoffman, and dig deeper into the lives of Chief Nelson and his son Detective Nelson. They decide to keep a trail on Chief Nelson's apparent new mistress, Heather Hoffman's rival network reporter. Hopefully she will come across some information that will assist their investigation. The team also decides to revisit some of Brenda Howell's former co-workers again. Perhaps some of them are no longer intimidated, or have changed their tune now that Brenda Howell has been granted full immunity.

Any and everybody who has something to say will be very valuable to this defense. After their lunch meeting, the team members disperse to their various assignments. Nick McLean has an important stop to make. He is going to sit in on Michael Petagnas' mock interview in preparation for Brenda Howell. McLean's presence is useful since he has spoken directly with some witnesses who are not cooperating. His input and insight will help give Petagnas enough of an edge to make Mrs. Howell feel the pressure of their words ... even in their absence.

CHAPTER 41

As Algernon Flowers wakes up and adds another notch to the day count on his cell wall, he feels a rush of emotion. For he knows that today his defense attorney, Michael Petagnas, is facing off against his former lover, Brenda Howell—a very crucial day in this case. Today's deposition is perhaps even more important than Howell's actual courtroom testimony during the trial. This is because every word Brenda Howell utters today goes on the record and can be used in trial, as opposed to her having the luxury of tweaking her testimony later to fit into the flow of the prosecution's case before the jury. If Algernon Flowers stands any chance of being cleared in this case, it needs to happen on this day, in that deposition room, with this particular prosecution witness.

Inmate Flowers paces in his tiny cell in an attempt to relax and slow his rapid heartbeat. His life, his future, his everything comes down to this deposition, yet it is out of his control. All he can do is sit in the enclosed green brick walls and hope for the best ... for Michael Petagnas' best.

.   .   .

Hazel Flowers hasn't slept much at all. In fact, she purposefully set her alarm clock to go off every hour on the hour so that she can say a prayer for Michael Petagnas as he faces Brenda Howell in her deposition. Ms. Flowers is hoping that this David and Goliath story ends the same as the one in her recent Bible study. At 9:30 this morning, the time of Brenda Howell's scheduled deposition, some of Hazel Flowers' Bible study group members are coming over to her home to pray and sit together. The weight of today's deposition of the prosecution's star witness is heavy, but the load is lightened by the support of some loyal and dear friends.

.   .   .

Private investigator Nicholas McLean is taking the morning off to play a few rounds of golf. He can't stand the thought of what today's deposition means to this case that he has poured his blood, sweat and tears into. He can't seem to relax. His mind is constantly racing with endless thoughts pertaining to his overall job performance. Has he failed Algernon Flowers and his family? Did he get enough information for Michael Petagnas to work with? Nick McLean wishes he had more time ... more time to dig deeper—to search wider—to push harder. However, time is not on his side. Within thirty minutes, Mrs. Brenda Howell is going to take the witness stand in the most pivotal deposition in this case. Whatever McLean and his team have done—all of the information that they have provided to the defense attorneys, it is either going to suffice, or fall short. Whatever is going to happen in this morning's deposition is now out of McLean's control. All he can do is play a few holes of golf to distract himself from the anxiety. As Nick McLean drives his first ball, all he hopes is that Michael Petagnas hits a hole in one in that deposition room.

.   .   .

Prosecutors David Edwards and Raul Henderson enter the deposition room with their new paralegal. Their expressions reveal the seriousness of the moment as they move quietly to their seats with almost a sense of reverence. They won't admit it, but their entire case is riding on this deposition. However Brenda Howell is presented to the jury during the trial will be irrelevant compared to what happens here today. Her every word will be on official record and available for the crafty defense attorney to use at will. Prosecutor Edwards will have the opportunity to question his witness first. His hope is that this will give him the opportunity to relax Mrs. Brenda Howell prior to her confrontation with the man who will basically be suggesting that she murdered her own child in cold blood. Edwards knows that whatever happens in this room today after his initial contact with Brenda Howell is out of his control. Has he prepared her enough to face the most notorious trial attorney of this era? Has his offer of immunity given her the sense of peace and confidence he needs her to have? Is his entire case against Algernon Flowers going to crumble before his eyes today? David Edwards does know that whatever happens today, it is completely out of his control at this point.

·   ·   ·

The only person that has any sort of control as to what this case will look like after this morning's events is Michael Petagnas. He enters the deposition room with his partner, Steven Didia Sr., and lead paralegal, Sandy Ward. Like everyone else in the room, their countenance truly reflects the severity of the moment. As last-minute prep, Petagnas looks over his notes on Brenda Howell, a thick binder full. He is confident, yet questions his overall preparation for this most important deposition. Has he looked at every angle? Has he thought of every theory possible? Has he laid enough traps to corner this woman he views as a professional liar and con artist? Is there any more information he could have gotten from his investigator that would unlock a major key to clearing his client? Will this moment define the outcome of this case? Will Petagnas fail Algernon Flowers, who put his life and complete trust into his hands? Will the very smart Brenda Howell have an explanation for even her most radical and unorthodox behavior? Michael Petagnas leans over to his partner, Steven Didia Sr., and confirms something from his notes. It's as if Petagnas is seeing something for the very first time. He appears enlightened. He almost smiles as he circles and highlights a point from his notes on Brenda Howell. One thing is for sure, whatever happens in this deposition room today, it is very much under the control of Michael Petagnas.

.   .   .

As Mrs. Brenda Howell enters the deposition room, there is a certain confidence to her walk. She is alone, however her parents and husband are waiting outside. She can feel their support and it shows in her face as she takes her seat. She waves and smiles at the prosecutors, but does not make eye contact with the defense.

Brenda Howell is sworn in and asked to state her name for the official record. After a few preliminary housekeeping items from the prosecutors to instruct her as to obtaining clarity for the court reporter, the deposition of Brenda Howell—the mother of Deja Howell—is underway. The prosecution questions her as to her marriage pre-Deja, and during the life of Deja. They ask her to describe the dissolution of her marriage to Detective Howell, and how she came into a relationship with Algernon Flowers. Mrs. Howell has nothing bad to say about Algernon. He was good with Deja and she never witnessed him harm her in any way. She also maintains that Deja never seemed afraid or appeared uncomfortable around Mr. Flowers. In fact, Brenda Howell says that she never noticed signs of any physical abuse or of any other kind for that matter. Throughout her deposition she has nothing negative to say about Algernon Flowers. In actuality, if she does, then it would appear to a jury that she was neglectful in leaving her child around someone she viewed as potentially abusive or a danger in any way. Brenda Howell chooses her words carefully. Finally when asked if she believed that Algernon Flowers murdered her daughter, Howell responds as if she doesn't want to think he would, but that she believes so now. With that said, the prosecution turns Brenda Howell over to the defense. Michael Petagnas opens his binder and drops his pen as he prepares to address Mrs. Brenda Howell for the very first time.

CHAPTER 42

Michael Petagnas politely and officially introduces himself to Mrs. Brenda Howell. She remains rather stone-faced, but makes eye contact with him. Petagnas briefly recaps what Mrs. Howell just testified to, as a way to establish any inconsistencies in her story. It is Petagnas' experience that when testimonies or statements are coached or rehearsed, after the initial questioning, once asked to re-establish the sequence of events, the coached or rehearsed statement becomes altered. He does this now to have it documented by the court reporter as a part of the official court record. Although there are slight revisions to her prior statement, this is far from the 'ah ha' moment needed to free his incarcerated client. However, this seems to lull Brenda Howell into a false sense of security, as she thinks that this line of questioning is Petagnas' A-game.

Brenda Howell has become so comfortable that she is now making eye contact with Petagnas throughout her responses.

Michael Petagnas knows now that he has her exactly where he wants her. Howell even smiles with Petagnas as he speaks politely and gently. Everything about her demeanor and body language suggests that she appears to have gotten past the worst of this deposition, and that she has everyone in the room eating out of the palm of her hand. That all changes when Michael Petagnas opens his binder to a page that has the blueprint layout of Brenda Howell's South Rocky apartment.

"Mrs. Howell, I was looking at your statement, and that of Algernon Flowers. One of the similarities in both versions of events is that on the morning in question, you carried Deja from her bed into the living room-kitchen area, is that correct?" asks a still-gentle Michael Petagnas.

Brenda Howell almost appears to have been stung by this question, as she loses the eye contact she once maintained with the laid-back defense attorney. With her eyes now diverted between the prosecutors and a balled-up tissue in her hand, she carefully responds.

"Yes, as I remember it, I carried her from her bed and took her into the living room-kitchen area," Howell replies.

"I was wondering if you can tell us why you passed the front door and didn't carry her downstairs to the car, to drive her to the hospital ... did you know she was beyond medical help ... that she was already deceased?" asks Petagnas as he looks at the blueprint of the apartment layout.

Prosecutor David Edwards doesn't like where this is heading, but he must allow this line of questioning. Brenda Howell doesn't like it either, and her cocky facial expression turns defensive.

"I don't know why—I guess in the moment I wasn't really thinking straight," replies Mrs. Howell.

"I understand that. As a parent myself, I can only imagine the panic of discovering your child unresponsive," adds Petagnas.

He looks for a page in his binder and then refers to it.

"According to the employee records at Weinstein Elementary, you were one of six teachers that are recognized by the board of education as CPR certified. There is a mandatory requirement that you and the others maintain regular training to keep your certification."

Petagnas looks up from his binder, as all eyes are on him … even Brenda Howell's.

"Your trainings are all up to date, and back in September you were called into the school cafeteria when a student passed out. You performed CPR until the paramedics arrived. In fact, you were credited with saving that child's life," Petagnas continues gently as Brenda Howell nods affirmatively. "So why is it that when you went into Deja's room, did you not even attempt to try to resuscitate your own daughter?" asks Petagnas.

After looking over in the direction of the prosecution, Brenda Howell responds, "I don't know … I wasn't thinking."

As Michael Petagnas flips through his binder, he continues to engage Mrs. Brenda Howell gently.

"Well let's go back to the night before. You decided that it was a good idea to leave Deja at home because she was sick and you didn't want to wake her up. Then when you returned home with Algernon Flowers, he brought it to your attention that Deja threw up on her pillow. Yet you were still concerned about him waking her up. In fact, you quickly and quietly got him out of her room so that you could clean her up," Petagnas says as Brenda Howell listens closely. "Being certified in CPR, and a certified specialist for the school, shouldn't you have attempted to wake her up to make sure she was not choking on any vomit? I mean it was all over her pillow, was it not?" asks Petagnas to Mrs. Howell, who is now very much on edge.

Brenda Howell's answers seem to maintain a similar pattern now.

"I don't know, I guess I wasn't thinking," she replies.

"Now I'm talking about the night before, not when you were in a panic the next morning when she was pale and cool to the touch as both you and Mr. Flowers stated … even then, that night you didn't think it would've been a good idea to wake her to make sure she was OK?" asks Petagnas.

Again Brenda Howell only offers a simple response. "I don't know, I didn't think about it."

Petagnas continues his line of questioning.

"If it were a student in your classroom, face down with a puddle of vomit coming from her mouth, wouldn't you make sure she was OK? Would you not check the back of her throat to make sure she wasn't choking on any of it?" he asks.

"I guess I would," replies Brenda Howell.

"You said that you carried Deja to the bathroom to clean her up. You didn't wake her up to make sure she was responsive, because you didn't want to wake her?" asks Petagnas.

"Correct," replies Mrs. Howell.

"Was this the first and only time that you've left Deja home alone while you went out?" asks Petagnas.

"Correct," replies an agitated Brenda Howell.

Petagnas flips through his binder once again. This action now seems to incite nervousness on the part of Brenda Howell as she anticipates his next point.

"Back to the morning after ... so you just watched as Algernon Flowers attempted to perform CPR on Deja as he had to be coached by the 9-1-1 operator?" asks Petagnas.

"Correct," replies Mrs. Howell.

For the next ninety minutes Michael Petagnas questions Brenda Howell as to her actions and behavior on the morning in question. All of her responses are brief, and offer little detail or additional information. Petagnas also attempts questions that require more than a yes-or-no response.

"Why would you continue seeing Algernon Flowers in a romantic way if you thought he hurt Deja?" asks Petagnas.

"I don't know," replies Brenda Howell, offering nothing more.

Her half-hearted reply, or lack of an explanation seems to trouble even the two prosecutors sitting in the room. After a short pause to make eye contact with Brenda Howell, Michael Petagnas continues.

"When you were questioned by Homicide Detective Hunter, you told him that Algernon Flowers noticed the bruising on Deja's lower abdomen, not that the ER doctor pointed them out to him. Were you deliberately trying to throw Algernon onto their track … to make them also look at him as a suspect?" asks Petagnas.

"I don't know, I don't think that was my intention," replies Brenda Howell.

"Because initially you were the suspect, correct?" asks Petagnas.

"Correct," Brenda Howell replies.

Once again Michael Petagnas flips through his binder. He stops at a page and pauses for both effect and recollection.

"Mrs. Howell, you also told Detective Hunter that Algernon found Deja unresponsive and alerted you. However it was you that called him and asked him to wake her up, is that correct?"

"Yes," Howell replies.

"Well how did you know that she wasn't awake already?" Petagnas asks and then waits for an answer from the now-defensive Brenda Howell.

"I don't know. I don't remember," she replies as she looks at Prosecutor Edwards, hoping he will say something or end this deposition.

Brenda Howell is visibly uncomfortable and wants nothing more to do with Michael Petagnas. However, Petagnas is not done. In fact, he pauses and suggests they break for lunch as he has more questions for Mrs. Howell. Both sides agree to break, and decide to reconvene in an hour.

·   ·   ·

After lunch, all involved parties return to their previously occupied seats. It is apparent that Brenda Howell used her lunch break to consult with prosecutors and her attorney. Every question she is now asked by the defense, her response is simply: "No comment." Even when Michael Petagnas asks about the history of domestic violence between her and her husband, she offers no comment. Brenda Howell offers no further comment about anything and this irritates Petagnas. Finally after nearly an hour of this seemingly pointless back and forth, he ends his portion of this deposition.

"I have nothing further at this time," says an annoyed Michael Petagnas.

Brenda Howell is excused, but takes the opportunity to roll her eyes at Petagnas as she struts out of the room. These two shall meet again in front of a jury. For now, Petagnas feels that he has gotten enough, or as much as he is going to get out of this witness.

For Prosecutor David Edwards, he sees some areas of weakness in his case against Algernon Flowers. He knows that he must strengthen his case before this goes before a jury at trial. Both the prosecution and defense teams dismiss and go their separate ways to prepare for the next pretrial date. As for the defense, the hope is to get an actual trial date soon. For the prosecution, they are vying for more time.

.   .   .

Less than an hour after the deposition, Prosecutor David Edwards is already on the phone with Brenda Howell's lawyer. He is scheduling another mock trial cross-examination to further prepare this very valuable prosecution witness before she is placed on the witness stand in front of the jury. Edwards understands that today was merely a warm up for Michael Petagnas and that his line of questioning may differ completely by the actual trial. Prosecutor Edwards needs his star witness to perform better in front of that jury if he is going to maintain his perfect winning record.

Michael Petagnas is pleased with what he was able to get from Mrs. Brenda Howell, although he really wanted more. Both Petagnas and his partner Steven Didia Sr. see holes and extremely vulnerable areas in the prosecution's case against Algernon Flowers, however they also know how unpredictable a jury can be. The men and women on the jury are going to want someone to pay for the murder of a little girl, and the only person on trial for that murder is their client.

CHAPTER 43

Algernon Flowers has a love/hate relationship with going to court. He *loves* the fact that he gets out of his cell for a couple of hours. He *hates* that he then has to sit in another cell at the courthouse and is fed stale bologna sandwiches. He *loves* that he gets to ride in the back of the sheriff's van, even though it contains no widows—the sensation of moving and the sound of the highway is relaxing and calming. He *hates* the sounds of other cars and pedestrians going about their lives, as it reminds him of the life he once enjoyed. He also *loves* the fact that every court date brings him a step closer to finally getting his day in court. He also *hates* the fact that every court date brings him a step closer to finally getting his day in court. What Algernon Flowers simultaneously loves and hates about getting his day in court is the fact that it can go either way ... *for* him or *against* him.

Before Algernon Flowers can go to court today he is searched, handcuffed, and shackled at the ankles. He is then loaded into the back of a cargo-style van with gated compartments resembling that of a mobile animal kennel. The van leaves the loading dock area of the Local County Jail. Algernon can see that it is a sunny day by the sunshine beaming through a crease in the back door. He hears the rubber tires moving along the gravel roadway that leads from the wooded area where the jail property sits toward the downtown area where the courthouse is. When the van comes to a red light and reaches a complete stop, Algernon can hear the brakes and idle engines of surrounding vehicles, and faintly, even some car radios nearby. He feels he is so close to the world that he is now isolated and alienated from. A part of him would like windows to see life going on outside of his current situation, but another part of him also welcomes the covering from others seeing him chained and shackled like an animal in his orange jail jumpsuit. As is the case with animals, their caged environment offers both the feeling of isolation and safety at the same time. Algernon is not sure which of the two he prefers anymore.

Michael Petagnas is unaware that his client, Algernon Flowers, is being taken to court in a neighboring county on an *unrelated*—yet *related* charge. Unrelated because it has *nothing* to do with his current murder charge. Related because it has *everything* to do with his current murder charge. Other than this case, Algernon Flowers has no prior criminal history. This is another fact that doesn't sit well with the prosecution when presenting an already-weak case to a jury. If they can get the jury to view the defendant as a criminal, then perhaps that jury will then convict that 'criminal' based on a combination of the weak evidence and the defendant's prior record. The prosecution found a possible way to achieve this.

With some digging, they discover on one occasion prior to his arrest, Mr. Flowers was swimming in a private pool in an apartment complex where a friend lived. A nosy neighbor, presuming that Algernon didn't live there due to his ethnicity, called the police. When the police officer arrived, he said he asked Algernon if he was a resident, and Algernon told him that he was. When he asked for his name, Algernon gave him the name of his friend who actually lived there. The officer saw that name on one of the mailboxes and left the scene, seeing nothing suspicious about Algernon. Now out of sheer desperation, prosecutors have found this officer and are charging Algernon Flowers with lying to a police officer and trespassing.

The first step is to bring these charges against Algernon Flowers. The next step would be to explain the charges to Judge Warren Jackson in hopes that he will allow the prosecution to bring this officer to court as a witness to testify that Algernon lied to him.

． ． ．

When Michael Petagnas learns that his client, Algernon Flowers, has been taken to another county to be officially charged with a crime, he is surprised. During his time as a prosecutor, he never sank this low to take a defendant away without first notifying his attorney that the client is being hit with an additional charge. When Petagnas speaks with the district attorney's office, they tell him that since it was unrelated to this case, they didn't see the need to notify him. However, Michael Petagnas knows they are going to make it become related to this case, eventually.

When Michael Petagnas questions the police officer, he gets a totally different response than what he was expecting. The officer explains to Petagnas that Algernon Flowers stated his friend lived there, and the officer then asked him what his friend's name was. When given the name of the friend, the officer then checked to make certain that the person, in fact, lived in that apartment complex. Since there appeared to be no crime or mischief occurring, the officer left. With that version of the story, and a statement from Algernon's friend who knew that Algernon was using the pool, Michael Petagnas goes to the neighboring county and gets the 'lying to a police officer' and 'trespassing' charges dropped.

Realizing just how desperate the prosecution is becoming, Michael Petagnas is more determined than ever to dig up more evidence of a cover up, and if there is, in fact, any police involvement. Petagnas puts a call in to Nicholas McLean.

. . .

When private investigator Nicholas McLean gets off the phone with Michael Petagnas, he decides to assemble his team. It once again becomes an all-hands-on-deck approach with one goal in mind, and that is to locate Heather Hoffman and find out what exactly her baby blanket story is all about.

. . .

As for Michael Petagnas, he and his team are dissecting the testimony and deposition of Brenda Howell and the other prosecution witnesses. They are starting to see a clear picture and a commonality of inconsistencies and flaws within the totality of the prosecution's case. The next step is to lock in a trial date, finalize a witness list, and then prepare to pick a jury.

. . .

As for District Prosecutor David Edwards, he would like to take more time. Not because he is grossly unprepared and has limited evidence, but because if he can delay this trial until after the elections, then that puts less pressure on him. Winning or losing a big case will not be a factor when the voters enter the polls if the case is still in pending status. Edwards sees this more like tackling one major project at a time. Defeat his opponent Nancy Groover and get re-elected, then he can concentrate all of his efforts and energy on taking on his former boss, Michael Petagnas, in the Algernon Flowers murder trial.

. . .

As for Algernon Flowers, sitting in a cell at the Local County Jail has become freakishly comfortable. He is almost more comfortable in his cell than out among people. He is becoming an anti-social rat of sorts, dwelling in his 'hole,' only coming out to attend court and then returning to his 'comfort zone'— his cage. This is the life he is getting used to, and he is losing sight of what life is like outside of his confinement. Before, his only therapy was the countless mail he received from friends daily. But eventually, over time, the number and frequency of mail has dropped significantly. Algernon Flowers is feeling forgotten and left alone to rot here behind bars while life goes on without him.

PART II
THE TRIAL

CHAPTER 44

Winter turns to spring and spring gives way to summer—summer to fall, then back to winter. This continuous cycle of ever-changing seasons is symbolic of human life and the need to evolve and grow. As time has evolved in Rocky Beach, Florida, there are many changes with the seasons, yet many constants as well.

David Edwards defeated his opponent Nancy Groover in the district elections. He maintains his office and continues to lead his team of prosecutors in Local County. Also, Rocky Beach Police Chief Donald Nelson has won his bid for re-election and remains in his office. Both Prosecutor Edwards and Chief Nelson have won over the public with their general work in their respective offices and within the Local County community.

Life has gone on in Rocky Beach. Several cases have come and gone in the court system. No one really talks much about the Algernon Flowers case except the occasional question of,

'What ever happened with that case?' from time to time. Brenda Howell has permanently relocated out of Local County, and her husband, Detective Frank Howell, has been transferred to another department that operates outside of Rocky Beach. The city of Rocky Beach has a new mayor who is working closely with the chief of police and the local community leaders.

Relationships are also susceptible to the element of change. Chief Nelson's wife has filed for divorce and it is rumored he is currently dating the much younger Channel Eight News reporter he is often seen with on his off days. Steven Didia Jr. and Jennifer Forde have both passed the state bar and ethics examinations and are now engaged to be married. Steven Jr. popped the big question during a dinner to celebrate their success of passing the bar exam. Now between planning their wedding and both working full-time as attorneys at the law firm of Petagnas & Didia, the young couple is living their dream, but not getting enough sleep to truly enjoy it. Steven Jr. and his fiancée Jennifer are not allowed to work on, or contribute to, the Algernon Flowers case due to Jennifer's history with the prosecution of the case. However, they are handling other smaller cases that come through the office. Both Steven Jr. and Jennifer possess the qualities of great trial attorneys. They often discuss starting their own law firm one day.

Michael Petagnas and his wife are pregnant and expecting their third and fourth children. The Petagnas household will soon consist of two adults and four children when the twins arrive. Petagnas and his wife have been interviewing for a nanny to help with the two older children. Michael Petagnas has been working on the Algernon Flowers case over the past nineteen months and is looking forward to finally getting this thing in front of a jury. After months of mock trials and extensive research and preparation, Michael Petagnas and his team are ready to defend Algernon Flowers' life in court. Although the Flowers family has long since run out of money, their initial retainer being depleted within the first few months, Petagnas and his office are pretty much representing Algernon for free.

Private investigator Nicholas McLean and his team are also working for free. The past year and a half has been brutal. The investigators have been running into roadblocks at every turn. No cooperation from the police or the chief's office, and no sign of Heather Hoffman, who is now officially considered a missing person. Their surveillance of Detective Peter Nelson has turned up no leads as to Hoffman's whereabouts. The playboy detective has many girlfriends he visits and takes on trips, but nothing leading to Heather Hoffman. Even with the time that has come and gone, Nick McLean has not been able to convince Deborah Long, Angela Crowell or Audrey Richardson to provide any more information, or to agree to testify against their friend and former co-worker, Brenda Howell. If there is going to be a victory for the defense in this case, it will have to be done with the information and evidence already provided by McLean and his team.

Over the past year and a half, Hazel Flowers has sold her daycare center and is currently thinking about putting her home up for sale as well. The stress of a pending trial has taken its toll on her business and her entire life. Today Ms. Flowers gets a visit from Sandy Ward. Sandy is returning some of Ms. Flowers' dishes. Feeling guilty for not being able to continue to pay for her son's legal fees, she turned to the only thing she loves as much as her family, and that is cooking. Hazel Flowers sold items from her garage and used the money to buy food and cook large meals every Friday for the entire staff over at the Law Offices of Petagnas & Didia. Sandy is returning the dishes from yesterday's big feast. Normally Sandy would return the dishes on the following Monday, however with the trial set to begin this coming Monday and the office expecting to be busy, she is stopping by on Saturday afternoon. Her visit is not only to return the dishes, but to also offer moral support to Ms. Flowers. After nineteen months of waiting, the trial date is finally here and Sandy knows that it won't be easy for Ms. Flowers to have to sit outside of the courtroom and not be allowed to support her son. Still not understanding why the prosecution would list her as a witness and cause her to have to wait outside with their other witness, Hazel Flowers has so many unanswered questions. She tries not to have animosity in her heart for anyone, but her patience is tried every day when it comes to the people and actions involved in the police department and district attorney's office. Unable to sleep or eat, Ms. Flowers is looking forward to her sister and cousins traveling from New York City to represent her by sitting in the courtroom in her absence. She knows that her son Algernon will be happy to see all of his family sitting behind him in court. As Sandy Ward prepares to leave, she gives a few words of encouragement to Ms. Flowers. In a surprise twist, it is Hazel Flowers who actually encourages Sandy. Ms. Flowers tells Sandy how much she appreciates all that she and the team have done in her son's defense. Even when they could no longer pay, the team fought long and hard for Algernon and she will never forget that.

.　　　.　　　.

Algernon Flowers marks another notch on his green cell wall. Today marks day number five hundred and eighty-four that he has spent here in the Local County Jail. He has put on several pounds, his beard is now thick and has many grey hairs, and his hairline is receding. His body shows all the signs of extreme stress and inactivity. He is almost unrecognizable—photos of him now and five hundred and eighty-four days ago would appear to be two different people. Today he is getting a visit from the jailhouse barber who will give him a haircut and a shave in preparation for his trial this coming Monday. Algernon's mother sent a suit for him to wear to court. He is allowed only one, so she made sure it was his favorite. She selected the one he wore in the photo on his CD cover. Just in case this is the last dress suit he ever wears, she wants it to be the one he wore when he recorded the album and made his life-long dream come true. When Algernon goes down to the transfer room to try on the suit, it no longer fits him since he has put on so much weight. His choice is to either wear an orange jumpsuit—which in the eyes of the jury makes a defendant already appear guilty, or old, miscellaneous clothing items donated by a thrift store.

Algernon is able to find a blue dress shirt, navy slacks, and a tan blazer that all fit him. Once he has his haircut and shave, he will be ready for his date with the jury on Monday morning. Now how does one sleep when he is going on trial for first-degree murder in less than forty-eight hours? He does not sleep at all.

.   .   .

Early Sunday morning, Michael Petagnas and Nicholas McLean visit Algernon Flowers at the jail. Petagnas is present to discuss last-minute details and to prepare Algernon mentally for what is going to take place tomorrow morning. McLean is present to support Mr. Flowers—the man he now calls 'friend.'

Michael Petagnas explains that the first order of business will be the selecting of the jury—a process called 'voir dire.' This is when a random pool of selected jurors will enter the room and both the prosecution and defense get to ask certain questions about their background—family and personal history—their views on the death penalty—whether they have ever been the victim of a crime, or anything that may influence them either way during this trial. Both sides can agree on a juror or strike a juror with each side getting six strikes. Once a jury of twelve, plus two alternates, has been selected, opening arguments will then begin.

After going over a few more details and general trial format information, Petagnas and McLean leave. Tomorrow is the day that all three of these men have been preparing for. Not one of them will get any sleep tonight, but adrenaline and nerves will keep them going throughout the entire trial. Michael Petagnas will go home and review deposition transcripts for the prosecution's first few witnesses. Algernon Flowers will return to his cell and wait to be taken to the courthouse in the early-morning hours. As for Nick McLean, he is still on the prowl. He has been tailing Detective Peter Nelson and his silver sedan, and tracked him to a remote location a few miles west of Rocky Beach. Nelson has visited this location in the past, now McLean is going to try to find out why.

CHAPTER 45

Private investigator Nicholas McLean puts his SUV in park and turns off the engine. He grabs a flashlight from his glove box and also his concealed firearm. He slides the small handgun into the waistband of his jeans and exits the vehicle. The beam from his flashlight is the only available light for miles. The sounds of crickets and other small animals fill the dark, secluded wooded area off the back highway as McLean walks cautiously. His flashlight beam bounces back and forth as he is not even sure what it is he is looking for exactly. In the stillness of these dark, abandoned woods, the resonating sound of every small branch or leaf that makes contact with McLean's shoes is amplified intensely. This is the area that the shady detective driving the silver sedan visited on more than one occasion. Was he merely having an adventurous rendezvous with one of his many girlfriends—or perhaps something much more sinister?

One thing is for certain: this remote and creepy location is the perfect spot to hide something.

As McLean steps carefully through the thick brush, he navigates around litter and other items that were dumped and discarded off the back highway. Occasionally, the sounds of nature around him are interrupted by the noise of a passing truck or car along the desolate highway road behind him. Some sort of small animal startles McLean as it runs across his shoe. Instinctively, he aims his flashlight in the direction of the quick-moving animal and catches a glimpse of its grey, bushy tail ... and something else. McLean holds his light on a certain object as he squints in an attempt to focus and see closer. He decides to move toward the object that caught his eye.

As Nick McLean gets closer, he is looking at what seems to be a pile of dirt and small sticks. At first glance it appears to be some sort of home built by animals, however this home has one very distinct feature that captured McLean's attention. Sticking out from the dirt and sticks, McLean can see a piece of clothing and human hair. Realizing that he may have just stumbled upon a shallow grave, he carefully backs away as to not further contaminate any evidence. As he backs away with his flashlight still shining on his discovery, he reaches for his firearm. After clearing the thick brush, he points his flashlight toward his vehicle and quickly retreats to it. Once McLean is in his SUV he locks the doors, and with his firearm still in his hand, he dials 9-1-1. After the first ring, McLean hangs up— realizing that if there is a connection to what he just discovered and the police chief's son, then calling the police may not go over well for him. McLean decides to drive to a nearby gas station off the highway and use a payphone to call anonymously, and report a possible body found buried in the woods.

Algernon Flowers sits up in his jail cell. He cannot seem to fall asleep. The anxiety and nerves keep his heart and mind racing. Within a couple of hours he will go before Circuit Court Judge Warren 'Hangman' Jackson in his first-degree murder trial. Understanding that sometimes innocent people are wrongfully convicted only to be proven innocent years later, Algernon does not want to be a part of that statistic. There is another statistic that is more frightening to Mr. Flowers ... Prosecutor David Edwards has never lost a case, and his conviction rate for murder cases is one hundred percent. With a jury that is going to want someone to pay for the death of a little girl, things should be easy for Prosecutor Edwards to maintain his perfect record. However, Algernon Flowers is represented by one of the best trial attorneys in the country, who also happens to have a perfect record in murder cases. As these thoughts swirl around in Algernon's head, he wants to sleep but cannot. Sleep or no sleep, very soon the heavy iron door to his tiny cell will roll open and he will be transferred to the courthouse to face the judge and jury.

After Nick McLean's anonymous call to 9-1-1, it is not the Rocky Beach PD, but the Local County sheriff's deputies to first arrive on the scene. One by one, various law-enforcement officials arrive to the wooded area. Within an hour of the 9-1-1 call, the entire area is swarming with homicide and forensic personnel from different Local County agencies. With sirens and floodlights now lighting up the once dark and quiet area, Nick McLean drives by in his SUV to peek and observe from a distance. He pulls over and notices several evidence collectors in full white covering, combing through the area, while officers corner off the area with yellow crime scene tape. Moments later a medical examiner's van arrives, and two men load a large black body bag into the back of it. McLean is startled by a knock on his window. He rolls down his window and notices a sheriff's deputy informing him that this is a crime scene and that he has to vacate the area. McLean obliges. As he slowly pulls away he keeps his eye fixed on his rearview mirror, and sees a news van arriving on the scene.

.   .   .

Before the sun comes up, the door to Algernon Flowers' cell rolls open. He is already up and ready to go. He takes the walk down the long corridor toward the inmate transfer area. When he arrives, he is stripped and then allowed to dress in the donated thrift store outfit he put together. Once he is dressed, he is handcuffed and shackled at the ankles, then carted off in the back of a windowless van. Next stop, the Local County Courthouse.

As the van navigates the commute, Algernon cannot hear any other vehicles. With it being so early, not many cars are on the road, and with his heart pumping out of his chest drowning out anything else, he is shut in from the outside elements and life beyond the van walls. It takes approximately fifteen minutes to arrive from the jail to the courthouse. Once the van carrying Algernon Flowers arrives, the roll-up gate is lifted to allow entry. The van enters the underground garage area, and the gate is rolled back down before the inmate is taken out.

As Algernon Flowers walks, he takes very small steps due to the chain that is shackled to his ankles. The chain drags along the ground for the duration of the long walk from the garage to the holding cell just outside of courtroom number nine. Once placed and secured in the cell, Algernon Flowers' handcuffs are removed and he is given a brown paper bag, which contains his breakfast. Jelly and toast with two boiled eggs. There is also a small plastic container of apple juice. Even if this were a more delightful meal, Algernon Flowers has no appetite at all—for he is merely a few steps away from the courtroom, where in the next couple of hours he will be tried for first-degree murder. All he can do is sit on the wooden bench and try to be comfortable with the ankle shackles still on while he waits to be brought into the courtroom.

.   .   .

When Michael Petagnas sits at his table to enjoy the lovely pretrial meal his wife prepared, he is shocked to discover that his trial—the trial of Algernon Flowers—is not the front-page story in the morning paper. The biggest trial of his career has been over shadowed by the discovery of a woman's body in a shallow grave just outside Rocky Beach last night. The unidentified remains are currently being processed, and the initial belief is that they may have been buried over a year ago, but weather and animals may have caused them to partially resurface over time. As Petagnas reads the article, his phone, which is set to a timer to exit 'do not disturb' mode, vibrates as he gets notifications. He looks at his phone and sees that he has missed several calls from Nick McLean. When Petagnas listens to the voicemail from McLean, he learns that the woman's hair color and clothing match that of the missing reporter from Channel Thirteen News, Heather Hoffman. The body is far too decomposed to draw that conclusion, but further tests should soon reveal the identity of the remains. Michael Petagnas knows that the process and testing to positively identify a badly decomposed body can take weeks or even months, so he doesn't even assume that this discovery will in any way have an impact on his case. It is, however, a good distraction from the media blitz that the start of Algernon Flowers' trial would've gotten. Petagnas finishes his breakfast and gets in his car to drive to the courthouse.

· · ·

Hazel Flowers hasn't slept much in the past few days. She is up early and dressed as she awaits the rest of her family to arrive into the kitchen. Ms. Flowers cooked a huge breakfast so that her family that has traveled from all over the country to support her and her son Algernon can be fed. Although she cannot be present on the front row behind her son, Hazel Flowers will have plenty of family and friends present for moral support during the first-degree murder trial. Dressed in her favorite dress suit, Ms. Flowers can only hope that the prosecutor will call her to testify early so that she can then sit in the courtroom after her testimony is complete. However, she knows that in reality she will not be called at all, and that listing her as a potential witness is just a ploy by the prosecution to keep her from the courtroom, which they hope will further discourage Algernon

Flowers—just another thing that she cannot allow to place negative thoughts in her head. She is staying positive and upbeat to symbolize her support and represent peace, as she fears her son will be terrified facing the judge and jury with his life on the line. As family members begin to enter the kitchen, Hazel Flowers does what she does best, and feeds everyone before the start of a very important day. After breakfast, the family gathers for a quick prayer before leaving. It takes several minivans and carloads to get the entire family to the courthouse. As the Flowers' caravan makes its way to the Local County Courthouse, a feeling of solidarity can be felt even among the spectators that watch them file out of the parking lot and into the crowded courtroom.

·　　　·　　　·

As Prosecutors Edwards and Henderson enter the courtroom, they are surprised to see the large number of supporters seated on the right side of the room behind the defense table. Some spectators had to be turned away due to insufficient seating. On the left side of the courtroom behind the prosecution table, there are a few local media reporters that are covering the case for local newspapers, some of Brenda Howell's family members, Detective Frank Howell and Police Chief Nelson. Prosecutors Edwards and Henderson shake hands with Detective Howell and Chief Nelson as they pass by on their way to their seats at the prosecution table.

Michael Petagnas enters the courtroom alone. His partner, Steven Didia Sr., is already seated in the first row directly behind the defense table, along with Sandy Ward, Steven Didia Jr., Jennifer Forde, and two other defense staff members. Petagnas walks down the center aisle to intimidating glares from Detective Frank Howell and Chief Nelson. He is no stranger to the hate and intimidation tactics, however he is not quite sure as to the lengths these lawmen will go to make a point. Petagnas takes his seat on the left at the two-man defense table. The seat on the right is reserved for the defendant, Algernon

Flowers, who is still in a holding cell. When the judge is close to exiting his chambers, the court officers will bring Algernon Flowers from the holding cell, remove his shackles, and allow him to enter and take his seat next to his attorney. Following Mr. Flowers' arrival, the judge will enter and all will rise. The tension continues to mount as everyone in the now-packed-to-capacity courtroom is waiting for the defendant and the judge to enter. The sound of muffled voices conversing with anticipation can be heard out in the foyer, where Nick McLean is walking. He is just arriving after an eventful night. He enters the courtroom and sees the rest of his investigation team that worked the Algernon Flowers case. One of his interns, who has been holding a seat for McLean, gets up and exits the courtroom, allowing McLean to join investigators Rachael O'Toole, Helena Wang, and Brent Patterson. Chief Nelson turns around and glares at Nick McLean. He then whispers something to another officer seated directly behind him. The officer then looks back at McLean and quickly returns his eyes to the front of the courtroom. McLean notices the awkward exchange. He refuses to be intimidated.

·   ·   ·

Algernon Flowers feels like a rookie quarterback waiting in the locker room before starting in his first Super Bowl. He is nervous and anxious as he prepares to face his more experienced opponent. Having been sitting and pacing interchangeably in the holding cell for the past three and a half hours, he has created more of a panic within himself. The waiting and not knowing what is going on just a few steps away beyond the door to courtroom number nine is enough to make him dizzy. His hope is that he does not pass out inside the courtroom, but a combination of nerves, lack of sleep, and lack of nutrition makes even standing up a daunting task. He sits on the wooden bench in the holding cell, and tries to breathe slowly and deeply. Within moments of relaxing, the door to the courtroom swings opens to the sound of jingling keys. Algernon Flowers opens his eyes and sees one of the court officers. It is time to enter the courtroom. This means that the judge is almost ready, and his murder trial will officially begin. The court officer opens the cell door and removes the shackles from Algernon's feet. Algernon is then directed to the door that leads to courtroom number nine.

CHAPTER 46

When Algernon enters courtroom number nine, the large number of people seated in the gallery overwhelms him. Every eye is on him as he makes the nerve-racking walk to the defense table. When he imagined his life and dreamt of making music that influenced the world, he didn't think that his celebrity status would instead be as a criminal defendant in a high-profile murder case. He pictured himself walking out onto a stage to the screams and cheers of adoring fans, not to the scrutiny of media and prosecutors looking to see him go down for an unthinkable crime.

During the walk—short in distance, yet long in duration—Algernon makes eye contact with family members near the front row and avoids it with the opposite side of the courtroom, as he doesn't want to see Prosecutor Edwards, who is trying to convict him of first-degree murder by any means. Algernon is greeted by his defense attorney, Michael Petagnas, as he sits next to him. With Petagnas on his left as a buffer between the prosecution table and himself, Algernon Flowers looks over to the left—past the prosecution—toward the empty jury box. Soon the fourteen chairs will be filled with men and women who have never met Algernon before today, yet will somehow decide his fate.

Directly behind Mr. Flowers sits Jennifer Forde, who is flooded with emotion. This is the first time she has been this close to the man that she was once helping Prosecutor Edwards send to prison or death. She still feels strongly, now more than ever, that they have the wrong person on trial fighting for his life. Jennifer wipes a tear from her eye as she looks over to the back of Prosecutor Edwards' head. She wishes that he would look closer at the evidence in this case. Her eyes make their way back over to the back of Algernon Flowers, and she can see him visibly trembling with fear. This is no monster—no murderer … this is a frightened young man who got caught in a trap that he never saw coming. Jennifer's heart goes out to this defendant, and she can only hope that one day she will get the opportunity to defend someone similar in her career. It is in this moment that her new passion and purpose are realized. She will not stand by and allow someone, regardless of social or economic standing, become just another innocent life or a second victim to a flawed and imperfect system.

The courtroom deputy yells out "All rise!" as the judge makes his way out of his chambers and onto the bench. Everyone in the courtroom stands to their feet until the judge is seated and the court deputy announces for all to "Be seated."

The Honorable Judge Warren Jackson looks across the packed courtroom and sees that all parties are in place. He calls the session to order. He explains to the gallery of observers that he will in no way tolerate the ringing of cell phones, or any photography whatsoever—also, no disruptive outbursts of any kind. Judge Jackson then goes into some preliminary legal formats before the day's proceedings begin. During the entire time the judge has been on the bench, he has yet to make direct eye contact with Algernon Flowers. It is not until the judge addresses the defendant directly that their eyes meet.

"Is the defendant clear on this?" asks Judge Jackson.

"Yes, your Honor," replies Algernon in a soft, shaking and breaking voice.

.   .   .

Today is day one of the first-degree murder trial, also known as 'Jury Selection Day.' The first pool of potential jurors files into the courtroom and take seats in the jury box. The Judge then addresses them and offers brief instruction. The Judge informs the potential jurors that this is a first-degree murder trial, and that the defendant, Algernon Flowers, is charged in the beating death of a child. This is important for the judge to establish in his initial address, because his first question to these potential jurors is: "Are you prepared to see and hear testimony in this type of case, and can you be fair and impartial?"

This is usually when a high percentage of potential jurors openly admit that they cannot be fair or impartial, or are not comfortable sitting in on a case like this—of this magnitude and nature. In this particular case, three potential jurors ask to be excused. The judge allows them to return into the general jury pool so that they may perhaps be called to sit in on a less intense case, such as a civil suit or slip and fall case. For the men and women who say that they can be fair and impartial in this case, and are prepared to hear and view evidence disturbing in nature, the judge then asks his second question: "Are you comfortable with recommending a sentence in this case, even if it means the death penalty?"

Like the first question, again some are not comfortable with this so they are excused. Once Judge Jackson has potential jurors that are comfortable with both of his questions, he then allows the prosecution and defense to question each potential juror. They ask questions relating to family background and profession, such as if there are any law enforcement in the family—or any family members ever charged with a crime.

They also want to clarify how each potential juror views crime, and whether they themselves have ever been the victim of any crimes. This is important to the defense because if a juror has been a victim of a violent crime where the assailant was never apprehended, he or she may take unresolved anger out on the defendant in this unrelated case. One other very important question that is asked to the potential jurors is: "Do you know the defendant or the family of the victim?"

As the morning goes on, jury pool after jury pool is brought in. Judge Jackson addresses them and offers his two opening questions. Then the remaining potential jurors endure more questions by both the prosecution and defense. One gentleman answers "yes" to the question of knowing the defendant. He worked for a temp-agency where Algernon Flowers applied for a job when he was raising money to fund the recording of his CD. The man remembers the name because of its uniqueness. He adds that Algernon was very polite and friendly. Needless to say, the prosecution elects to 'strike' this man as a potential juror in this case. They do not want anyone inside the jury room that will speak well of the man they want to paint as a ruthless monster.

The entire first day of this trial is taken up by attempting to seat a jury of twelve and two alternates. In the small community of Rocky Beach, there are lots of people who have either heard of this case prior and have already formed an opinion, or have a problem sitting in on a murder trial where the victim is a young child.

By early evening, the prosecution and defense have finally reached the required number necessary for a jury, and can now begin opening statements. However, since it is so late in the day, Judge Jackson decides to hold off on opening statements until 9 A.M. tomorrow morning. Before releasing the jury for the night, he instructs them to avoid reading or watching any news coverage of this case, and not to discuss it with anyone—not even among themselves. At the end of testimony and closing arguments, when the trial has entered the deliberation phase, then they may discuss this case among themselves. After the jury is dismissed, the judge gives further instruction to both the prosecution and defense before ending the day's session. The entire courtroom rises as the judge returns to his chambers. Algernon Flowers is taken back to the holding cell where he is shackled, cuffed and then transported back to the Local County Jail. Day one was nerve racking, but opening statements begin tomorrow. That is when Prosecutor Edwards is expected to start strong, just as he learned from his former boss, Michael Petagnas. Algernon is expecting tomorrow to be a much tougher day in court. As he rides in the back of the windowless, county transport van, he replays the events of the day over in his head. He will probably not sleep again tonight, as he will stay up seeing the faces of the men and women that will be deciding his fate. Day one is in the books, and Algernon Flowers' emotional tank is already on empty.

CHAPTER 47

Day two in the Algernon Flowers first-degree murder trial is set to get underway, as the defendant enters courtroom number nine wearing the same clothes from day one. Algernon Flowers greets his attorney as he takes the seat next to him. At one point, Michael Petagnas gets up from the defense table to speak with his associates seated in the row directly behind them. Petagnas' absence eliminates the buffer between Algernon Flowers and Prosecutor David Edwards. Algernon can feel Edwards to his left, but keeps his focus forward and locked onto the bench in the front-center of the courtroom. This awkwardness seems to last forever, until finally broken up by the voice of the courtroom deputy yelling "All rise!" as the judge takes his place on the bench.

Today begins opening statements in the first-degree murder trial, and if County Prosecutor David Edwards has learned anything from his former boss Michael Petagnas, he will be starting strong with character-damaging allegations. It is rumored that when Mr. Petagnas was the district attorney, while in the middle of his opening statement, some defendants and defense lawyers would wave the white flag and beg for a plea deal. The opening statement is a very powerful tool, especially for the prosecution who gets to go first in painting a descriptive picture of their case. This is the first impression that the jury gets of the defendant. Some cases are won in the opening statements alone. Both David Edwards and Michael Petagnas understand and live by this.

Judge Jackson addresses both sides and those seated in the courtroom gallery before bringing in the jury. The prosecutors, defendant and defense attorney stand as the jury enters. In what seems almost like the entrance of a sacred ceremonial processional, the twelve-member jury and two alternates quietly walk in and file into the jury box. Each juror is assigned a number and a seat. Once they are seated, the judge goes over his daily instruction and then the session begins.

"Is the prosecution ready? Is the defense ready?" asks the judge.

Both sides acknowledge that they are prepared to proceed, and then the judge opens the floor for the prosecution to go on with their opening statement. The first-degree murder trial of Algernon Flowers has now officially begun.

Prosecutor David Edwards stands and walks to the small podium near the jury box. He places some typed pages containing his opening statement on top of the podium and gives them a quick glance. He then buttons the jacket of his grey pin-striped suit, and addresses the men and women of the jury.

"Ladies and gentlemen of the jury, we are here today because a little girl—three-year-old Deja Howell, was brutally and viciously beaten. This child received a beating so severe that her injuries ultimately caused her death. A beating inflicted by that man, the defendant," exclaims Prosecutor Edwards as he points directly at Algernon Flowers.

Prosecutor Edwards explains to the jury the brief history between Mr. Flowers and the child's mother, Brenda Howell, as well as the encounter with police after the suspicious death.

"You will hear from the Rocky Beach homicide detective who interviewed the defendant as he explains how cocky and arrogant the defendant was," continues the well-polished prosecutor as he reads from his notes.

Each time he refers to Mr. Flowers, Prosecutor Edwards uses the term 'the defendant' as his voice dramatically elevates with volume and intensity. Edwards also makes it a point to gesture in the direction of Algernon Flowers with each reference.

"When Brenda Howell went to work that morning, she thought her little girl would be safe with the man she fell in love with ... yes, Brenda Howell was in love with the defendant," Edwards says as his voice continues to fluctuate to match his points.

"You will hear testimony from the county medical examiner that will show the extent of little Deja's injuries suffered at the hand of the defendant, Algernon Flowers," concludes Edwards as he finally addresses Algernon by his actual name.

After taking up nearly two full hours with his opening statement—after giving the jury a list of all the possible testimonies that they will be hearing over the course of the trial—after thanking the jury for their time—after unbuttoning his suit jacket, David Edwards has completed his opening statement, and returns to his seat. Prosecutor Ramon Henderson gives his co-council a nod of approval for his very thorough delivery.

Judge Jackson then turns to the defense and informs them that it is now their turn to give an opening statement. Michael Petagnas stands but doesn't step away from the defense table. He is standing out of respect while addressing the judge.

"If it pleases the court, your Honor, at this time the defense will hold off on giving an opening statement, and rather chooses to save it for later in the trial," states a very confident Petagnas.

Every news reporter in the room begins to write in their notebooks as Petagnas sits. Prosecutors Edwards and Henderson look at each other as neither one of them expected this to be Michael Petagnas' first strategic move. They are not sure what his overall defense strategy is, but it makes them a bit nervous. By forfeiting their opening statement until the end of the prosecution's case, Petagnas keeps his defense strategy to himself. He offers no alternative theories, and is not required to offer any evidence until after the prosecution rests their case. The prosecution will get a rebuttal case to follow the defense's case, however the extent of damage that may be inflicted by Petagnas at that point is not a risk Prosecutor Edwards is comfortable with. In Michael Petagnas' opinion, the opening statement from the prosecution, though emotionally stirring, did not offer anything solid tying Algernon Flowers to this crime, nor why he is even considered a suspect except for his demeanor in the eyes of detectives and a weak and tainted medical examiner's report. Petagnas feels that there is no need to give an opening statement in return, but rather to poke holes in the prosecution's case, and reveal to the jury how wrong the indictment against Mr. Flowers was in the first place. Hopefully the jury will look past the emotions in this case, and apply the common-sense factor.

Even Judge Warren Jackson is a bit surprised the defense is holding off with their opening statement. However, he is prepared to move on.

"Is the prosecution ready to call their first witness?" asks the judge.

Prosecutor Edwards' assistant has to scramble to the back of the courtroom gallery, and out into the hallway to see if the first witness is prepared. They weren't expecting to have to call their first witness before lunch, but with the defense not using up any of their opening statement time, the prosecution's first witness is way ahead of schedule.

When David Edwards gets word that his first witness is ready, he makes the official declaration.

"The prosecution calls Mr. Earl Wallace to the stand!" states Prosecutor Edwards.

The emergency medical technician, Mr. Earl Wallace, enters courtroom number nine from the main doors at the rear of the gallery and makes his way down the center aisle. He then moves toward the left, walks past the jury, and enters the witness stand. Before taking his seat, he raises his right hand and is sworn in by the courtroom deputy.

"Do you swear that the testimony that you are giving here today is the truth, the whole truth, and nothing but the truth to the best of your knowledge and understanding?" asks the deputy.

"I do," replies Mr. Wallace before sitting.

Prosecutor Edwards asks the EMT to give and spell his full name for the official court records, after which he is asked to share his background and training with the jury. Once Mr. Wallace is through addressing the jury, Prosecutor Edwards asks him to share what he remembers on the morning he was called to the Brenda Howell's apartment. Earl Wallace's testimony doesn't differ much, if at all, from his taped deposition from over a year ago. He basically offers the jury a picture of what it was like in the apartment as a first responder. Earl Wallace is not here to give his opinion as to what he thinks happened, but rather to help place the jury on the scene. After a few questions from Prosecutor Edwards, the defense has their opportunity to cross-examine the prosecution's witness. Michael Petagnas stands yet remains at the defense table. He doesn't even take the time to button his navy blue suit jacket. He has only one question for prosecution witness number one.

"Mr. Wallace, you stated that you have no opinion as to what happened to this little girl—basically Mr. Flowers was performing CPR when you arrived, and that you had difficulty placing the breathing tube down the unconscious victim's throat, correct?" asks the calm and very eloquent defense attorney.

"That is correct," replies Mr. Wallace.

Following the witness' response, Michael Petagnas states to the judge, "The defense has nothing further, your Honor," as he lowers himself into his seat.

Being the experienced trial lawyer he is, and seeing that this witness brings nothing to offer the jury that suggests his client is the killer, Petagnas doesn't want to cloud the jury with useless information and minor details that will only confuse them later in the deliberation room. Also, the longer each prosecution witness takes on the stand, the more weight the jury subconsciously holds to the prosecution's case in their minds. By eliminating the uninfluential witnesses quickly, Petagnas hopes to save the bulk of time and energy on the more 'cross-examination-worthy' witnesses.

Judge Jackson addresses the prosecution.

"Re-cross?" he asks.

"Nothing at this time, your Honor," replies Prosecutor Edwards after checking with his co-council.

The judge then asks both sides if the witness may be excused. If neither side intends to recall this witness later in the trial, then he can be released from the witness list. Earl Wallace exits the witness stand and courtroom number nine as he is officially excused.

It is not even time for lunch yet and already the judge is ready for the prosecution's second witness. The prosecution calls its next witness—Ms. Patricia Gaddis.

Patricia Gaddis, who lived in the apartment directly below Brenda Howell's at the time, enters the courtroom from the main entrance and walks toward the witness stand. Like the witness before her, she is sworn in and then asked to state and spell her full name for the record. She then gives a little of her background to the jury. Patricia Gaddis' testimony is also very similar to her deposition. Basically she tells the jury that on the morning in question, she heard a loud thump, followed by footsteps moving quickly above her. Shortly afterwards, the ambulance arrived on the scene. Gaddis is shown a photo of the apartment complex to offer the jury a better idea as to exactly where she was in relation to Brenda Howell's apartment. After a few questions from Prosecutor Edwards, Ms. Gaddis is cross-examined by the defense.

Michael Petagnas stands, and again remains behind the defense table. This time his does button his jacket as he has two questions for prosecution witness number two.

"Ms. Gaddis, you testified that you don't recall exactly what time it was, but that the sun was up and you were having coffee already when you heard the loud thump—and shortly afterwards the ambulance arrived, correct?" asks Petagnas.

"Correct," she replies.

"You also mentioned hearing footsteps moving quickly. Would it make sense to you that when Mrs. Brenda Howell returned home, and the two adults discovered the unresponsive child, the loud thump could then be the slamming of a door against the wall upon being frantically opened, and the foot-steps being that of the two adults rushing to relocate the child to the room where they attempted to assist her?" asks Petagnas.

Before Ms. Gaddis can respond, Prosecutor Edwards leaps out of his seat and objects.

"Objection! Calls for speculation, your Honor," states Edwards.

Before Judge Jackson can even rule on the objection, Michael Petagnas withdraws the question.

"Withdrawn, your Honor," politely exclaims the defense attorney.

Mr. Petagnas doesn't need Patricia Gaddis to answer that question. For the question is actually more of a statement and a theory, therefore no answer is needed. The jury now has an-other perspective of this witness' testimony. Petagnas' hope is that the common-sense factor will begin to kick in, and the men and women on this jury would find that his theory bet-ter explains what this neighbor heard as opposed to what the prosecution wants them to conclude. The timing of the noises Ms. Gaddis heard coincide with the two adults moving around frantically shortly before the ambulance arrived, rather than to suggest that the thump was associated with the initial beating of the small child, and that one adult was then chasing the three-year-old around the apartment.

Michael Petagnas continues to address the judge. "Nothing further for this witness, your Honor!" he states as he takes his seat.

Neither the prosecution nor defense has any intention of recalling this witness again, so she is dismissed. The prosecution's next scheduled witness is the emergency room physician on duty the morning that Deja Howell was brought in to the hospital. In similar fashion, as with the two witnesses before him, Dr. Richard Mason makes his way to the witness stand and is sworn in. He is then asked to state his name for the record and to describe his medical background and training for the jury. Before asking Dr. Mason a question, Prosecutor Edwards gets one detail out of the way. He asks the judge to inform the jury that this witness knows the family of the defendant, and is not testifying as an expert witness, but just to contribute information as to his contact with the victim on the morning in question, and the state of mind of the victim's mother. It is Edwards' hope that the jury would view Brenda Howell as the grieving mother, and what better witness to bring this point out than someone who is not only a professional, but one who also knows the defendant in this case. The judge obliges.

Dr. Mason's testimony offers nothing more than what is already in his deposition, and he cannot give an opinion either way as to what he thinks happened to the victim, other than the obvious bruising as signs of some sort of trauma. Mason testifies that he saw Algernon Flowers in the ER and asked him if he had any knowledge of the bruises on the victim's lower abdomen, just as he testified in his deposition. However, Prosecutor Edwards' follow-up question to Dr. Mason is about his opinion of Brenda Howell during his initial interaction with her.

"Doctor Mason, as a medical doctor who has had to inform people as to the passing of a loved one on a regular basis, would you say that, in your opinion, Mrs. Brenda Howell's grief was genuine?" asks Edwards.

"I would say it seemed authentic," replies the doctor.

David Edwards takes it a step further. "And would you say that Mr. Algernon Flowers seemed calm?" asks the prosecutor.

"Yes, I would say that he was calm," Dr. Mason replies.

The prosecution has nothing further, so the judge turns the witness over to the defense. Michael Petagnas appears relaxed as he stands, buttons his jacket, and crosses his arms before addressing the witness. He has three questions for prosecution witness number three.

"Dr. Mason, during your deposition you mentioned that the call came in from the ambulance as a 'full bus.' What does that mean?" asks Petagnas.

"That is code for a deceased body," replies the doctor.

"And you are a medical doctor—not a behavioral psychologist, correct?" asks Petagnas.

"Yes, that is correct. I am not a behavioral psychologist," replies the doctor.

"So it is safe to say then, that you are not concluding that by showing genuine grief, or maintaining a calm demeanor, or poised state of mind, in any way exhibits guilt or innocence, is that correct?" asks Petagnas as a follow up.

"That is correct. I am not suggesting that the behavior of any of the adults present determines anything," replies the doctor politely.

With a smile Michael Petagnas announces that he has nothing further, and takes his seat.

With nothing further from either side, or any intention to recall the witness, Doctor Mason is dismissed, and the judge decides to break for lunch. Judge Jackson addresses the jury with the usual instructions to not talk among themselves about this case, and to be back in one hour. The prosecution and defense stand up as the jury files out of the jury box and into the side door to the jury holding area where they will be provided lunch. After they exit, the judge tells the lawyers for both sides to return ready to proceed within the hour.

The courtroom deputy yells "All rise" as the judge vacates the bench and returns to his chambers. Algernon Flowers is then taken back to the holding cell where he is shackled and given a brown-bag lunch. Petagnas and his team head to the lobby to get lunch. On their way out of the courtroom, Michael Petagnas is met by the angry and aggressive stare of Detective Frank Howell. Noticing this, Steven Didia Sr. whispers to Petagnas, "I guess you're doing great!"

CHAPTER 48

During the lunch recess in the Algernon Flowers murder trial, private investigator Nicholas McLean gets word from one of his team members, Brent Patterson. Patterson has obtained exclusive information from the authorities that are looking into the human remains discovered in the wooded area off the back highway. Although it is early in the investigation, the initial (but unofficial) report is there appears to be a confirmed match to the missing news reporter Heather Hoffman, who went missing more than a year ago. McLean wants to know how, if at all, this ties into the Algernon Flowers case. If there is a connection, McLean and his team want to tie it together sooner rather than later, in the event it can save Algernon's life.

·   ·   ·

While eating his lunch, Prosecutor David Edwards flips through his questions for his fourth and very important witness, homicide detective Rodney Hunter. Uncertain as to the exact defense strategy of Michael Petagnas, Edwards wants to stay ahead of the game. Especially since this is the prosecution's portion of the trial, he doesn't want to have to play catch up against the gifted trial attorney seated just across the aisle.

.   .   .

Michael Petagnas has lunch with his team in the courtroom cafeteria. He has been approached by a couple of news reporters looking for a statement. However, Steven Didia Sr. plays the role of public relations specialist, and lets them know that Mr. Petagnas will not be offering any statements at this time. The defense doesn't want to create any more of a 'media-frenzy.' The body found in the woods over the weekend has taken much of the would-be press away from courtroom number nine, and Petagnas prefers it that way. He wants no distractions as he has a man's life in his hands.

.   .   .

Algernon Flowers tries two bites of the bologna sandwich from the brown-bag lunch and then decides to just eat the orange. He is too nervous to even complain about how hungry he is. He was sick to his stomach when the prosecutor gave his opening statement and called him a murderer while pointing directly at him. Algernon occasionally looks at the jury during testimony to see if he can gauge how they are processing each witness, but like in most cases, it's tough to try to read exactly what the jurors are thinking. However, when Michael Petagnas cross-examines the witnesses, Algernon feels as though it paints a more accurate picture of the actual events. The hope is that the jury is paying attention.

.   .   .

After lunch, all the parties reassemble in courtroom number nine. The packed gallery waits for the defendant, followed by the judge, to enter. As has become customary, all eyes gravitate toward the door, which leads to and from the holding cell, as Algernon Flowers enters the room. Once he is seated next to his attorney, the judge soon follows. When the judge recognizes that all are present, he instructs the courtroom deputy to bring in the jury. After his usual spiel of jury instructions, Judge Jackson allows the prosecution to call its next witness. The prosecution calls Detective Rodney Hunter.

As the tall, large-framed homicide detective enters and approaches the witness stand, he makes brief eye contact with Algernon Flowers, but neither of the men holds contact. This is their first meeting since the initial interaction over twenty months ago. It was Hunter that interviewed both Brenda Howell and Algernon Flowers the day that Deja Howell was pronounced dead.

After being sworn in, Detective Hunter is asked to give his name for the record, and then to share his experience, training and background in law enforcement to the jury. Detective Rodney Hunter is a professional trial witness. His eye contact, body language, and overall communication to the jury are what trial lawyers teach, and hope to have with every witness they call. Like the other three who testified before him, Detective Hunter's testimony is pretty much word for word as his original deposition. He speaks of his interview with both adults thought to be present when the victim was discovered, and how he and his team went about their investigation leading up to the arrest of Algernon Flowers over a month later. One thing that Detective Hunter offers that doesn't sit right with Petagnas is the fact that Algernon's demeanor was suspicious to him. This is the first time that Detective Hunter has used the term 'suspicious,' so Petagnas makes a note of it. Algernon Flowers sits to the right of his attorney and has also been taking notes since the trial testimony began at 9 o'clock this morning. After a few questions from Prosecutor Edwards, Judge Jackson turns the witness over to the defense for cross-examination.

Michael Petagnas stands, buttons his suit jacket, and for the first time during the trial, steps away from the defense table.

He carries his binder with notes and approaches the podium. He slides the podium back so that he is side by side with the prosecution table, and in direct line of sight to the witness stand. He is directly positioned between the witness and the jury, and aligned with the prosecution table in a perfect ninety-degree angle. This is to create the feeling of a tennis match, whereby the jury looks back and forth between the witness and the attorney questioning the witness. It is Petagnas' experience that this positioning will keep the members of the jury engaged and attentive. Essentially, by aligning himself with the prosecution table, this offers the jurors the ability to see him, the witness, and also catch the reaction of the prosecutors—all in one fluid motion.

Michael Petagnas officially and directly addresses the jury for the first time. He introduces himself and reminds them that he is representing Algernon Flowers. He also thanks them for being attentive and considering all of the evidence. This has a dual purpose—number one: to remind them to pay attention, especially to this particular witness; and number two: this reminds them that the 'defendant' has a name, and deserves the consideration of their time to consider all the evidence before rushing to judgment. Petagnas is now ready to engage the well-polished homicide detective.

"Detective Hunter, you used the term 'suspicious,' which you didn't mention in your deposition. Can you tell the court when Algernon Flowers officially became a suspect in this case?" asks Petagnas.

"They were both considered suspects," Detective Hunter maintains, referring to Algernon Flowers and Brenda Howell.

"Dr. Richard Mason testified earlier that he informed Algernon about the bruises on Deja's lower abdomen. You stated here today and in your deposition that Brenda Howell told you it was Mr. Flowers who noticed the bruises, correct?" asks Petagnas.

"Yes, she did say that," replies the detective.

"Did that seem to point your investigation in the direction of Algernon Flowers more so than Mrs. Howell?" Petagnas asks while making eye contact with the jury to make sure they are focused.

"Well, yes. That did make us want to talk to him, sure," replies Detective Hunter.

"Detective Hunter, when did you decide to take photos of Brenda Howell's hands?" asks Petagnas as he flips the page in his binder.

This question seems to have the full attention of the jurors as they look at the tall detective—awaiting a response from him.

"Well, I noticed that when she saw photos of the bruises, she closed her hands and placed them under the table on her lap. That is what prompted me to ask to see her hands, and then I noticed the broken fingernail and large diamond cluster rings," replies Detective Hunter.

Prosecutor Edwards whispers discreetly to his co-council Ramon Henderson. It is obvious that neither of them like the direction this interaction is going. The quick-thinking Michael Petagnas shifts the podium slightly. This movement creates just enough of a distraction to pull the jurors' attention over toward his direction in hopes that they pick up on the expressions of the two prosecuting attorneys. Petagnas briefly pauses to allow the moment to sink in before continuing.

"The broken fingernail and diamond cluster rings on Brenda Howell's hands caused you to photograph them?" asks Petagnas for both clarity and effect.

"Yes, that is why I took photographs of her hands," replies Hunter as he is now responding while looking directly at Petagnas, and no longer making eye contact with the jury. The once-polished prosecution witness is now completely disengaged from the jury.

"Did you take photographs of Algernon Flowers' hands?" asks Petagnas as he walks behind the prosecution table.

"No, I did not," replies the detective.

Petagnas reaches behind the prosecution table looking for something. He finds it—a large, blown-up copy of the photo that Detective Hunter took of Brenda Howell's hands on the evening in question. Petagnas begins to carry the large two and one-half by four and one-half-foot photo toward the witness stand. This causes an immediate objection from Prosecutor Edwards.

"Objection! Excuse me, your Honor, but is the defense presenting evidence?" Prosecutor Edwards asks the judge.

Michael Petagnas stops in his tracks, which is directly front and center of the jury box. He is holding the large photo up, facing the jury, as he address the judge.

"Your Honor, this is THEIR evidence—a photo taken by THIS prosecution witness. I am just getting confirmation that this is, in fact, the photo we are talking about," states Petagnas, still wisely displaying the photo to the jury.

Each juror is staring at the photo, some even turning their heads slightly as they study it. Michael Petagnas doesn't actually care if the judge rules in favor of the prosecution. The photo's image of Brenda Howell's right hand with large protruding rings, and the way the broken fingernail is chipped, will not be something this jury will soon forget. The defense hopes that when the prosecution's expert witness, the county medical examiner, takes the stand and shows photos of the bruises on Deja's body, the jury will mentally match up the two. Petagnas feels that even his young children are smart enough to match up the shapes of Brenda Howell's rings to the shapes of the bruises on the victim, and he hopes that at least one of these jurors is smart enough to as well.

Judge Jackson, who also seems quite intrigued by the photo, peeks over his glasses at the witnesses, and then makes his ruling.

"Objection sustained! Mr. Petagnas, if you are prepared to begin the defense's case and start introducing defense evidence you are free to do so," states the judge.

As Petagnas respectfully turns around to return the photo to the prosecution's stack of evidence, he transfers it from his left hand to his right so that it is still facing the jury, as some of them are still looking at the photo. After returning the photo, Michael Petagnas returns to the podium to continue his cross-examination of the homicide detective.

"Detective, you mentioned that Mr. Flowers' demeanor seemed suspicious. What exactly do you mean by that?" asks Petagnas.

"I mean he just came off as arrogant," replies Detective Hunter.

"Was it arrogance, or confidence—like a person who knows that he has absolutely no involvement in what he is being accused of?" Petagnas asks while gesturing toward his client seated alone at the defense table.

"I am not sure what the difference is, but arrogant was my word of choice," states a defensive Rodney Hunter.

Petagnas already feels that he has achieved all that was necessary with this witness, however he wants to clear up one more thing in front of this now very attentive jury.

"Detective Hunter, isn't it true that Brenda Howell was grilled by you until her husband, Detective Frank Howell, showed up and ended the interrogation?" asks Petagnas in the most assertive vocal tone he has used thus far.

Detective Hunter looks at the prosecution table before answering—almost as if he is expecting an objection.

"Yes, we spoke with Mrs. Howell, and her husband came in and ended the interview," replies Detective Hunter.

"Nothing further, your Honor!" exclaims Petagnas as he grabs his binder and returns to his seat next to Algernon Flowers.

There is no redirect from the prosecution, but the defense makes a request that Detective Hunter remain available to be recalled if need be. Detective Hunter is allowed to leave for now. Judge Jackson addresses the courtroom and the jury.

"Due to the lateness in the day, and since the next sched-uled witness is expected to take up quite a bit time, we are going to adjourn and reconvene at 9 o'clock tomorrow morn-ing," announces the judge.

He then gives the jury instruction to not discuss the case to anyone, and to avoid any social media or coverage of this case, before dismissing them. After the judge strikes the gavel, he retreats to his chambers. Algernon Flowers is then taken to the back and placed in the holding cell. He will be transported back to the Local County Jail. After a grueling day of testi-mony, it will be another sleepless night for this defendant.

CHAPTER 49

It has been several days since Hazel Flowers has seen her son Algernon. Every morning she takes the drive with her family to the Local County Courthouse. However, when they enter courtroom number nine, where the Algernon Flowers murder trial is taking place, Ms. Flowers has to go and wait in the witness holding room with the other prosecution witnesses. This is difficult for her on various levels. She is not only missing her son's trial, the most impactful event of his life, but she is also sitting among men and women who are actually here to testify against her son—one person in particular, Josephine Young. Josephine is close friends with Brenda Howell, and just so happens to be married to a musician that has performed with Algernon in the past. Having ties with both Brenda Howell and Algernon Flowers, it was Josephine Young who was instrumental as a mutual contact between the forbidden lovers during the homicide investigation. Mrs. Young and her husband once housed

Algernon and Brenda Howell, allowing them a place for one of their occasional meetings. Josephine and her husband lived within a few miles of Brenda Howell's parents, which made it an ideal spot for the forbidden lovers to join.

It was the county medical examiner that was scheduled to testify next for the prosecution, but due to a death in her husband's family, Josephine Young will be accompanying him out of state, therefore will be giving her testimony early. She will be testifying next. Mrs. Young knows Ms. Hazel Flowers from seeing her at musical events where both her musician husband and Algernon have performed together. Mrs. Young waves at Hazel Flowers from across the room. Ms. Flowers waves back to be polite, but feels awkward about it. She feels like she is literally surrounded by the enemy.

Day three of his first-degree murder trial—second day of actual testimony—and Algernon Flowers sits in the holding cell just outside of courtroom number nine with eyes bloodshot red from lack of sleep. Mr. Flowers waits for the court officer to bring him into the courtroom. Both his nerves and adrenaline are keeping him from passing out from sheer exhaustion. Still wearing the same, and only, courtroom clothes he has available, Algernon holds his legal notepad, which he uses to take notes during his trial. He will not get a pen until he enters the courtroom. He has thoughts that he would love to write down, but they will have to wait.

Out in the courtroom gallery, people are still filing in when private investigator Nick McLean enters. He and his staff are technically and officially off the case, as the case is now in the trial phase, however they all are here to support Michael Petagnas and Algernon Flowers. They have all grown quite attached to the Flowers family, and McLean himself has developed both a bond with, and respect for, Algernon. To have this magnitude of stress placed on a person's mind, yet to remain strong and maintain sanity is worthy of McLean's respect. No matter what happens in this trial, neither Algernon Flowers nor Nick McLean will ever forget each other.

The entire gallery grows silent, and all eyes gravitate to the door to the right as the defendant enters the courtroom. Everyone can visibly see the weariness and emotional fatigue that Algernon Flowers is experiencing. He appears almost twice his age, and steps gingerly, like he will faint at any moment. He doesn't even have the strength to look up and see the supportive faces of his family seated in the gallery. He sits next to his attorney and offers him a rather frail handshake. Noticing his client's depleting health and overall state of physical weakness, Michael Petagnas gets candy from Sandy Ward, who is seated directly behind the defense table. He offers the spearmint candy to Algernon in hopes that the sugar will assist in giving him a temporary boost of energy.

"All rise!" is the call from the courtroom deputy as the Honorable Judge Warren Jackson enters the room and takes his seat on the bench. Michael Petagnas almost has to hold his client up, as the young man's weak knees can barely hold his body steady. Once Judge Jackson takes his seat, everyone is seated and then the judge summons the jury. This is another time in which Algernon Flowers must endure the challenge of standing—for the ceremonial entrance of the men and women that will soon decide his fate. Once the jury is seated in the jury box, the judge gives his usual instruction, and then has the prosecution call its next witness.

Mrs. Josephine Young enters the overcrowded and tension-filled courtroom, and approaches the witness stand. She is sworn in and then asked to spell her name for the record, and then give her background to the jury. She, like Brenda Howell, is a school teacher. Mrs. Young is very well spoken, and very well educated. Her testimony is that during the period between the death of Deja Howell and the arrest of Algernon Flowers, she assisted Algernon and Brenda Howell in arranging secret romantic meetings. The one thing in particular of her testimony that Prosecutor Edwards wants to hammer home is Josephine's opinion of one specific event. During the time before Algernon's arrest, he purchased roses for Brenda Howell—not a dozen—but one for each day since the day they met, which added up to almost seventy by that time. Mrs. Young says in her testimony that she felt that gesture made Algernon seem suspicious. The roses were sent through a mutual contact, Algernon's friend, and Brenda's god-brother: Larry Thomas. After her direct testimony, Judge Jackson offers Josephine Young to the defense for cross-examination. Unsure as to why the prosecution even called this particular witness in this case, Michael Petagnas actually thinks about not even asking her a single question on cross examination. He decides he should at least address the one point that Prosecutor Edwards was trying so hard to make seem relevant, which is more than likely a filler to confuse the jury into thinking that the more witnesses the prosecution puts on the stand, the more true the charges against the defendant must be.

Michael Petagnas stands to his feet, but doesn't bother to step away from the defense table.

"Mrs. Young, does your husband ever buy you roses?" asks Petagnas, almost appearing irritated.

"Well, yeah. On special occasions," replies Josephine Young.

"Does that make him suspicious, or romantic?" asks Petagnas.

"Romantic ... but my husband wasn't suspected of murder when he sent me roses," snaps Mrs. Young with a touch of attitude and sass.

This response makes Michael Petagnas feel the need to continue further with this witness.

"Wasn't Brenda Howell also suspected in the same murder? Because according to earlier testimony from Detective Hunter, both Brenda Howell and Mr. Flowers were considered suspects," fires back Petagnas.

"I guess so," replies Mrs. Young.

"You thought it strange or 'suspicious' that Algernon purchased roses for the woman he was dating, and whom at the time he was then living apart from ... did you also find it strange or 'suspicious' that if he is suspected in the murder of her daughter, that Brenda Howell was still making arrangements to see him romantically? It was you who assisted in one of these meetings was it not?" asks a semi-fired up Michael Petagnas.

"Well, I guess I didn't look at it that way," responds Mrs. Young.

Michael Petagnas takes his seat as he declares, "Nothing further, your Honor!"

Prosecutor Edwards feels the need for a redirect, to regain the focus on Mrs. Young's original opinion, and not lose her value in the eyes of the jury.

"Redirect, your Honor!" states Edwards as he stands to his feet. "Mrs. Young, in your opinion, did the defendant buying all of those roses seem excessive?" asks Edwards.

"Yes, it did. I thought it was quite strange," replies Mrs. Young.

Feeling as though he has made the point that he needed to make, Prosecutor Edwards takes his seat, "That is all, your Honor," he concludes.

Prosecutor Edwards wants to state in his closing arguments that Algernon did this 'out-of-the-ordinary' gesture out of guilt, and make it seem significant. Edwards has a hidden agenda. His hope is that this action on the part of Mr. Flowers will counter against what he believes the jury, and everyone else, thinks about Brenda Howell's actions following the death of her daughter. He needs this testimony to do so.

Michael Petagnas, still not seeing anything of significance that this witness has to offer, decides to end this once and for all.

"Re-cross, your Honor!" declares Petagnas, who is already standing and ready.

His demeanor is that of a cowboy in an old Western movie as he stands, guns holstered, loaded and ready to draw.

"Mrs. Young, you cannot testify that Algernon buying roses for his girlfriend makes him guilty of murder, can you?" asks Petagnas.

"No, I cannot," replies Mrs. Young.

Petagnas is already in his seat before she completes her answer to the question.

"Nothing further, your Honor," he concludes.

Prosecutor Edwards decides that it is best to excuse the witness, because at this point she cannot offer anything further, and he doesn't want the skillful Michael Petagnas to defuse the minimal value of her testimony any further.

With nothing further from either side, or the intent to re-call this witness, Josephine Young is excused and released. The judge has the prosecution call its next witness.

"The prosecution calls Doctor Abigail Lee," announces Prosecutor Edwards.

Dr. Lee, the Local County medical examiner, enters the courtroom and takes the witness stand. Next to Brenda How-ell, this is the prosecution's most valuable witness. Dr. Lee is sworn in and then asked to spell her name for the record and then to share her background, experience and training with the jury. Once she has completed her recital of credentials, Prosecutor Edwards asks the judge that she be listed as, and received as, a credible 'expert witness' in the field of pathology. The judges obliges and then addresses the courtroom. He warns those in the gallery that this witness will be showing images of the autopsy performed on the young victim, and if they do not wish to view them, they can be excused at this time. A handful of observers in the gallery take this opportunity to exit.

CHAPTER 50

Dr. Abigail Lee has served in the Local County Medical Examiner's Office for many years—even back when Michael Petagnas was the district attorney. In fact, she has testified as a medical expert on some trials prosecuted by Michael Petagnas in the past. Today, Dr. Lee is under direct examination by Prosecutor David Edwards, testifying as the prosecution's medical expert. Dr. Lee explains to the jury that in her opinion, the cause of death in this case is 'blunt force trauma.'

"Non-penetrating trauma or blunt force trauma refers to physical trauma to a body part, either by impact, injury or physical attack," explains Dr. Lee as she directly addresses the jury.

She goes on to explain how she was able to arrive at this conclusion, by examining the tissue and cells during the autopsy.

The lights in courtroom number nine are dimmed, as this present prosecution witness will begin showing photos of the autopsy conducted on the victim. Michael Petagnas walks over to the end of the jury box, near the prosecution table, in order to get a good look at the large mobile screen on which the images will be projected. He carries a notepad to take notes as well.

As Dr. Lee shows images of the actual autopsy she conducted on Deja Howell, she explains what is being displayed in each frame. She defines which organ or tissue sample is on the screen, and gives her description for its function and what it was able to tell her about how this victim died. As the jurors look on, some find it very difficult to view, even looking away at times. The most difficult image of all is the full-body photograph of the little girl's lifeless body sprawled out on the shiny metal table. To the jury it brings everything into perspective as to why they are all here—the murder of this innocent child. This surely creates feelings of anger, sadness, and above all—a need and desire for justice. At the conclusion of Dr. Abigail Lee's photo presentation, the lights are returned to full illumination, and Petagnas returns back to his seat at the defense table.

As the men and women of the jury seem to be allowing their eyes to readjust to the bright florescent lighting in the courtroom, Michael Petagnas can't help but notice some, if not most, of them looking over at Algernon Flowers. Petagnas can only imagine that they are looking at the giant 'bull's-eye' on his client as the only person they can hold responsible for causing the damage in the very disturbing photos that they just had to witness. Clearly there is a need for justice, and unfortunately for the defense, there is only one defendant in this case. As Prosecutor Edwards wraps up with Dr. Lee, he inquires as to her opinion regarding the time of death.

"In relation to the extent of the injuries, I would say that death would have occurred within a couple of hours," states Dr. Lee while looking at the jury.

The prosecution is done with its direct examination of its medical expert. Judge Jackson decides that this would be a good time to take a break for a fifteen-minute recess. He dismisses the jury and then he heads back to his chambers. Algernon Flowers is then taken back to the holding cell where he will wait to be brought back into the courtroom.

Michael Petagnas in not very fond of the timing of this recess to be directly after such a presentation by the prosecution's medical expert that has, without a doubt, angered the jury. Although this break is short, it will allow the images of the deceased little girl to sit in their minds as they subconsciously direct their rage at the defendant. Petagnas doesn't view Dr. Lee's testimony as very damning to his case, however he is concerned that the jurors have probably decided to convict someone for this murder, and there is only one option for them.

. . .

Algernon Flowers is brought back into courtroom number nine after the short break in testimony. The judge takes his seat on the bench and the witness, Dr. Abigail Lee, returns to the witness stand. The judge reminds her that she is still under oath and then gives the order to bring the jury back in. Once the jury is seated, the judge gives his usual instruction and then turns the floor over to Michael Petagnas for the defense cross-examination.

Clearly familiar with one another, Petagnas and Dr. Lee exchange polite and professional greetings. The last thing this experienced trial attorney wants to do is have this witness bring back any photos that will only further upset and anger the jury. With his client as the only defendant in this case, that will only backfire. Dr. Lee has already said it all as to '*HOW*' this little girl died. She suffered a beating that caused severe internal injuries. Instead, he focuses on what the medical examiner did NOT say, and that is '*WHEN*' this little girl died. Standing at the podium facing the witness, Petagnas begins his cross-examination of the prosecution's medical expert.

"Dr. Lee, you spoke extensively and at great length as to the cause of death, being blunt force trauma in the abdominal area. Is it your opinion that the time of death is a couple of hours after sustaining these injuries?" asks Petagnas.

"Yes, that is correct. Within a couple of hours of sustaining these injuries," replies Dr. Lee while making eye contact with the jury.

"That would be what time, in your opinion?" asks Petagnas.

"About two hours, maybe three," replies Dr. Lee.

"No, not how long after the injuries ... Let's say your testimony is that this victim died two to three hours after sustaining these injuries ... Can you tell the jury what time the injuries were inflicted?" asks Petagnas.

"I can only testify as to what my medical opinion is, and that is that death occurred within two to three hours after these injuries were sustained," replies Dr. Lee.

"So can you tell this jury exactly or approximately when that was as far as what time—8 o'clock—9 o'clock?" asks Petagnas.

"That I cannot say with absolute medical certainty," replies Dr. Lee.

"So if these injuries were sustained at 10 o'clock P.M., your opinion, according to your formula, would tell us that death occurred then around midnight or 1 o'clock in the morning?" asks Petagnas for clarity.

"According to the severity of the injuries, yes ... two to three hours after sustaining these injuries," replies Dr. Lee.

Petagnas flips through his binder as he offers another theory.

"Dr. Lee, could it be possible that if some of these injuries were sustained earlier in the evening, and then perhaps later that night further injuries were inflicted ... would that change your theory as to how long it would've taken death to occur?" he asks.

"Are you asking if the victim were to have received injuries in an initial beating, and then a second?" asks Dr. Lee for clarification.

"Yes, can you tell the difference between injuries from an initial beating, and further damage inflicted by a secondary beating, if they were a couple of hours apart?" asks Petagnas.

"I'm not sure I fully understand your question," states Dr. Lee.

"OK, if the victim suffered a beating at, let's say, 8 o'clock in the evening, and is left, bleeding internally … the injuries from that beating may not have caused death within two to three hours. But if, let's say, there was another beating that took place around midnight, would the injuries from the combination of the two beatings then change the time of death in any way?" asks Petagnas.

"Yes, that would definitely alter the time it would take for death to occur," replies Dr. Lee.

Michael Petagnas knows the prosecution is going to object to this next question, but it is one that he doesn't actually need an answer to. He only needs the jury to hear it for consideration later when Brenda Howell gets on the witness stand. With his binder closed and already in his hand as he expects an objection, Michael Petagnas offers a final question to Dr. Lee.

"So if this child was beaten for whatever reason in the evening, and threw up from that beating—let's say to her abdomen—then as punishment for throwing up and making a mess, receives a second beating … "

Before Petagnas can complete his question David Edwards is on his feet.

"Objection!" yells Prosecutor Edwards.

Because this is the defense cross examination of a prosecution witness, Petagnas can only ask questions related to what the witness has testified to, or what has already been testified to during trial testimony to this jury. The fact that Deja Howell threw up blood and was allegedly ill has not been testified to at this point. This will not come up until Brenda Howell takes the stand. In most murder trials, the prosecution likes to close with the medical examiner as its final witness. It is a strong finish to get the jury angry by autopsy photos right before heading into deliberation. However in this case, the prosecution elected to put its medical examiner on early in order to get the 'anger factor' inserted before Brenda Howell takes the stand and the defense offers another theory. The throwing up of blood and a beating to the abdomen seem too coincidental for most logical people. The prosecution needed to get the medical examiner's testimony in first.

Michael Petagnas is already halfway to his seat at the defense table when the judge gives his ruling.

"Objection sustained!" exclaims Judge Jackson.

"Nothing further, your Honor," states Petagnas as he takes his seat.

Prosecutor Edwards conducts a brief redirect to re-establish the prosecution's theory, and try to lock down a more accurate timeframe from Dr. Lee. However, like the defense medical expert Dr. Harvey Walters, Dr. Lee can only place most of the injuries within at least eighteen hours prior to the pronouncement of death. That wide window takes away from the prosecution's original opening statement that Algernon Flowers caused these injuries in the hour and a half that Brenda Howell left the apartment to go to work. In addition, Dr. Lee via Michael Petagnas has now opened the door that suggests that there may have been injuries or a beating prior to the 'fatal injuries' or a secondary beating. Prosecutor Edwards is not sure whether this confuses the jury, and if so, is it favorable to his case or the defense? Uncertain as to where exactly his expert's testimony rests with the jury, David Edwards takes his seat.

During the defense's re-cross examination, Michael Petagnas has Dr. Lee reiterate the highlighted point that he feels helps his client.

"Dr. Lee, so once again you are saying that you cannot place the time of fatal injury nor the time of death within the hour and a half to two-hour window that Algernon Flowers was left alone with the victim, correct?" asks Petagnas.

"That is correct. I cannot place the fatal injuries or time of death within any window or timeframe other than the 18 hours I mentioned earlier," replies Dr. Lee.

After the re-cross by the defense, the prosecution and defense are done with this witness, and Dr. Abigail Lee is dismissed.

Judge Warren Jackson dismisses the jury for lunch and then retreats back to his chambers. Algernon Flowers is taken back to the holding cell and given a bag lunch. At the request of Michael Petagnas, Mr. Flowers is given a vegetarian meal with extra fruit. Petagnas hopes the higher nutritional value will give his client some much-needed energy. Petagnas then joins his team for lunch in the courthouse cafeteria.

CHAPTER 51

The afternoon lunch break begins to wind down in the Algernon Flowers first-degree murder trial. Private investigator Nicholas McLean sits with his team in the gallery of courtroom number nine. As spectators and key players alike continue to file in, McLean can't help but notice the absence of Rocky Beach Police Chief Donald Nelson. Neither Chief Nelson nor his son, Detective Peter Nelson, has been present since Monday morning. McLean observes Detective Frank Howell entering the courtroom, along with two other plain-clothes detectives, as they make their way down the center aisle toward the front, behind the prosecution table. The defense private investigator is unable to put his finger on exactly why he has such a knot in his stomach, but McLean knows he does not trust this trio that has been sitting in the same seats throughout the entire trial. Frank Howell, in particular, has been eyeballing Michael Petagnas, and McLean suspects Petagnas should watch his back. If this jury were to find Algernon Flowers not guilty, and Petagnas presents enough evidence for the media to report that perhaps Brenda Howell had something to do with her own daughter's death, the public outrage would create quite the pressure for the arrest of Detective Howell's wife, and mother of their now one-year-old son. This scenario would also not fare very well for newly re-elected District Attorney David Edwards, who granted immunity from prosecution to Mrs. Howell. A first-degree murder conviction of Algernon Flowers is the only way that this can end well for the Howells, the Rocky Beach Police Department, and the Local County District Attorney's Office. When Nick McLean looks at Detective Frank Howell, he doesn't seem to be the type of person willing to allow anything to come between his happy family and right now, the one thing standing in the way of a conviction against Algernon Flowers is confidently walking back into the courtroom.

As Michael Petagnas walks down the center aisle toward the defense table, he can feel the burning glare of Detective Frank Howell and his companions. Petagnas doesn't make eye contact, even as the three pairs of eyes follow his every step with angry and intimidating looks. Private investigator McLean has seen enough and decides to have his partner, Brent Patterson, the former Navy SEAL, stick by Michael Petagnas when he exits the courtroom, and to also escort him daily between his home and the courthouse.

Algernon Flowers is brought back into the courtroom and takes his seat next to his defense attorney. Michael Petagnas can see that by eating a healthier lunch, his client has regained some strength. This is important, because Algernon Flowers may have to testify in his own defense, and he needs to be sharp on the witness stand during cross examination against the crafty David Edwards.

Shortly after 1 o'clock P.M., Judge Warren Jackson re-enters the courtroom and takes his seat on the bench. After inquiring as to all parties being present and prepared to go forward, the judge calls the jury back in. Once the jury is seated and given their usual instruction by Judge Jackson, the prosecution calls its next witness: Mrs. Harriet Blake.

Mrs. Blake, the school secretary at the Richard M. Weinstein Elementary School, makes her way down the center aisle and to the witness stand. She is sworn in and then asked to state her name for the record and to briefly share her background for the jury. This witness is important for the prosecution in order to establish that Brenda Howell was, in fact, at work on the morning in question, which would mean that Algernon Flowers was alone with the victim.

After explaining to the jury her function at the school, and her basic normal everyday activities, Harriet Blake tells what she remembers from the morning in question. She remembers that Brenda Howell stopped in the office on that morning and asked her for the time. She does remember it was out of the ordinary for Mrs. Howell to stop by the office that early, or at all in the mornings, but Mrs. Blake did not think anything of it at the time.

After the prosecution is done with its direct questioning of the witness, the defense has the opportunity to cross-examine. Michael Petagnas has only two questions for this witness. He stands, but doesn't leave the defense table. It is this body language that offers to the jury an impression of insignificance, and low esteem of this particular witness for the prosecution. However, Petagnas finds value for the defense.

"Mrs. Blake, are you aware that Mrs. Brenda Howell asked several other coworkers for the time, around the same time that morning?" asks Petagnas.

"No, I was not aware of that," replies Mrs. Blake politely.

"And to your knowledge, is there a large clock located in the office where Mrs. Howell met you and asked for the time?" Petagnas follows up.

"Yes, there is," replies Mrs. Blake.

Petagnas takes his seat as he announces to the judge, "Nothing further, your Honor."

Mrs. Blake is excused. For the rest of the afternoon, prosecutors Edwards and Henderson take turns questioning employees from the Richard M. Weinstein Elementary School where Brenda Howell worked at the time of her daughter's death. These witnesses are called in to place Brenda Howell out of her apartment for over an hour and a half on the morning in question. With every witness that is called, Defense Attorney Michael Petagnas has only two questions during a brief, yet effective cross-examination:

Question number one: "Are you aware that Brenda Howell asked several other school employees for the time within the small hour and a half timeframe?" Question number two: "Did she say why she was leaving to go back home so soon?"

Every witness responds in the same fashion: "No" to both questions from Michael Petagnas.

The prosecution's strategy appears to be backfiring, as the jury begins to see Brenda Howell's actions as an attempt to create an alibi, rather than random people placing her at work at a certain time. At the end of the final witness from the school, the prosecution informs the judge that its next witness is Mrs. Brenda Howell and she is expected to take up a significant amount of time. Both the prosecution and defense agree to recess until tomorrow morning. The judge agrees, and dismisses the jury and then announces that court will adjourn and reconvene tomorrow at 9 A.M. sharp. With the strike of his gavel, the judge retreats back to his chambers, and Algernon Flowers is taken back to the holding cell to await his transfer back to the Local County Jail.

Michael Petagnas is met by defense investigator Brent Patterson, who will be his acting bodyguard for the remainder of the trial. All parties exit courtroom number nine with overwhelming anticipation of tomorrow's proceedings. The prosecution will call Brenda Howell to the stand—the very witness they expect to put the nails in the coffin of Algernon Flowers. All of the local news reporters that have been present during the trial write about this highly anticipated prosecution star witness for tomorrow morning's headlines. Both David Edwards and Michael Petagnas will prepare for the most important testimony expected in this entire trial.

.   .   .

Tonight, like every other night since the trial began, private investigator Nicholas McLean and his team of investigators visit the home of Hazel Flowers. They have dessert and peppermint tea with Ms. Flowers and her family. The support is great for the mother of Algernon Flowers. She is forced to sit in the room with the other prosecution witnesses, where she doesn't feel any love or support. Missing her son's trial is very hard on the supportive mother who has always attended her son's concerts and music recitals. Now during his most difficult hour, when he needs her support the most, she cannot sit behind him in the courtroom. As McLean does every evening, he is filling Ms. Flowers in on all the courtroom happenings. She knows that he is only telling her what she wants to hear to give her confidence and hope in the case, but she loves the time of positive energy after spending the entire day surrounded by prosecution witnesses. The one witness she wishes she could meet is first up on the stand tomorrow—Mrs. Brenda Howell. Hazel Flowers has yet to meet the woman at the center of this entire ordeal, and didn't even know that her son Algernon was dating her. Ms. Flowers knows that if the relationship was getting serious, her son would have, like he does with all the girls he dates, brought her home to dinner for the 'Mom test.'

Brenda Howell has been receiving celebrity treatment, and therefore not having to endure sitting in the stuffy room with the other prosecution witnesses. She has been sitting in a private room with her infant son, and a prosecution-provided nanny, while her lawyer sits in the courtroom. Tomorrow Brenda Howell will reach the climax of her spotlight.

CHAPTER 52

Algernon Flowers sits in the back of the windowless van being transported to the Local County Courthouse—his usual predawn ride in the same clothes for the fourth day straight. However, today he will be seeing Brenda Howell for the first time since his arrest five hundred and eighty-eight days ago. He has so many questions for her, but only Prosecutor Edwards and Michael Petagnas will be permitted to ask the questions.

.   .   .

Michael Petagnas drives to the county courthouse as the former Navy SEAL turned private investigator, Brent Patterson, follows in a car behind. Today is the apex of this trial. The medical examiner testified and showed very disturbing autopsy photos to the jury yesterday. Today, the only other person that could have caused those fatal injuries will be testifying against Algernon Flowers. The prosecution will undoubtedly paint Brenda

Howell as the grieving mother of the child that was taken away from her at the hands of the defendant. Brenda Howell: the former elementary school teacher—wife of a police detective—an educated and attractive woman who has now given birth to another child—initial murder suspect turned star prosecution witness. This is going to be an uphill battle and the 'make it or break it' in this trial for the defense. The life of Algernon Flowers depends on what happens in courtroom number nine today.

Prosecutor David Edwards enters the courtroom realizing that everything comes down to the testimony of today's witness. Many following the trial feel that Michael Petagnas has successfully poked holes in every prosecution witness' testimony to this point. Some may even argue that he has already established enough reasonable doubt. However, the winner of today's head-to-head battle between David Edwards and his former boss will walk away with his perfect trial-winning record intact. During yesterday's gut-wrenching testimony of the prosecution's expert witness, Dr. Lee, Prosecutor David Edwards could feel the anger and rage of the jurors. He senses they are ready to convict someone for the brutal death of the young victim in this case. To his advantage, there is only one defendant in this trial. His mission for today is simple: make Brenda Howell connect with this jury as a mother ... for jurors view mothers as protectors, not murderers. During the jury selection process, the prosecution deliberately and purposefully sought out mothers and parents, since they would be less likely to picture any mother hurting her own children. Today, David Edwards is going to ask Brenda Howell to look those parents and fellow mothers in the eye, and tell them that she did not murder her young daughter.

·   ·   ·

Brenda Howell requested that her lawyer, Kelly Sloan, stand near the witness stand during her testimony, to coach her on which questions she should exercise her Fifth Amendment right by not answering. However, prosecutors think having her lawyer visibly present during trial testimony will raise suspicion with the jurors as to why she lawyered up if she isn't being charged and has nothing to hide. Instead of standing by her side, Brenda Howell's lawyer comes up with a simple formula as to which questions not to answer: *avoid ALL questions coming from Michael Petagnas.*

. . .

The anticipation of today's courtroom action can be felt throughout the entire gallery. The atmosphere is similar to a major sporting championship matchup as local news reporters and other observers enter early to claim their coveted seats. Defense Attorney Michael Petagnas enters the arena of courtroom number nine, and for the first time in this trial, feels like he has to overcome the most tremendous odds, since he is limited to only cross examining Brenda Howell on questions asked by prosecutors during their direct examination. Petagnas would love to have some of the witnesses that his private investigator found, but they would have to be called during the defense's case ... if they even cooperate at all. Petagnas doesn't expect the experienced Prosecutor Edwards to walk his star witness into a trap. Petagnas will have to be patient, and wait for any opportunity to expose the injustice in this case.

. . .

Algernon Flowers is led into the courtroom and sits at the defense table. Shortly thereafter, Judge Warren Jackson enters and takes his place on the bench. Before bringing in the jury, there is a matter the judge wants to deal with. It has been brought to his attention that two of the jurors were talking about the case in the lobby. Apparently someone overheard them, and that someone came forward. The judge sends for the man who overheard these two jurors discussing the case. The no-nonsense judge gives the jury specific instruction at the start of every session, and at the end of every day. One major point of the judge's instruction to the jury is to never discuss the case, even among themselves. The time for discussion is during the deliberation phase. The judge wants to get to the bottom of this to avoid any tainting within the jury, any cause for a mistrial, or reason for a later appeal.

The main door at the rear of the courtroom creaks open and a slim, well-dressed young gentleman makes his way down the center aisle. His countenance is that of duress, as he tries to ignore the many pairs of eyes that are showering upon him; some with looks of hopeful anticipation, while others with looks of betrayal and disappointment. His name is Larry Thomas. He is the god-brother of Brenda Howell, and a friend of Algernon Flowers. It was Larry Thomas who introduced Mr. Flowers and Mrs. Howell after Brenda asked to meet the handsome man on the cover of the CD. Although he is torn between his loyalty to the two people he knows quite well, he wants to do the right thing. He alerted the courtroom deputy as soon as he witnessed the two jurors communicating in the lobby. The judge asks Mr. Thomas to get on the witness stand and be sworn in by the deputy. Now under oath, Larry Thomas is asked by Judge Jackson to tell exactly what he heard.

"Two female jurors were talking in the lobby, and one said to the other: 'It's a shame what he did to that little girl,' as she shook her head in disgust," testifies Mr. Thomas while never losing eye contact with the very stern judge.

When asked by the judge to identify the juror who made the statement, Mr. Thomas walks over to the jury box and points to the empty chair assigned to juror number six. In an attempt to discredit Mr. Thomas, Prosecutor Edwards repeats something similar, and asks him if that's what he heard. However, Mr. Thomas restates, verbatim, what he said originally. In a second attempt to discredit and confuse Mr. Thomas, Prosecutor Edwards points to another seat nearby and asks him if he is sure that the talkative juror was sitting there. Mr. Thomas corrects Prosecutor Edwards, and again points to the chair that is assigned to, and has been occupied by juror number six. Judge Jackson has heard enough, and finds Larry Thomas to be credible. Mr. Thomas is excused, and avoids any eye contact with the men seated at the prosecution or defense tables as he lowers into a seat in the rear of the gallery.

Prosecutor Edwards does not want a juror who is already sold on the guilt of the defendant to be excused, but now it is out of his control. In addition to the twelve main jurors, there are two alternates in the event the judge needs to excuse the two jurors who were engaging in discussion about the case— with a formulated opinion—before considering all the trial evidence and testimony.

Judge Jackson calls in juror number six only. The African-American woman seems puzzled as to why she alone has been called into the courtroom. Judge Jackson asks her to sit in her usual seat, and she takes the place pointed out by Mr. Larry Thomas. Next, the irritated judge asks her about the discussion she may have had with another juror, but the woman adamantly denies it. The judge doesn't want to risk leaving grounds for appeal, but he is not sure if that statement is enough to persuade the other juror in any way. Judge Jackson decides to warn juror number six to not discuss the case with any of the other jurors, and then excuses her to return back to the jury room.

Michael Petagnas stands to state on record that he has an objection to the judge allowing that juror to remain on the jury. He feels she has already made her decision based on some of the trial testimony, and is not going to be fair and impartial. The judge recognizes Petagnas' objection, but announces that he is allowing juror number six to remain on the jury for the duration of the trial. Michael Petagnas objects again, this time the judge scoffs him at.

"Your objection is noted, Mr. Petagnas, and this court has ruled! Now please be seated so that we may continue!" he barks.

Michael Petagnas takes his seat, deflated, feeling like he is fighting a war he cannot win. He has already managed to irritate the judge, which is no way to begin the morning. He thinks his client is getting a raw deal with a tainted jury, and now the prosecution's star witness is about to take the stand to cause further damage.

Judge Jackson gives the order to bring in the entire jury, and offers his usual instruction—only this time with a little more emphasis concerning discussions amongst themselves, which is still not of much consolation to the frustrated defense attorney.

After the morning's minor delay, the prosecution is ready to call its next witness. Prosecutor David Edwards stands confidently, as if being mounted upon his one hundred percent conviction rate. Almost with his chest sticking out a bit, he makes his declaration:

"The prosecution calls Mrs. Brenda Howell!"

CHAPTER 53

When Mrs. Brenda Howell makes her way down the center aisle of the courtroom, she keeps her eyes to the floor, appearing meek and humble. She passes her husband, Detective Frank Howell, to her left as she walks to the front of the courtroom. She splits the prosecution and defense tables without even the slightest peek over toward the man that is accused in the murder of her daughter. When she reaches the witness stand, she remains standing to be sworn in. In this moment, for a split second, her eyes drift in the direction of the defendant—her former lover, Algernon Flowers. These two haven't seen each other since Algernon's arrest nineteen months ago. After being sworn in, Brenda Howell speaks softly, with the body language of a frail flower, while stating her name for the record. She is then asked by Prosecutor Edwards to tell the jury her relation to Deja Howell.

"She was my daughter," states a semi-tearful Brenda Howell in a soft voice.

Michael Petagnas tries not to smirk at this award-worthy performance. Algernon Flowers wasn't sure what emotion he would experience when he finally saw and heard from the woman whom he now realizes set him up. He is surprised at what he actually feels. The woman he once viewed as pretty and sweet all those months ago now appears very different. When he looks at her now, all he can see is her ugly, wicked and evil soul. It is as if a spell or a curse has been lifted from him, and his eyes can finally see the true nature of her being. This actually makes him feel even more foolish for falling into her web of deceit.

Prosecutor Edwards asks Brenda Howell to explain to the jury how she and her husband met, and how little Deja coming into their lives made them complete. Mrs. Howell tells of how becoming a mother changed her life in so many positive ways. She gives the history of her troubled marriage at times, but states she and her husband never stopped loving each other.

While sharing her background, Brenda Howell pauses periodically to wipe tears from the corners of her eyes. Michael Petagnas has his eyes set, not on Brenda Howell, but on juror number two. Juror number two is an older woman who happens to have a successful practice as a psychotherapist in Rocky Beach for over thirty years. She is the second closest juror in proximity to Brenda Howell on the witness stand, and she is eyeballing her intensely, focusing on her eyes. As a trained professional, she is noticing the 'grieving' mother is producing no actual tears. The other important fact that juror number two notices is that Mrs. Howell doesn't look in the direction of her former lover, Algernon Flowers, nor her husband, Detective Frank Howell. In the professional opinion of juror number two, Brenda Howell should be looking at both men with two completely different emotions: Algernon Flowers with anger and heartbreak, and Frank Howell apologetically ... with feelings of guilt and embarrassment for bringing the man who is charged with their daughter's death into their lives. Juror number two is reading body language and other nonverbal signs, not just listening to emotionally moving words. On the other end of the jury box, another female juror is almost in tears, and Michael Petagnas can see that she is clearly eating up this performance.

After several general family and personal background questions, Prosecutor David Edwards asks Brenda Howell to go into the details of the morning she went to work and left her daughter alone with the defendant. The night prior is purposefully and intentionally omitted by David Edwards, as to avoid allowing Michael Petagnas the opportunity to cross-examine her about leaving the child unattended, and change how the jury perceives her. Michael Petagnas picks up on this right away and makes a note of it.

Brenda Howell states she went to work and then realized that she didn't have a class, so she went back home. Upon arriving back home, Brenda states she called the defendant and asked him to bring Deja downstairs so she can take her to the daycare near the school. After getting off the phone with the defendant, she waited in her vehicle, which was parked downstairs. Soon after, the defendant was waving her in from the second floor landing outside her apartment door.

"He was telling me that he thinks something is wrong with Deja," recalls a soft spoken Brenda Howell.

She goes on to explain that she turned the engine off, and ran upstairs into the apartment. She went into Deja's room and saw that she was pale, her lips blue, and she was cool to the touch. Brenda claims she then ran with the lifeless child in her arms, and laid her on the floor in the living room/kitchen area. She recalls the defendant being on the phone with 9-1-1. The defendant then performed CPR on Deja as instructed by the 9-1-1 operator. Soon the ambulance arrived, and emergency medical technicians came in and took over as they attempted to revive the unresponsive toddler. They then took her to the hospital.

Michael Petagnas notices Brenda Howell is not mentioning anything about telling the EMTs that Deja was sick over the weekend, or that she threw up in her bed the night before. The quick-thinking defense attorney turns around to the row directly behind him and passes a note to his paralegal, Sandy Ward. After reading the note, Sandy Ward pulls the forensics lab report from the defense evidence files. She passes it forward to Mr. Petagnas, who continues to take notes while listening to Brenda Howell's account of the events as they unfolded.

.   .   .

Through the morning recess, and up until the lunch hour, Brenda Howell is on the witness stand testifying in the first-degree murder trial of her former boyfriend, Algernon Flowers, who is charged in the beating death of her three-year-old daughter. The prosecution has one final question for its star witness.

"Mrs. Howell, did you kill your daughter?" asks Prosecutor Edwards bluntly.

Looking directly at the jury, Brenda Howell replies softly, "No, I did not."

Prosecutor Edwards is satisfied with the testimony of Brenda Howell. He feels she has successfully connected with the jury as a mother who loved her daughter and loves her family. The undefeated prosecutor takes his seat with confidence and gets a nod of approval from his co-council, Ramon Henderson.

Judge Warren Jackson decides to break for lunch before going into cross-examination by the defense. The jury is instructed to not discuss the case, and that testimony will resume after lunch. The jury is dismissed, and the judge retreats to his chambers. Algernon Flowers is taken back to the holding cell and Michael Petagnas and his team assemble in a huddle on the two front rows of the now-empty courtroom gallery.

Back in the holding cell, Algernon Flowers looks at the notes he was taking during the trial testimony of his former girlfriend. He made points of all of the things that he feels are important for his attorney to bring up during cross examination.

He feels that she has deliberately altered the version of events to suit her best interests and make her look like the victim—even more so than the actual victim in this case.

Upon the request of their client, Michael Petagnas and Steven Didia Sr. arrive in the courtroom holding area. They are meeting with a frustrated Algernon Flowers who is going over all the notes he has taken during Brenda Howell's testimony. Petagnas and Didia Sr. listen, but then Steven Didia Sr. interrupts the panicked defendant.

"Al, relax. Michael is going to rip her to shreds during cross-examination. That soft-spoken victim act is not going to last long. Her true colors will be revealed," proclaims a confident Steven Didia Sr.

This is a very crucial and pivotal moment in this trial, where total trust and confidence must be present between a defendant and defense attorney. Algernon Flowers knows that his life depends on what happens with Michael Petagnas and Brenda Howell next in this trial. He must place his total trust in his attorney … it is his only option at this point. Michael Petagnas assures his client that he will approach the prosecution's star witness with caution for the jurors who are now sympathetic to the mother of the young victim. He also vows to go for the jugular if and when the opportunity arises. It is a tough position for Algernon Flowers to be in, but he cannot just yell out 'LIAR' in the courtroom, as he would like to. He must be patient and allow his skillful and experienced attorney to expose all the lies to the jury.

After the lunch break, everyone is reassembled in courtroom number nine. The judge enters, and Brenda Howell is back on the witness stand. Judge Jackson calls the jury in, and things are ready to get underway. Before the judge turns the witness over to the defense for cross examination, he calls the prosecutors and Michael Petagnas over near the bench for a quick sidebar. Joining the prosecution and defense is Kelly Sloan, lawyer for Brenda Howell.

Neither the jury nor those in the gallery can hear what is being discussed. After a few brief moments of discussion, the prosecutors and Petagnas return to their respective tables, and Kelly Sloan takes her seat on the front row behind the prosecution table. The judge then addresses the jury to inform them that Mrs. Brenda Howell is exercising her Fifth Amendment right to not answer any questions from the defense. He goes on to explain to them that this is her legal right, and that they should not read anything more into this decision. One juror in particular—juror number two—immediately wrinkles her brow. She, along with another juror and some courtroom observers, finds this odd. Michael Petagnas was expecting this, and actually hoped for it. This will allow him to refer to all of Brenda Howell's words spoken at her deposition several months ago—even the parts that she so conveniently left out of her testimony here today.

Judge Warren Jackson gives the floor over to Michael Petagnas for defense cross examination of the prosecution's star witness. If Petagnas were a canine, he would be salivating as if the prosecution just left a large T-bone steak in front of him. This is the moment he has waited over a year and a half for: The moment to finally confront Mrs. Brenda Howell in front of the jury in his client's first-degree murder trial. His entire career flashes before him as he evaluates this moment and files it among his most important to date.

The life of Algernon Flowers comes down to this moment, and Michael Petagnas intends to give his client the best fighting chance possible. Sandy Ward hands Mr. Petagnas a large binder, which contains Brenda Howell's entire deposition and initial statement to police. Petagnas pats his nervous client on the back as if to say, 'Trust me, I got this,' and then carries the large binder over to the podium. He then calmly and politely addresses the prosecution's star witness with these words:

"Good afternoon, Mrs. Howell. I'm very sorry for your loss. I just have a few questions regarding your version of events."

CHAPTER 54

Michael Petagnas opens his large binder and adjusts the podium for comfort and positioning. He wants to make sure the jury can easily see him, Brenda Howell, and the prosecutors. However he is blocking the direct sightline of Brenda Howell to her husband seated directly behind him. He is not expecting a response to any of his questions, so he reads directly from Mrs. Howell's deposition.

"Mrs. Howell, do you remember meeting with the prosecution team along with some of my staff and me several months ago during your deposition?" asks Petagnas.

He doesn't need an answer from this witness, just the open door allowing him to introduce her words from the deposition into evidence and to the jury. Brenda Howell sits quietly, looking straight ahead. She doesn't answer, so Petagnas continues.

"Well during that deposition you mentioned, as you did here today, that you parked your car downstairs from your apartment and called Algernon Flowers to ask him to wake Deja up and bring her downstairs. Is that accurate?" asks Petagnas. Again Brenda Howell doesn't respond.

"OK, well I will read your statement," continues Petagnas as he reads from his binder. "'And so I parked and then called Al to ask him to wake Deja and bring her downstairs ...' Do you recall those words?" he asks, only to get no answer from the uncooperative witness.

"Well how did you know that Deja wasn't already awake?" asks Petagnas.

He is not expecting any response so he uses this opportunity to rattle off questions to which the jury would want answers:

"You mentioned that after Mr. Flowers waved you up and said something is wrong with Deja, you then turned off your engine. So you were already parked instead of waiting in the fire lane or by the sidewalk?"

"In your testimony here today you made no mention of what you told the EMTs when they asked you what was wrong with Deja. Do you recall in your deposition saying ... 'I told them that she had been sick and threw up on her pillow the night before'?"

There is still no response from Brenda Howell. This allows Petagnas to refer to her deposition response.

"'I fed her Salisbury steak and she threw up the gravy—it was brown like the gravy.' Do you recall that statement?" Still nothing from the witness, so Petagnas continues:

"Well if Deja was sick the night before, why not—since you were already parked—why not go upstairs to check on her yourself? Why call Mr. Flowers from downstairs and ask him to wake her?"

With each unanswered question, the entire jury, especially juror number two, is looking intently at Brenda Howell. They are definitely wondering what the answers are to these questions, as Michael Petagnas continues to fire away:

"Do you know if Deja threw up before you left, while you were gone, or after you returned from picking up Mr. Flowers the night before 9-1-1 was called to the residence?"

"When you left your sick three-year-old daughter alone in bed, do you even know if she was lying in the puddle of dark-colored vomit before you left the apartment?"

"In your deposition, when I mentioned that the lab found that Deja threw up blood and not just Salisbury steak gravy, you replied that sometimes children have blood in their stool and vomit, do you recall saying that?"

As Petagnas continues to fire away question after question, he hopes that Brenda Howell doesn't decide to eventually break her silence and disrupt the rhythm. He can tell the men and women of the jury are creating their own answers to these questions:

"Can you explain to the jury why you carried Deja past the front door, instead of rushing her to the hospital in your car?"

"How long, approximately, would you say it was that Deja was home alone when you drove from South Rocky to Rocky Beach to pick up Mr. Flowers ... for at least forty minutes, give or take?"

"Do you recall during your deposition when I asked you if anyone else had access to your apartment, since you made an extra set of keys, and you said that you forgot where you put them?

"Mrs. Howell, why wouldn't you take Deja with you when you left to go to work that morning, since her daycare is close to your school? Is it because she was sick?"

"You mentioned here today that you left work after only a short time because you realized that you didn't have a class. If you did have a class, when were you going to get the chance to take Deja to the daycare?"

Michael Petagnas continues to throw questions like a fighter throwing punches in the ring:

"During your deposition, when I asked you about parking in the front staff parking space and in reverse, you said that you wanted to be able to leave quickly to get Deja and take her to the daycare ... When or how were you planning to do that if you actually did have a class?"

As if they are watching a tennis match, the men and women of the jury move their heads and eyes back and forth from the witness stand where Brenda Howell sits to the podium where Michael Petagnas stands. For the next two hours, Petagnas outlines his entire case by simply asking questions that Brenda Howell refuses to answer. The tide has shifted, and Prosecutor Edwards can feel it. The jury now has more questions than sympathy for Brenda Howell. Judge Warren Jackson cannot admit it, but even he wants some of these questions answered. Brenda Howell has the right to not answer any questions, but sometimes no response IS a response.

It is Petagnas' next question that the jury and the entire gallery will like an answer to, however there's still no response from this witness.

"Mrs. Howell, why would you continue to meet Algernon Flowers for romantic and intimate meetings if you thought that he did something harmful to Deja in the hour and a half that you left the two of them alone?"

Every reporter, every spectator, every person present is now at the edge of their seat. Many sitting behind the prosecution table grow more agitated with each unanswered question.

Michael Petagnas continues. "I asked you back in your deposition if Deja ever appeared afraid of Mr. Flowers, or ever said he hurt her, or if you ever noticed any bruises while bathing her, or anything like that, and you said no, and that he has never hurt her to your knowledge ... do you recall that?"

"Do you remember telling Detective Hunter that Algernon Flowers noticed the bruises, and not that the emergency room physician pointed them out to him?"

"My partner, Steven Didia, asked you if you made a statement to the effect that, 'If you can't have Deja, no one would' after your husband threatened to gain sole custody due to your arrest for domestic violence?"

Prosecutor Edwards puts a stop to that question.

"Objection, your Honor! The criminal history of the witness is not relevant here," argues Edwards.

"Your Honor, I'm just referring to the witness' deposition, and that question was asked and answered, but I will withdraw the question," offers Petagnas.

He flips through his binder as he continues to bombard Brenda Howell with the tough questions:

"Mrs. Howell, do you recall me asking you during your deposition about your relationship with Deputy Ronald Garzero, the safety officer at the school?"

Detective Frank Howell in particular does not like this question, and even physically shifts in his seat behind Petagnas. Some jurors look in his direction when this question is posed.

"How many people did you ask for the time that morning?" Petagnas asks a stoned-face Brenda Howell.

The time is approaching 3 P.M., the usual afternoon recess. Petagnas is on a roll and decides to finish strong before the judge calls the break. He wants to maintain the momentum he has going, while he holds the jury's undivided attention. He decides to ask the question the jury members have been asking themselves ever since they saw the photo that the homicide detectives took of Brenda Howell's hands:

"Mrs. Howell, how did you break your fingernail?"

With that asked, he waits momentarily … just long enough for the moment to get awkward—as if perhaps Brenda Howell will finally respond to a defense cross examination question—long enough for the eyes of the jurors to pierce through this witness.

"Nothing further, your Honor!" Petagnas exclaims as he closes his binder and walks back to the defense table.

As expected, Judge Warren Jackson calls the afternoon recess. He excuses the jury and then informs the prosecution and defense to be prepared to resume in twenty minutes. After the judge leaves the bench, Algernon Flowers is taken back to the holding cell. Michael Petagnas sits at the defense table looking at his notes. Did he forget anything? Did he cover all the important facts? Has he established enough reasonable doubt to clear his innocent client? These questions race through his mind as he sits alone. Steven Didia Sr. takes the defendant's seat next to Michael Petagnas and puts his arm around his partner and friend.

"Well done, Michael," he says encouragingly. "Now let's bring it home."

CHAPTER 55

After the twenty-minute afternoon recess all parties are back in place. Prosecutor David Edwards has a tough decision to make. He can ask Brenda Howell some of the same questions that Michael Petagnas left open for the jury's interpretation, and allow Brenda Howell to answer, but he is not sure of some of her answers. He also doesn't want to leave some questions out and allow the jury to speculate even further. If he does a redirect examination, he also opens the door for the defense to re-cross. His other option is to get this witness off the stand before any further damage to his case can be inflicted. The prosecution chooses not to redirect.

After an entire day on the witness stand, Brenda Howell is dismissed. With that, Prosecutor Edwards announces: "The prosecution rests, your Honor."

Unsure of how the jury sits after Brenda Howell's testimony, David Edwards second-guesses his choice to close with her as opposed to the medical examiner. His hope now is to make up some ground during the defense's case. Perhaps Algernon Flowers, who is very eager to tell his side of the story, will take the stand in his own defense, and it would be Edwards' opportunity to try to make him look bad during cross-examination. However, since the burden of proof is on the prosecution, Mr. Flowers is not obligated to testify. Prosecutor Edwards feels he has put on the best case he can with what he has to work with.

At this time, after the prosecution rests its case and has called its final witness against Algernon Flowers, the defense has the opportunity to present its case. However, Michael Petagnas requests a sidebar, to speak outside of the jury's presence. The prosecution and defense meet at the judge's bench. The court reporter is present as well to document the sidebar. Michael Petagnas announces to the judge that he will like to file a motion for acquittal. This is shocking to the prosecution and a bold move by the defense. Without presenting a shred of evidence, or calling a single witness, Petagnas will like the court to acquit Algernon Flowers due to his belief that the prosecution failed to prove its case against his client. Judge Jackson decides he will hear Petagnas' motion, and then make his ruling. If the court denies the motion, Petagnas will be prepared to carry on with the defense's case, and call his witnesses.

Judge Jackson dismisses the jury and asks them to return tomorrow morning at 9 A.M.. Once the jury is out of the room, Prosecutor Edwards informs the judge that the prosecution needs time to prepare a rebuttal of the defense's motion, as this is unexpected to them. The judge decides to dismiss early and reconvene in the morning, at which time he will hear the defense's motion and allow the prosecution to argue against it.

With a strike of the gavel, the judge exits back to his chambers. Reporters scramble out of the courtroom to report the latest developments. Algernon Flowers is taken back to the holding cell to await transfer to the Local County Jail. Michael Petagnas, who, with his team, is the only one not surprised by his move, already has his case law and argument for tomorrow's motion. Prosecutors Edwards and Henderson, however, have a lot of homework to do tonight.

.   .   .

Back at the Flowers' home, Hazel Flowers and her family are having dinner with their usual guests—Nick McLean and his team. As they discuss the events of the day, Ms. Flowers has many questions for those who were present in courtroom number nine.

"What does that mean exactly?" asks a confused Hazel Flowers.

McLean goes on to explain that when the prosecution fails to prove its case against a defendant, the defense can file a motion of acquittal. It is rare and most often denied, but Michael Petagnas feels strongly that they did not meet their burden of proof against Algernon Flowers. If the judge denies the defense motion, then Mr. Petagnas will have to continue on with his case to jury.

.   .   .

Back at the Local County Jail, Algernon Flowers is in his orange jumpsuit and walking to his cell. The correctional officers have been following the case in the media, and are suddenly treating Mr. Flowers with respect. It appears as though the cross examination of Brenda Howell and her silence has spoken loudly. Although the local media still reads as 'prosecution-friendly,' those who view objectively appear to have a different perspective.

Tonight Algernon Flowers will try to sleep and dream about tomorrow's motion. Knowing that it is a long shot, and no judge in the history of the Local County judicial system has ever granted such a motion, Algernon envisions the possibility of 'what if?' What if Judge Hangman Jackson becomes the first judge to grant a motion of acquittal—and in a first-degree murder trial at that? It is farfetched, but what else is an inmate to do … except dream?

.   .   .

Michael Petagnas will also try to sleep well tonight. He feels that he has given Algernon Flowers a fighting chance and has done everything in his power. He is sitting up in bed reviewing the report of the defense medical expert, Dr. Harvey Walters. If and when the judge makes his ruling, if the motion is denied, Petagnas must be prepared to call the first witness for the defense—that will be Dr. Harvey Walters. The physical evidence in this case actually favors the defense, so Petagnas is prepared either way with however the judge rules.

.   .   .

In a small cottage-style home in a golf community bordering West Rocky Beach, Audrey Richardson is meeting with Sandy Ward from Algernon Flowers' defense team. Ms. Richardson has been closely following the trial and has been wrestling with herself as to what she should do. She reached out to the law office of Petagnas & Didia and was put in contact with Sandy Ward. Audrey Richardson has powerful testimony regarding Brenda Howell's strange activity on the morning her daughter was taken to the hospital. Her window in the Richard M. Weinstein Elementary School office allowed her to witness Mrs. Howell sitting in her car and nervously looking at her cell phone. Ms. Richardson thinks Brenda Howell seemed in no rush to get to her classroom, as she testified to. After hearing all the anti-defense news reporters saying that Mr. Flowers could go to prison for the rest of his life if convicted in the case, Audrey Richardson can no longer sit in hiding and do nothing. She wants to offer her testimony as a defense witness.

Although the defense is hoping Dr. Harvey Walters' report will be enough to clear Algernon Flowers of murder, it is always good to have an extra bullet in the chamber. Audrey Richardson tells Sandy Ward of the threats and intimidation she received from Rocky Beach Police detectives. She explains that she left town earlier during the investigation, after giving her original statement to a local detective.

"He drives a silver sedan with dark tinted windows," Richardson tells Sandy Ward.

Audrey Richardson goes on to inform the defense paralegal that after she gave her story, she felt that because it wasn't what they wanted to hear, they didn't want her to testify. She is coming forward now because she can't live in fear, nor can she live with herself if an innocent man goes to prison or gets the death penalty while she says nothing. Sandy Ward takes the trembling hand of the frightened Ms. Richardson.

"You are very brave, and on behalf of Mr. Flowers, I want to say thank you for your help," says a grateful Sandy Ward.

Sandy then takes out a small voice recorder from her bag and holds it between her and Audrey Richardson. She is going to need a full statement and will have to give the prosecution a copy as well in order to add Ms. Richardson to the defense witness list. Sandy Ward presses the red record button on the voice recorder and allows Audrey Richardson to finally get her story off of her chest.

.   .   .

It is late in the night, and Michael Petagnas' co-council is still working as he listens to an audio recording emailed to him from Sandy Ward. After hearing what Ms. Richardson has to say, Steven Didia Sr. feels her testimony would be very useful to the defense, and instructs Sandy Ward to begin the process of adding Audrey Richardson to the defense witness list.

One thing Steven Didia Sr. doesn't quite understand is why some of the Rocky Beach Police detectives would want to prevent such important testimony from being considered in this case. There must be something deeper going on, but he doesn't want to bring this up to Michael Petagnas until after tomorrow morning's very important motion hearing. For now, he will make sure Prosecutor Edwards and Judge Jackson know the defense has acquired another key witness.

CHAPTER 56

It is early on Friday morning and day five in the Algernon Flowers trial, however this is not the biggest story in today's Local County newspaper. The Flowers' trial has taken a back seat to a newly developing story. Authorities have reason to believe the human remains found in the woods last weekend are that of missing news reporter Heather Hoffman. They are still awaiting DNA testing and dental records to confirm this and positively identify the body, but articles found on and near the body suggest this, and support the belief that it is, in fact, Ms. Hoffman.

Private investigator Nicholas McLean has an inside source close to the investigation into the mystery of the human remains. According to his source, the victim hid a mini USB flash drive in the waistband of her underwear—probably in an attempt to conceal it from whomever wanted to kill for it. The discovery of the flash drive is not public knowledge, but

McLean has learned that it contains folders and files all saved under one title: 'BABY BLANKET.'

·   ·   ·

Algernon Flowers takes his morning ride in the windowless van to the Local County Courthouse. This is the fifth day of his trial and his clothes are starting to smell. He perspires in the back of the stuffy van to and from the courthouse, and in the warm holding cell as well. The collar on his shirt is blackening daily and the armpits have permanent sweat stains. Algernon can not wait until his attorney presents evidence and witnesses in his defense. He wants the world to know that he did not do the horrible thing he is accused of. After sitting quietly, and having to listen to the entire prosecution case and their witnesses speak, all Algernon Flowers wants at this point is a voice—a voice to state his case—to tell his side of the story.

Michael Petagnas walks into courtroom number nine and takes his seat at the defense table. He has heard the news report about the authorities believing the remains in the woods are that of Ms. Heather Hoffman. Petagnas wonders how that relates to this case. He knows there is some connection due to Nick McLean's investigation, but to what extent? Though it concerns him, Michael Petagnas cannot allow it to be a distraction from today's mission. Today he is going before the court in a motion hearing to acquit Algernon Flowers of the first-degree murder charge.

Every defendant has a constitutional right to a jury trial. This right can be waived, and the court may try the case. However, even in a jury trial, the defendant has the right to take the case away from the jury and have it decided by the trial judge. This is done through a motion for acquittal, which may be granted if there isn't enough evidence to support a conviction. This procedure protects the defendant from an improper or irrational jury verdict. If the court grants an acquittal before the jury returns a verdict, the defendant cannot be tried again for the same crime because double jeopardy protection attaches.

Algernon Flowers is brought into the courtroom, and shortly thereafter, Judge Warren Jackson takes his seat on the bench. For today's hearing, the jury is not needed, so they are waiting out in the jury room until after the motion hearing is complete and trial testimony resumes. Since this is a defense motion, Michael Petagnas will present first, to be followed by a prosecution rebuttal.

Michael Petagnas stands at the defense table and addresses the court:

"If it pleases the court, your Honor, the defense on behalf of the defendant, Algernon Flowers, will like to be heard on this motion of acquittal. It is our opinion, and I am sure that the court will agree, that the prosecution has failed to meet its burden of proof in this case. Mr. Flowers has been held without bail awaiting trial since his arrest nineteen months ago, yet the evidence in this case is merely circumstantial at best, and even most of that points to another theory altogether. Had Algernon Flowers been related to a Rocky Beach police detective, would he have been indicted in this case? The defense believes not. If the court carefully examines the evidence and testimony in this trial, we are confident that your Honor would agree that not only has the prosecution failed to meet its burden of proof, but also, at the least, there should have been another defendant in this case. Let's review the testimony and evidence submitted by the prosecution.

"The emergency medical technicians arrive on the scene, and the body of the victim is already cold, discolored, and rigor mortis is already setting in. This goes against the prosecution's theory that the victim sustained injuries by Algernon Flowers in the hour and a half window that Brenda Howell was out of the apartment. The bruises on the victim match the shapes of Brenda Howell's diamond cluster rings, and Homicide Detective Hunter even noticed this and the broken fingernail on Brenda Howell's dominate hand, which prompted him to photograph her hands. If we go back to the night before, according to Brenda Howell, the victim was sick and had been throwing up. Yet she leaves this sick three-year-old home unattended while she takes a twenty-minute drive each way to pick up Mr. Flowers. When Algernon Flowers notices that Deja is lying in bed with a pool of dark brown vomit coming out of her mouth, Brenda Howell rushes him out of the room and proceeds to clean up. Mr. Flowers never sees the child conscious or moving on her own the entire time from the night Brenda Howell picked him up, nor the next morning when Brenda Howell mysteriously arrives from work and calls Algernon Flowers to ask him to wake the victim—the sick three-year-old that she left alone the night before, and left again before the sun came up the next morning—leaving the sick three-year-old with her boyfriend, who is asleep. What makes her think that after driving all day and into the night from Nashville to Rocky Beach, and then being up late with her, that Algernon Flowers would wake up before the sick three-year-old? If Brenda Howell thought she had a class that morning, what time was she expecting to return back home to care for her sick three-year-old? Also, your Honor, if there was more than a night light in Deja Howell's room the night when Algernon Flowers noticed the pool of vomit she was lying in, he would have noticed that it wasn't Salisbury steak gravy that she threw up, but as the forensics lab has confirmed from testing the pillow case—it was blood. Is this all a coincidence that the child has bruises in the shape of her mother's rings—her mother has a broken fingernail on her dominant, or punching, hand—and the child is also throwing up blood? Talk about circumstantial evidence. Even Brenda Howell's behavior when arriving to work early and asking several coworkers for the time—even in the short time she was there, to ask for the time on even two occasions would be strange. During a weekday morning commute, it is almost a thirty-minute drive from Brenda Howell's apartment to the Richard M. Weinstein Elementary School—almost an hour round trip, which means that Mrs. Howell was only at work for approximately a half hour! A half hour and she asks over half a dozen people for the time. Not to mention she took the first parking spot, closest to the main office, a spot usually

reserved for the elderly staff members—perhaps to be seen ...
AND Brenda Howell backed her car into that spot, as to make
a speedy exit. The defense would argue that all these add to another possible theory, one that this jury will never hear, because
there is only one person charged with this crime. If I may, your
Honor, I will like to submit to the court the defense's theory as
to what happened to the victim here in this case.

"On or around that weekend—on Sunday, perhaps after
an argument with her estranged husband, Brenda Howell took
her rage out on the couple's three-year-old daughter. Whatever
it was that triggered the beating of little Deja Howell, she began
to exhibit some symptoms, like vomiting. Brenda Howell could
not take the child with bruises and other signs of abuse to the
hospital, especially since the three-year-old could speak well
enough to tell the doctors what happened to her and who did it
to her. Brenda Howell's husband has already threatened to take
full custody of the child due to Brenda's history of domestic
violence. Instead of seeking medical attention for Deja, Brenda
Howell hoped that the child would sleep off her injuries. However, with the child's condition continuing to decline, Brenda
Howell needed a Plan B ... and Plan B is now sitting in the defendant's seat. There were countless calls and text messages to
Algernon Flowers' cell phone from Brenda Howell constantly
checking on his travel status and his estimated time of arrival.
Brenda Howell needed another adult in the apartment to take
the fall—someone trusting and available. With her husband
out of town and planning to return the following evening,
she needed to act quickly. There is no doubt that Deja Howell
would have told her father, Detective Frank Howell, that her
mother, Brenda Howell, hurt her. If Deja Howell was going to
survive her initial beating, there is no doubt in my mind that
Brenda Howell would have inflicted more injuries to the child
in order to silence her. Brenda Howell saw her teaching career,
her reputation, her freedom, her life all being snatched away
if Deja Howell told her father or a doctor that 'Mommy beat
me' ... The decision for Brenda Howell to sacrifice Algernon

Flowers—a man she had only been seeing for two months—was an easy choice.

"Phone records show that Brenda Howell became irate and annoyed whenever Mr. Flowers responded with a later time of arrival. When he finally got to Rocky Beach, he had no transportation to get to Brenda Howell's apartment. This was the universe attempting to save this innocent man from being framed and caught up in the drama that is now his reality. Brenda Howell had no Plan C, or any other options. She needed Algernon Flowers in her apartment. Only problem was, she couldn't present the fatally injured child to him ... Deja Howell could't sit up in a car seat with her abdominal injuries. Brenda Howell then took the chance of leaving the three-year-old alone in her bed, appearing to be asleep. Brenda Howell was not concerned that her injured, or 'sick,' as she claims, child would wake up while she was gone, because she knew that Deja Howell was not waking up—and was never waking up again.

"After arriving back at her apartment with Plan B, Brenda Howell then used the power of seduction as a distraction. After having sex twice, and making strong frozen drinks with lots of alcohol in them, Brenda Howell expected that after driving the entire day, and the combination of sex and alcoholic drinks, Algernon Flowers would fall asleep and not notice the state of the injured child. However, Mr. Flowers went to check on the child when Mrs. Howell was fixing a second alcoholic beverage, which SHE never drank any of, by the way. Mr. Flowers noticed the pool of blood, which in the night light appeared to be dark brown ... another time that the universe was trying to save Algernon Flowers from this fate. Had he thought it was blood there is no doubt he would have insisted that they take Deja to the hospital. However, instead, Brenda Howell gave him another drink and rushed him out of Deja's room, and back to her bed.

"Early the next morning, perhaps Brenda Howell realized that little Deja Howell was no longer breathing and was now cold and blue. She needed to get out of the apartment so that Algernon Flowers was alone with the body. When she arrived at school, she backed her car into the first spot. She got there before the other staff did so that spot was available. This was important because she planned that when Algernon Flowers woke up and saw the lifeless body of the victim, she could be seen rushing from work to the hospital. That's why she asked so many different coworkers for the time ... Brenda Howell was establishing an alibi. She needed people to say that she was at work when her daughter's body was discovered by Plan B. Unfortunately for Brenda Howell, she wasn't getting a call from Algernon Flowers soon enough and grew impatient. Did he discover the body yet? Were there police at her apartment looking for clues? Had she covered her tracks? As these thoughts and questions raced through the mind of Brenda Howell, she couldn't take it anymore, so she decided to return home. When she arrived, she didn't see any crime tape or police activity. So she decided to park and wait a little longer. After a while, she decided to call and wake Algernon Flowers to ask him to wake Deja and bring her downstairs. This is when Algernon Flowers let her know that something was wrong with Deja. There is a reason Brenda Howell carried Deja's body past the front door, with no intention of getting her to the hospital. There is a reason Brenda Howell didn't attempt to revive her daughter with CPR ... Brenda Howell knew that it was far too late. Your Honor, all of the testimony here, and the physical evidence, supports another theory other than Algernon Flowers murdering this child within the short window that Brenda Howell left him alone with the body. Neither the county medical examiner, nor our own medical expert can put the injuries and time of death in a smaller window than eighteen hours. All of the evidence and testimony in this case better supports this defense theory, rather than the prosecution theory. If anything, all the prosecution has proven here, over the course of this trial, is the fact that Deja Howell died, and that her death was caused by injuries from a vicious beating. Nothing they've offered says that Algernon Flowers caused those injuries. In fact, one with common sense would argue that the evidence supports and suggests otherwise.

"So, your Honor, the defense asks that the court grant this motion of acquittal based on these facts and the lack of evidence tying Algernon Flowers to this first-degree murder charge. The jury is going to act on human emotion and impulse to make someone pay for what happened to this little girl. However, since the only available target happens to be an innocent man, what other choice are they given? We are asking that the court make this decision based on the facts and evidence in this case, and consider and weigh all the testimony. We are confident that your Honor would rule in favor of the defense. Thank you."

CHAPTER 57

After presenting his motion to the court, Michael Petagnas takes his seat. It is obvious why he retired from the district attorney's office with a one hundred percent conviction rate. Some observers in the courtroom gallery wonder, if Michael Petagnas were still the district attorney here in Local County, would Brenda Howell have been the defendant in this case, or would her ties to the Rocky Beach Police Department still give her an unfair advantage?

It is now time for the prosecution to argue against the defense motion. The current district attorney, David Edwards, stands and buttons his jacket. He has no intention of waving the white flag here. He wants to continue with the trial in hopes of getting a conviction and maintaining his perfect record.

"Your Honor, let us not take this case out of the hands of the jurors. We do feel that the prosecution has provided this jury with enough to make a reasonable decision," states Prosecutor Edwards.

He argues that his case is strong enough to at least go into the deliberation phase. It is Edwards' hope that the emotions of the jury would cause them to convict Algernon Flowers in spite of a less-than-stellar prosecution case. On the other hand, Michael Petagnas wants the court to make the decision so that emotions are taken out of it, and common sense, and the weighing of evidence, actual facts, and trial testimony are considered in determining the fate of his client. Michael Petagnas also offers case law where in another case, the prosecution failed to meet its burden of proof and the court granted a motion of acquittal.

Both sides argue back and forth in favor of and opposed to, respectively. After a couple of hours in, the judge decides to bring in the jury and dismiss them for the day. They are told to return on Monday morning at 9 A.M. Judge Jackson wants the rest of the day and the weekend to consider both sides in this motion for acquittal. He wants to read up on case law and review the evidence and testimony in this trial before making his ruling. The prosecution and defense are also told to report back to court on Monday morning at 9 A.M.

With the strike of his gavel, the judge disappears back to his chambers. Algernon Flowers is ushered to the holding cell to await transportation back to the Local County Jail. After a long and emotional week of trial, it will be an even longer weekend, as Algernon waits to hear what Hangman Jackson decides.

With the early dismissal, Michael Petagnas uses the afternoon to meet with his team to strategize. If the judge denies their motion, they will have to proceed with their case. Petagnas is planning to open up with the same statement he offered the court in his motion of acquittal hearing. He plans to offer alternate theories that make more sense when put together with the circumstantial and physical evidence as well as trial testimony. Steven Didia Sr. is also giving Michael Petagnas another tool to add to his arsenal—the testimony of Audrey Richardson. Ms. Richardson's testimony will help support Petagnas' theory of Brenda Howell's strange and out-of-character behavior.

In addition, the defense medical expert, Dr. Harvey Walters, is prepared to take the witness stand and confirm the wide window of time in which Petagnas argues is when Deja Howell received her fatal injuries. Petagnas believes that the initial beating took place on that Sunday, and since all the nail salons were closed, Brenda Howell couldn't get her broken fingernail repaired. It also fits in with the medical expert's report. The defense team prepares to begin its case on Monday morning.

. . .

Private investigator Nicholas McLean is visiting Algernon Flowers at the Local County Jail. Not as a member of his defense team in the interview room, but as a friend in the non-contact visitation booth. Separated by thick glass, the two men discuss the trial proceedings thus far and how they both hope for the best outcome. McLean opens up to Algernon and shares how inspirational he has been to him—his strength to withstand so much over the past nineteen months, and still manage to smile. Also, the love Algernon has for his family—his love for his nieces and nephews despite his separation from them at the moment. He missed birthdays, graduations, holidays, two Christmases, and even the funeral of his dear aunt. This all helps Nick McLean with his own family. He hasn't visited his sister and brother-in-law in Chicago in almost three years, and he now has a newborn nephew that he has yet to meet. The story of Algernon Flowers has motivated McLean to want to possess great inner strength, and surround himself with love—both from the people he loves, and the things he loves to do. On the other side of the thick glass, Algernon Flowers has been inspired by the tenacious and persistent Nicholas McLean—he works so hard and fights tooth and nail for someone who could never repay him ... It is these qualities that Algernon can only hope his nieces and nephews will grow up to possess. The men align their fists against the thick glass as a symbol of their mutual respect and unity.

McLean exits the booth so that Hazel Flowers can visit her son while there is still available visitation time remaining. Algernon is happy to share the events of the day with his mother, who is unable to sit in on the trial. The mother and son have much to talk about and catch up on. For Hazel Flowers, it is great to see her son smiling. She knows that Michael Petagnas will put on a great defense case, but it is natural for her to worry. She masks her fears and concerns with distracting conversation about all the family members that are in town for the trial. Having yet to see her son in his courtroom clothes, Ms. Flowers will look forward to finally getting to sit in the courtroom on Monday, now that the prosecution's case is over and she is no longer considered a potential witness. It will be the first time in almost two years that she will see her son in something other than the department of corrections' orange jumpsuit. When their visit is over, Algernon Flowers returns back to his cell and Ms. Flowers goes back home to spend the very long weekend with her family. It has been good for her to be surrounded with so much love and support.

．　　　．　　　．

At the end of the day, Michael Petagnas and his team have wrapped up their preparation of the defense case layout—the best sequence of witnesses and evidence that they feel will be most effective to the jury. For now they will call it a night and be ready for Monday morning. Steven Didia Sr. has the firm pay for a hotel room in an undisclosed location for Audrey Richardson, who is terrified of being retaliated against for offering her testimony. Didia Sr. wants nothing to go wrong over the course of the weekend and is taking no chances with this important defense witness.

．　　　．　　　．

Saturday and Sunday seem to drag on forever for all the parties involved in the Algernon Flowers first-degree murder trial. Since the trial began, this is the first break or days off, and everyone can feel the tension. Sunday's schedule for Hazel Flowers and her family is to attend regular church service and then return home for the usual large Sunday afternoon family feast. Although Algernon has not been there for quite some time, the presence of so many out-of-town family members visiting fills a void at the table. After dinner, the family listens to Algernon's CD and shares stories of the young man they all watched grow up.

The newest member of the usual Sunday afternoon family feast is investigator Nick McLean. He doesn't have any stories to share from when Algernon Flowers was growing up, but he shares about how the young man that he has come to respect and now calls 'friend' has encouraged him. Over the course of the entire case, McLean has come to learn that it is both Algernon Flowers *and* his family that are equally blessed to have each other. They have a great son, nephew, brother and uncle— and he has a great family and support system. The mighty inner strength of Algernon Flowers comes from the love he has for his family and their love for him.

CHAPTER 58

Early Monday morning, inmate Algernon Flowers wakes up in his tiny cell and notches day number *five hundred and ninety-two* onto the green brick wall. He then brushes his teeth and washes his face. Today begins the second week in his first-degree murder trial. He stands by the heavy iron cell door and waits for it to roll open. He is anxious to go to the inmate transfer area to change into his court clothes and make his way to the courthouse. Since he can't sleep, he chooses to stand and wait.

.   .   .

Michael Petagnas leaves his home and is met by his temporary bodyguard, Brent Patterson. As he did last week, Patterson follows Petagnas during his commute to the Local County Courthouse. Petagnas and the prosecutors were told to arrive early. Petagnas imagines this is so that they can get the judge's ruling out of the way and then bring in the jury to begin the

defense case. Michael Petagnas is rehearsing his opening statement in his car as he drives.

.   .   .

The defendant is usually at the courthouse three hours prior
to the start time given by the judge, so it is no surprise for
Algernon Flowers to be in the holding cell outside courtroom
number nine this early. However, he is confused when the deputy unshackles him and brings him into the courtroom almost
an hour earlier than the start time given by the judge. The clock
on the back wall of courtroom number nine reads 8:10 A.M.
Algernon Flowers notices it as he enters through the side door
near the holding cell. He also notices that only a handful of people are present in the gallery. Another distinct difference is the
presence of courtroom deputies. Throughout the entire trial,
there has only been one deputy present. This morning, there
are four—two standing in the center aisle, one near the defense
table, and another by the bench. The most out-of-the-ordinary
element, however, is the presence of Judge Warren Jackson,
who is already seated on the bench. Usually the judge comes
out after the defendant. It is obvious that the judge has called
an early meeting. When Algernon takes his seat, the judge begins to address the parties present.

"Now that the defendant, Mr. Algernon Flowers, is present, let us begin," announces the judge in his usual stern voice.

He goes on to explain how extensively he has reviewed the
testimony and evidence in this case. He carefully and repeatedly
considered all the elements.

"I looked at the video of Mr. Flowers' interview with homicide detectives, and I kept seeing a young man who, from the
beginning, has denied any knowledge or involvement in what
happened, and even after being interrogated by some of the
best and most experienced detectives using all of their tactics,
he never once changed any elements of his story, even when
asked in different ways," adds Judge Jackson.

He continues to refer back to the defense theory presented during the motion hearing, and if it were presented to this same jury, it would absolutely make for a much stronger argument.

"I am agreeing with Mr. Petagnas in that the prosecution has failed to meet its burden of proof in this case. I am granting the defense's motion of acquittal!" declares the judge.

Algernon Flowers isn't sure he heard correctly until he sees prosecutor David Edwards slam his pen down on the table in anger. Algernon hears some muffled cheers of jubilation and celebration from a few rows behind him. He recognizes one voice to be that of his sister Natasha, who usually gets to court early to save seats for the rest of the family. It isn't until Michael Petagnas places his arm around Algernon Flowers that he fully realizes what has just happened.

"You have been given an opportunity to do something great with your life ... don't waste it!" whispers a smiling Petagnas to his client.

The judge announces he has already dismissed the jury. He calls Algernon Flowers forward to the bench. With shaking legs, Algernon makes his way to the front of the courtroom. He stands before the judge with tears beginning to fill his eyes.

"Algernon Flowers, I hereby grant you this judgment of acquittal by the circuit and district court in the State of Florida," decrees Judge Warren Jackson.

The deputy near the bench hands Algernon a pen and the judgment of acquittal document to sign. The judge then announces to the deputies, "Mr. Flowers is to be released immediately from the custody of the Local County Department of Corrections!" With those words and a strike of the gavel, Judge Warren Jackson departs to his chambers.

Algernon Flowers is taken back to the holding cell for the final time. Michael Petagnas follows behind to talk with his client. Petagnas explains to Algernon that with the judicial acquittal, he can never be charged with this crime again. This is better than if the jury acquitted him, because then Prosecutor Edwards could appeal and retry him in the future.

"This is the best possible outcome," explains a satisfied Michael Petagnas.

.　　　.　　　.

Hazel Flowers is still en route to the courthouse when she gets the call from her daughter informing her that Algernon was just acquitted. She has still not seen her son during the trial, but now she will see him at home. She shouts for joy as she orders the caravan of family members to turn back and head home.

"I have to start to cook his favorite meals ... my son is coming home!" declares a jubilant Hazel Flowers.

Private investigator Nick McLean gets word from Steven Didia Sr. about the judge's ruling. The large, tough man breaks down sobbing in his SUV. He was hoping that what he was able to uncover would be enough ammo for the defense. Getting close to Algernon and the Flowers' family makes this victory all the more sweet. McLean calls the rest of his team to share the great news.

.　　　.　　　.

As Algernon Flowers is led out of the holding cell, he takes the walk down the long hallway leading to the underground garage. This time he rides in the back of a marked deputy's car—with windows. As the car carrying the newly exonerated man exits the garage, the morning sunlight is the brightest he can remember. The vehicle pulls up the ramp and comes to a stop at a red light, and Algernon looks over to his right where he can see the parking lot of the courthouse. There is a commotion that catches his attention. Detective Frank Howell has to be physically restrained. He appears to be yelling violently at Brenda Howell. Neither the detective nor Mrs. Howell was present in the courtroom for the judge's early ruling. There are several other people present in the area during the altercation. The deputy's vehicle pulls away, and Algernon loses sight of the parking lot. As the car drives toward the Local County Jail, Algernon Flowers is overcome with emotion, as this is the last time he will have to take this drive. Tomorrow, he will wake up in his HOME. After five hundred and ninety-two days of waking up in a tiny jail cell, he may not sleep tonight at all, but rather celebrate with his family all night long.

When Algernon Flowers arrives at the jail, corrections officers are shocked to learn that he is being released. Usually first-degree murder defendants are transferred to a state prison, not released to go home. This is such a new concept for them that they are quite unsure of the proper procedures. They decide to place him back in his regularly assigned cell and wait for a supervisor. It takes another half hour before the iron door is rolled open, and the supervising officer tells Algernon to pack up his photos and letters, because he is going home.

After making his way to the booking and release area of the jail, Algernon Flowers is given all of his belongings in a clear plastic bag. He is then released. Finally, Algernon Flowers steps outside of the county jail. When he arrives in the parking lot, he notices a car racing toward him. Before it reaches him, the passenger door flies open and his sister jumps out of the still-moving vehicle and leaps into his arms. This is the first time he has hugged a family member in more than nineteen months.

.   .   .

When Algernon Flowers arrives to the Flowers' residence, there are several cars parked in the driveway and along the street. When he exits the car, his mother, Hazel Flowers, greets him in the garage. As the mother and son embrace, a house full of family members surrounds them.

The first thing on Algernon Flowers' agenda is to take a long, hot shower and then eat his favorite dishes. This is a day he was unsure would ever come. He has to pinch himself to make sure that he didn't fall asleep in the holding cell and is dreaming the entire thing. When he is finally alone in the bathroom, he—the man who was on trial for murder and facing an uncertain future—collapses to his knees and cries tears of joy and gratitude.

.   .   .

The very next morning, Algernon Flowers would catch a flight to Atlanta, Georgia, where he would stay with some friends and start to rebuild his life. He vows to write a book about his ordeal, not only to share his side of the story, but as a writer, it would be a therapeutic release. It would be several years before Algernon could mentally and emotionally revisit this painful experience to write about it. Just as it took a wicked and evil woman to nearly ruin the young, trusting man, it eventually requires a loving, caring woman to fully restore and resuscitate him. Relationships and trust will carry brand new meaning to Mr. Algernon Flowers for the duration of his natural life.

.   .   .

Michael Petagnas remains undefeated as a trial attorney—not only because of his tremendous skill in the courtroom, but because when he decides to take on a case, it is because he believes in his client one hundred percent. It is easy to fight for what he believes in. Mr. Petagnas continues to keep in touch with Algernon, whom he stills calls, "young man" or "kid." Michael Petagnas remains an advocate for justice, and continues to fight for those who cannot fight for themselves.

.   .   .

Not much in the newspaper about Algernon Flowers, except for a couple of small articles that some of the prosecutor's reporter friends wrote about the trial. The bigger story is the positive identity of the body found in the woods. Authorities confirmed that the remains are that of Channel Thirteen News reporter Heather Hoffman. It seems that both Chief Nelson and his son Detective Nelson really enjoyed getting into Heather Hoffman's panties. Ironically, it is what she hid in her panties that did them both in.

The BABY BLANKET file on the USB flash drive found tucked in the waistband of Ms. Hoffman's underwear was full of secret audio recordings and photos—all of which suggest the chief and his son destroyed evidence and tampered with witnesses in the homicide investigation of Deja Howell. It also suggests that Brenda Howell was having an affair with her husband's coworker—the chief's son. Both Chief Nelson and his son are taken into custody, which sets in motion a state-appointed internal investigation of the entire Rocky Beach Police Department.

. . .

Nicholas McLean is sitting on his sister's couch in Chicago. He holds his baby nephew for the first time. McLean promised to visit his sister and brother-in-law as soon as the Algernon Flowers trial was over. Witnessing the close bond of the Flowers family has changed McLean's perspective. He loves his job and realizes from the Flowers case just how important what he does actually is. However, family is his number one priority from now on.

While sitting on the couch with his nephew and brother-in-law, McLean's sister enters the room, brings in his ringing cell phone, and hands it to him. McLean answers. It is Michael Petagnas. Petagnas has just taken on a new case. A wealthy man was found completely burned in his own bed, and now his wife has been charged with first-degree felony murder. However, Michael Petagnas thinks there is a lot more to this story, and that is why he needs the best private investigator he knows.

"Nicky, we could really use you on this. What do you say, one more?" asks a cool and confident Michael Petagnas.

Nicholas McLean looks down at his infant nephew, who almost appears to wink and smile at his uncle. McLean smiles, then lifts his nephew up toward his face and kisses his forehead.

CHAPTER 59

It is twenty-two years earlier, in the Brooklyn borough of New York City. The street lamps illuminate the sidewalk, still wet from a recent thunderstorm. A tall, muscular man exits the Brooklyn Medical Center on this chilly evening and looks for oncoming traffic before darting across the street to a twenty-four hour deli. As he approaches the side entrance of the deli, he notices a commotion coming from the adjacent alleyway. He sees three teenage boys kicking a younger teen that is cowering from their assault. The tall, muscular man doesn't hesitate to abandon his original intention or his own personal safety to leap into action and provide assistance to the outnumbered and overpowered youth.

"Hey, cut that out!" yells the tall man as he sprints down the narrow alleyway.

As he gets closer, one of the assailants turns defensively and displays a small pocketknife. The tall man doesn't even notice the weapon held by the young thug as he pushes the big-boned teen to the ground. The hand-held knife is dislodged, and slides underneath a green, iron dumpster. All three of the teen attackers flee at the rebuke of the tall man.

"Get out of here, you punks!" he barks.

The man then turns his attention to the young victim who has sustained some bruises but appears not to be seriously injured. The young man is sixteen-year-old Michael Petagnas. He struggles to get to his feet with the help of the tall, muscular man.

"Are you OK?" questions the man as he helps young Michael gather some personal items that were misplaced during the attack.

"Yes, sir. I'm OK. Luckily you were here to help. Thank you," replies a shaken but relieved young Michael Petagnas.

He goes on to explain to the tall, muscular gentleman that the three thugs attempted to steal the new motorcycle that his parents gave him as an early graduation present. After pulling into the alleyway to escape the rain, young Michael Petagnas was approached by the three would-be robbers. His refusal to hand over the keys is what led to the beating he received.

"Well, no bike is worth the value of your life. Next time just give up the keys," offers the heroic man as a piece of future advice. "Don't you want to make it to your graduation in one piece, young man?"

"Yes, sir!" replies young Michael Petagnas. "I'm going to the Port Orange University in Florida. I'm going to be a lawyer one day!"

The man extends his hand and offers his blessing. "Well, sounds like you've got a great head on your shoulders, kid. Try to keep it there. Good luck."

Young Michael Petagnas shakes the tall, muscular man's hand and smiles before getting onto his motorcycle and riding away. The man is Peter Flowers. He enters the deli and soon exits with a large, brown paper bag. He checks for traffic as he races back across the street and enters the hospital. He arrives back to his wife's room, located in the maternity ward, just in time to witness the birth of their second son—whom they uniquely name Algernon.

THE END

ACKNOWLEDGEMENTS

Many individuals have been influential in the development of this story & ultimately this book—

Special thanks to Michael J. Politis for assembling a talented staff which provided a powerful and impactful defense.

Many thanks to Private Investigator Nick Boccuzzi Jr. for his bravery in conducting a fearless investigation, which uncovered and exposed truth in a cluster of woven lies and corruption.

Infinite gratitude to my family, close friends, and everyone who believed in my innocence, for it is because of you all that any of this is possible.

To my dear nieces and nephews who have been extremely understanding of my complete absence during the writing stages of this novel – Uncle Al loves you!

To the special lady who allowed me to vent, and provided much needed emotional support during the difficult writing process of this literary work, thank you so much for revisiting the darkness with me, and inspiring me to dig deep within.

Special thanks to the talented Gary Cergol for designing powerful cover art.

Big thank you to my copy editor Susan "hawk eyes" Miller, who can spot grammatical errors from across the galaxy.

This book is dedicated to the many wrongfully accused men and women, who are left with the task of self-restoration while facing the uphill battle of trying to prove their innocence. I fight alongside you! Never Give Up!

ABOUT THE AUTHOR

Algernon currently resides in New York City, where he was born and raised. When he was only ten years old, Algernon penned his very first story entitled: "The Coin" which was a mystery thriller about a group of children that found a rare coin, and the troubles that followed them when word of their discovery got out. Mysteries and suspense thrillers were his favorite genre growing up. As an adult, Algernon enjoys all genres – From fiction to self-help and personal development.

After receiving a musical scholarship as a gifted jazz pianist, he went on to study music education, production & performance. After obtaining his BA, Algernon went on to take creative writing classes and attended writing workshops conducted by award winning authors in New York City, Orlando FL and Los Angeles CA.

Algernon has also written stage plays and screenplays as well as unpublished motivational books. Stage & Screen Plays include: Road To The Potter's House – Special Delivery I & II – Reality Check – Pick Of The Litter.

Algernon was arrested in FL and charged with first-degree murder for a crime he did not commit. After a trial, he was acquitted by the circuit county court and released. He struggled for several years after that incident in wanting to share his story, however it was a place far too painful to revisit. After years of writing classes and training, Algernon has finally written and released the novel JUST ANOTHER INNOCENT LIFE inspired by his own personal life story.

As a Motivational Speaker, Algernon has spoken to audiences on a variety of inspirational topics. In his signature message "Make It 'Till You Make It" Algernon shares his remarkable and courageous journey from being homeless and sleeping on the streets of New York City, to working on major television/film productions and creating the life of his dreams.

www.algernonwrites.com

www.ingramcontent.com/pod-product-compliance
Lightning Source LLC
Chambersburg PA
CBHW070214260626
47160CB00002B/548